MONSTER CAMP

MONSTER CAMP

CAMP

Sarah Henning

Margaret K. McElderry Books
New York   London   Toronto   Sydney   New Delhi

MARGARET K. McELDERRY BOOKS
An imprint of Simon & Schuster Children's Publishing Division
1230 Avenue of the Americas, New York, New York 10020

MARGARET K. McELDERRY BOOKS is a trademark of Simon & Schuster, Inc.
For information about special discounts for bulk purchases, please contact Simon & Schuster Special Sales at 1-866-506-1949 or business@simonandschuster.com.
The Simon & Schuster Speakers Bureau can bring authors to your live event. For more information or to book an event, contact the Simon & Schuster Speakers Bureau at 1-866-248-3049 or visit our website at www.simonspeakers.com.
Interior design by Irene Metaxatos
The text for this book was set in Stratford.
Manufactured in the United States of America
0323 FFG
First Edition
10 9 8 7 6 5 4 3 2 1
Library of Congress Cataloging-in-Publication Data
Names: Henning, Sarah, author.
Title: Monster Camp / Sarah Henning.
Description: First edition. | New York : Margaret K. McElderry Books, [2023] | Audience: Ages 8–12. | Audience: Grades 4-6. | Summary: When eleven-year old Sylvie joins a monster LARPing (a.k.a. live action role-play) summer camp, she finds herself in the performance of her life after realizing that she is the only human among real monsters.
Identifiers: LCCN 2022058104 (print) | LCCN 2022058105 (ebook) | ISBN 9781665930055 (hardcover) | ISBN 9781665930062 (paperback) | ISBN 9781665930079 (ebook) Subjects: CYAC: Camps–Fiction. | Role playing–Fiction. | Monsters–Fiction. | LCGFT: Monster fiction. | Novels. Classification: LCC PZ7.1.H46426 Mo 2023 (print) | LCC PZ7.1.H46426 (ebook) | DDC [Fic]–dc23
LC record available at https://lccn.loc.gov/2022058104
LC ebook record available at https://lccn.loc.gov/2022058105ISBN 9781665930055
ISBN 9781665930079 (ebook)

To my little monsters,
Nate and Amalia.
Okay, you're not that little
anymore but you get the
point. Love you.

The Worst First Day of Summer

Sylvie Shaw was a monster, and everyone knew it.

The type with glistening fangs, pale skin, and a thirst for adventure to go along with her taste for blood.

She didn't even try to hide it.

If anything, she flaunted that fact, arriving every single day to Evermore Middle School looking like she'd stepped straight out of her well-appointed casket. Black clothes guarding her skin—even on the hottest days—and huge sunglasses over her eyes to ward off the sun. Her hair was always down and parted in the center, emphasizing the widow's peak she maintained with care. In her hand, a glittery black tumbler emblazoned with a merry, fanged "You Suck" and filled to the brim with a sloshing red liquid.

Okay, that's not entirely true.

Sylvie arrived that way in her dreams. Because Sylvie

was actually a human who just liked to role-play as a monster.

A vampire, to be exact.

Sylvie was the founder of Evermore Middle School's first-ever Monster LARPing (aka live-action role-play) Club. Though her single dad wasn't *thrilled* with her love of LARPing, the club was Dad-approved, mainly because he was always bent on Sylvie hanging out with real live humans and not just sitting in her room, mainlining all the classic monster shows and movies—*The Munsters*, *The Addams Family*, *Dracula*, *The Invisible Man*, and every cartoon counterpart. Most of them were her mom's old DVDs, and so she wasn't sure why her dad didn't like her spending time with them, because in a way it was like spending time with her mom.

And for the last six years, they both very much missed spending time with her.

Anyhow, Ethan Shaw preferred Sylvie as she was.

He didn't like it very much that she pretended to be a vampire. It was annoying and completely cut into Sylvie's attempt to survive sixth grade by making every day an adventure in LARPing. So, Sylvie just made it so he wouldn't worry . . . by making herself a monster when he wasn't around.

Like in the bathroom at school before the bell.

Or in today's case: in her bedroom after he was safely across town at a construction site.

Sylvie the Vampire had somewhere to be.

Dustin had agreed to meet Sylvie in Evermore Glade Park for a summer LARP.

As a LARP partner, he had some very specific requirements about the LARPs he would engage in, particularly that he and Sylvie were always adversaries. It wasn't an ideal situation, though seeing as Dustin was the only person who'd joined her LARPing club . . . beggars couldn't be choosers.

But today was the first day of summer, and Sylvie had decided all bets were off. With the sun shining, no classroom confines, and seventh grade on the horizon, Sylvie hoped against all hope that she could finally convince Dustin to do a LARP where they were on the same team.

Perhaps hunting a rogue monster together.

Or a rogue human who wanted to use Sylvie's undead powers for no good.

Or any of the other common-but-cool scenarios in the dog-eared vampire novels Sylvie had on her bookshelf—ones she'd subsequently condensed and added to the three-ring binder she used for official LARP activities.

The point was, if Sylvie could convince Dustin to team up with her rather than kill her, they had options. And maybe, *just maybe*, by the end of the summer, they could convince others LARPing was fun too.

So, excited by the sheer possibility of it all—and bolstered by the fact that her dad had left for work at seven—Sylvie dressed in her best black jean shorts and black tank top; drew on her widow's peak with fresh, waterproof eyeliner; applied her sharpest stick-on fangs; and walked to the park with her binder full of LARPing scenarios for her vampire and Dustin's knight.

Sylvie arrived right at ten, but only saw a couple of moms and toddlers, no Dustin.

She plopped in the seat of a swing at the appointed playground and waited.

And waited.

By 10:10, Sylvie checked her phone. Nothing. By 10:15, she texted Dustin.

Hey. I'm here. Are you coming?

By 10:20, Sylvie was in the middle of digging a very nice ravine in the wood chips under the swings when a shadow fell over her from behind.

"If it isn't Draculette."

She knew that voice.

Sylvie whirled around to find Fisher Loggins, palming a basketball and wielding a grin that would make a hyena jealous.

Fisher had the unique distinction of thinking sixth grade at Evermore Middle School was totally fair because he had everything going for him. He was sporty. He was popular. And because of those things and the copious groundwork laid by his equally athletic big brothers, everyone from the kids to the teachers to the principal seemed to think he walked on water.

But that was because he was nice to the right people

and totally, utterly horrible to everyone else.

Particularly Sylvie.

Fisher was the reason Sylvie had stopped wearing her stick-on fangs at school. The second week of sixth grade, the grade A jerk nailed her in the face during gym-class dodgeball, and one of them went up her nose.

Then Mr. Sharp told her no more fangs in gym class. It wasn't fair because Mr. Sharp wasn't the one who lost a tooth to Fisher Loggins, and he didn't have to pay for them anyway. And even more unfair was the fact that Sylvie's schedule included gym every single school day, like it was math or English or something actually important.

But if Sylvie had learned anything about middle school, it was that literally nothing was ever fair unless you were good at a sport or at the top of the class or, in the case of total unicorns, both.

Sylvie was neither nor both.

And so, she'd spent her entire sixth grade year trying to recruit anyone who was also neither nor both to be a monster too.

Through LARPing.

Sylvie made some really rad posters, and even convinced Miss Tottenham to sponsor the Evermore Middle Monster LARPing Club. Except instead of creating a trove of character sheets and a band of monsters and misfits eager for regular quests and battles . . . the club had been less than successful.

All Sylvie had for her trouble was Dustin.

And now instead of Dustin, she had trouble brewing with Fisher.

Flanking him were his usual boneheaded minions, Kyle and Kiefer. Each of them held water bottles and blank expressions. They would have to pass Sylvie to get to the basketball court on the other side of the park. Just her luck.

Sylvie hugged her binder tighter and ground her Converse firmly into the wood chips. "Leave me alone, Fisher."

His smile only widened. "I'm just being nice. Helping a lonely girl by checking on her."

That was absolutely not what he was doing.

Sylvie's eyes narrowed. "I'm not lonely and I don't need your help."

"Of course you do," Fisher argued. "Where's your boyfriend? What's his name? Justin? Derek?"

"Dustin is not my boyfriend."

"Oh no, Draculette, did Dust-Mop break up with you? That's it, isn't it? You look like you want to fling yourself into the sun." He glanced at his buddies. "How about we help you out and give you a push?"

Before Sylvie could realize what he meant, Fisher chucked the basketball to free up his meaty hands as he and his minions converged on Sylvie's swing. She hadn't been holding on to the swing chains, but now she grabbed furiously with her right hand, her left clutching the binder with all the strength she had from her weekly climbing-gym jaunts with her dad.

"No! Hey, stop!" All three of them had hold of the chains now and were pulling her back as if to swing her up in a deep arc, sniggering like hoarse hyenas. "Stop!"

Sylvie started kicking. She nailed one of the minions in something fleshy. Kyle and Kiefer flew apart, giving Sylvie the sliver of space she needed to flee from the swing and onto solid ground outside of their tangled fence of limbs.

But in her escape, the corner of Sylvie's binder caught on somebody and jolted straight out of her hands and right onto the toes of Fisher's expensive high-tops. With some sort of soccer move—because of course he played *all* the sports—Fisher flipped the binder from the top of his laces into his outstretched hands.

"Did Dust-Mop get sick of playing pretend with you?"

"It's role-playing, not pretend—"

"Same thing, Draculette! You were going to meet him and play, weren't you? And then he stood you up. That's it, isn't it?" Fisher held up her binder as if it were proof—and it did say "Sylvie's LARP Book" on the side, so maybe it was. "You even brought your little guide. And then he just left you here!"

Sylvie gave him her best scowl. "That's mine! Give it back!"

Fisher's mean grin only widened, his blue eyes narrow slits. "You want it back? Pretend you're a killer vampire and *take it!*"

Sylvie was starting to get nervous. She leapt for the binder, but he swung it above his shoulder, out of reach.

Then, because he was truly a jerk, Fisher yelled, "Go long, Kyle!" and tossed her binder in a quarterback's perfect spiral in the direction of the picnic tables.

Kyle started running, and so did Sylvie. He was fast, but she was faster, darting ahead of him. Unfortunately, she was also a head shorter, and not classically athletic, so when they both leapt over the wooden railroad-tie boundary of the swing sets and onto the grassy lawn for the incoming binder, Kyle easily caught it.

Sylvie gritted her teeth and jumped again, trying to get a finger on the spine to tip it out of his hands. But Kyle was a good minion and immediately slung it right back to Fisher as Sylvie tumbled to the grass, still slick with morning dew.

She skidded to a stop just as Fisher caught her binder in his meaty hands. Triumphant, he hopped up onto the nearest picnic table and loomed over her.

"If this really is your manual to being a vampire, it's trash, Draculette. You can't fly. You aren't super strong. You don't even bite."

"It's not—" Sylvie heaved.

"I said I'd help you, and I will, because I'm a nice guy."

Then, with the grace of the Evermore Middle sixth-grade point guard that he'd been last year, Fisher shot her binder in a perfect arc . . . right into the nearest park trash can.

"Give up the ghost, Draculette. You're a terrible monster."

Quest,
Party of One

Sylvie didn't give up the ghost.

Or the LARP.

Even after Fisher had stalked off with his minions to the basketball court, laughing the whole way.

No, instead, she stood up and dusted herself off. Her knees were scraped up and stained green by the grass, and wood chips dotted her socks. But she clenched her teeth, pinned her eyebrows together, and marched over to the trash can.

Sylvie fished out the binder. A banana peel clung to the outside corner, and some of the pages bore the neon-green mark of the last of someone's Mountain Dew.

She didn't care. She had her binder back.

But . . . Sylvie didn't have her phone.

Upon further inspection, Sylvie saw it was back toward the swings, over the railroad-tie barrier and half-buried in wood chips. Sylvie rescued it, brushed off a fine layer of clingy debris, and was surprised to see it light up with a message—two, actually.

Both from Dustin.

Sylvie sunk to the bench of the same picnic table Fisher had climbed and read.

Oops. Forgot to text you. Got into the most awesome camp! Gonna hone my survival skills!

I guess phones aren't allowed. Later.

Sylvie stared at the screen. Her heart fluttered once in her chest and then began a slow slide into the pit of her gut. Without meaning to, one hand snaked up to the silver crescent-moon necklace at her throat—one last present from her mom—and her fingers rubbed along the edge.

The comforting motion calmed her like it always did, but she'd be lying to herself and the power of her mom's necklace if she said it made her actually feel better.

Dustin wasn't her boyfriend. He wasn't even her friend, really. But it still hurt that he had stood her up. He hadn't even thought to tell her where he was. If she hadn't texted him, she never would've known.

He'd arrived to her third LARP meeting with headphones on and carrying the latest iPhone in his palm like it was surgically attached. Before that day, she'd never said two words to him—the over-the-ear headphones didn't exactly invite conversation—yet Dustin knew what the club was, and he wanted to play.

At first, Sylvie was elated.

But after filling out a character sheet, which he'd titled "Knight of the Night," Dustin informed Sylvie that the only way he would play would be if he got at least one chance to kill a monster.

And that was how every LARP Sylvie Shaw ever did ended in her murder.

Specifically, Dustin, as Knight of the Night, wanted to role-play methods he picked up in the stupid game he was always playing on his phone: *Monster SLAY 3000*.

"SLAY" stood for something Sylvie never cared to learn. And even though she didn't exactly want to prance around as a vampire on the verge of a second death every single time she LARPed, at least she'd had someone to engage with.

This was like that first day of Monster LARPing Club all over again.

Big expectations. Same lonely result.

Suddenly, she had a lump in her throat, and tears pricked the edges of her eyes, hot and heavy. She couldn't LARP. Not alone. Not today.

Sylvie walked home as fast as she could. Through the park to downtown, past the clock tower, with a right turn at her street, with its ancient brick sidewalks and stately but marginally maintained Victorian homes. The one she shared with her dad was ahead, painted a whimsical cacophony of bright blues her mother had loved.

As she approached, Sylvie's drying eyes caught on the second-floor window—the one with the built-in seat where she'd cuddled up with her mom daily the summer Sylvie was five, sounding out words until she could actually, truly read them. That made her both want to cry all over again and distracted her enough that the toe of her black-and-white Converse All Stars snagged an uprooted brick.

For the second time in as many hours, the ground was rushing up toward Sylvie's face.

In one swooping toss, she sent the binder hurtling toward the safety of Mr. Mortimer's pristine lawn. Hands free, Sylvie got them out front just in time, her palms skidding on the bricks, her bent knees catching next, the rest of her body in a total heap after that.

For a long moment, Sylvie lay there, facedown and panting.

Then, all at once, she finally began to cry.

Big fat tears streamed out of her eyes and down her cheeks before leaping off the point of her chin to the stupid sidewalk below.

Heaving, Sylvie rolled over and rubbed at the tears with her forearms, hands too caked with dusty dirt to be of any use. Lips wobbling, Sylvie squeezed her eyes shut and pulled her knees to her chest.

"The first day of summer and it's already been the worst day of summer," she muttered under her breath, her voice doing a stupid, pitchy, trembly thing that was completely embarrassing.

Then it became even more embarrassing because,

with the snap of a twig to her right, Sylvie realized she wasn't alone.

If Mr. Mortimer caught her like this, her dad would be getting a frantic phone call as fast as her neighbor could run his fingers through the dial of his rotary phone. If it was someone else? Someone from school? That would be even worse.

Gritting her teeth, Sylvie's eyes snapped open to meet whoever had come across her in this shameful state. She first spotted her LARP binder sprawled open on Mr. Mortimer's lawn, and sitting on its mussed-up pages was the largest orange tabby this side of the Mississippi.

"Gunther," Sylvie sighed with relief to the cat, who blinked at her with his big yellow eyes, his enormously fluffy tail beating out a whole silent rant. "I'd appreciate it if you kept this between you and me."

Gunther's tail stopped swishing for a moment as if he were considering her request. He was the neighborhood cat—not really anyone's as much as everyone's. The Ortegas three houses down made sure he stayed up-to-date on shots, and everyone else kept him fed. Gunther probably had the best gig of any cat in Evermore, and he knew it.

Sylvie tried smiling at him. He tilted his big orange head. And then, in one fluid motion, he stood up, arched his back, and hissed.

"Well, geez."

Annoyed as much as she was disappointed, Sylvie bared her own fangs and hissed right back.

Gunther's eyes only narrowed further, and then, because apparently he didn't like a dose of his own medicine, the cat ran away.

Okay, now, officially, today was the first day of summer and also the worst.

Wallowing with Wednesday Addams

Magnus the ancient corgi met Sylvie at the door.

His smile, bark, and eternally erect ears gave away that he did not yet know this was the worst day of the summer. Additionally, he was the kind of corgi with a long tail, and that tail swished merrily as Magnus trotted behind Sylvie, who entered the house in a mood.

Her grumpy, stomping steps on the hardwood didn't deter him. In fact, Magnus happily watched Sylvie with his big, cataracts-cloudy brown eyes and not a hint of concern as she tried to shake off her terrible morning with a shower and a change of clothes.

As she dried her hair in front of the mirror, Sylvie forced her mouth into something that was more of a quivering grimace than a smile and saw that her stick-on fangs were still there. Straight and sharp and perfect.

It almost felt like a win.

"I'm a good monster, Fisher Loggins," Sylvie told her reflection.

For some reason, that made her want to cry all over again.

Magnus trailing, Sylvie made herself a fang-safe cheese sandwich, flipped on the little TV in her room, and popped in her mom's old DVD of *The Addams Family*.

The doggie took up position at her side, his short little legs splayed straight back as he lay on his tummy, knowing that Sylvie's next move was to plop into the massive beanbag chair nuzzled up against the foot of her bed and draw up the blanket there.

Sylvie patted Magnus on his graying head, took a bite of her sandwich, trained her eyes on the screen, and spent the rest of the day in someone else's world.

Sylvie's dad found her midway through the second movie in the 1990s live-action Addams Family redux, *Addams Family Values*.

He came in, removed his ball cap, and dropped into the roll-y chair at Sylvie's desk that was entirely too small for him. It squeaked under his weight, but he didn't flinch, as solid and stiff as his work jeans were after his construction foreman's shift.

With one look of his tired gray eyes, Sylvie wasn't surprised when instead of "Hey there, Syl-Bear," he greeted her with a question. He watched her with those eyes and asked in his stubble-rumbling voice, "Do you want to talk about it?"

That lump in Sylvie's throat was back, hard as a rock.

Her lips started trembling and tears were forming, hot and fierce, before she could look away.

Sylvie swallowed, trying to clear that roiling ball of sadness and frustration. It didn't work. To buy herself time, she paused the movie, right at the point when it becomes very clear that the Addams kids and all the other camp "misfits" are about to turn the pageant featuring the first Thanksgiving into a fiery lesson about mistreating others.

Dropping the remote in her lap, Sylvie rubbed Magnus's soft ears and didn't look her dad in the eye as she asked him a question in return. "How did you know?"

"Doesn't take twenty-twenty vision to see the storm cloud over your head. Heck, Magnus can probably make it out."

The very blind dog wagged his tail at the sound of his name and booped Sylvie on the arm with a wet nose.

Her dad had the kind of patience that meant he could sit there for hours, just waiting for her to finally spill. But Sylvie hated to waste his time like that, so she ripped off the Band-Aid and immediately launched into the whole sordid tale.

Being stood up by Dustin.

The convergence of Fisher and his minions.

How they stole her LARP binder and tossed it in the trash can.

Her whole body shaking, Sylvie drew her knees to her chest beneath her blanket, the beanbag sighing gently, and waited for her dad to say something.

He rubbed a hand through his brown hair, which had been matted into weird, forked lines by the hard hat he wore all day at work (there was a reason he rocked a ball cap after-hours). His fingers then moved to scratch at the stubble lining his chin as if in thought.

Finally, he said, "Maybe it's a good thing you can't LARP this summer, Syl-Bear. It'll give you a chance to try new things."

Talk about a stake through the heart.

"I don't want to try new things."

"Come on, sure you do! Isn't that the point of LARP-ing anyway? To have an adventure?"

Sylvie's mind answered: *Yeah, as a vampire.*

But Sylvie knew her dad didn't want to hear that.

Instead, she ran her tongue over her fangs and shrugged. Her fingers scrambled to the crescent moon at her throat. She held on for dear life to that little piece of silver as her dad talked through his thoughts, all of which centered on the idea that Sylvie shouldn't spend every minute of her free time pretending to be the undead.

"Right? It is," he said, answering his own question. "Let's figure out a way for you to have an adventure this summer."

When Sylvie didn't say anything, her dad slipped his hat back on his head and leaned toward her, his big, dusty elbows propped up on his big, dusty work jeans.

"Don't you want to do more than just sit in your room, watching the same movies for the thousandth time?" He gestured to the TV as if it were exhibit A in why Sylvie needed to get out more. "How many times have you seen this one? At least eight million viewings, right? Maybe eight million and two?"

Sylvie rolled her eyes.

"Dad, that's physically impossible."

"I don't know, my Syl-Bear is pretty special. If anyone could do it, it's her." He scrunched up his nose, and all his stubble scrunched with it. "That said, repetition isn't exactly an adventure."

Sylvie nearly snorted—he was totally showing his cards that he didn't know the first thing about adventure. Sylvie had definitely gotten that knowledge from her mom, along with every single iota of monster love. "Dad, quests are all about repeated forward movement."

Sylvie unpaused the TV. Wednesday Addams's revenge roared to life in a screaming chaos of burning torches and confused parents.

"How about camp?" he asked, very pointedly looking at Sylvie's little TV, but clearly only seeing Camp Chippewa and not the fact that Wednesday and Pugsley Addams had just put it to flame.

"Dad, have you ever watched this movie?" Sylvie cried, gesturing to the smoke on the screen. "They hated camp and destroyed it after pretending to cooperate. Would you like to set me up to be an arsonist?"

"It's a movie. It's not real life, Sylvie."

He tapped his temple. As if her brain couldn't tell the difference. Sylvie frowned.

"That's exactly why I want you to go to a camp, Syl-Bear." Her dad's voice was all hoarse, and he was looking at her with those big gray eyes and leaning so far forward in his chair, he might tip into Magnus's snoring jelly roll of a body. "I know you love your movies and your LARP-ing, but all of that's make believe. You need to make real memories with real kids and real fun."

Suddenly, the tears were back, threatening Sylvie's eyeballs. "Dad, I just told you all about the real, terrible memories I made today with real, terrible kids in real, terrible time."

Her voice was pitchy and hot, and the second she was done, that lump in Sylvie's throat rolled back into her windpipe, and she heaved. Tears formed faster.

"Well, those kids from the park won't be at whatever camp you pick. I'll make sure of it." Her dad was confident, but Sylvie frowned. "You don't know it, but you could have a new best friend out there, just waiting to meet you. All you have to do is show up and be yourself."

It was on the tip of Sylvie's tongue to tell him that being herself was exactly what had gotten her in trouble today. The real Sylvie was her fangs and her widow's peak and quests laid out neatly in a LARP. It was part of the reason she hadn't ever made up some funny LARP name like "Dustin, Knight of the Night," because "Sylvie the Vampire" was Sylvie.

But then something truly spine-tingling hit Sylvie square on the nose.

"Dad, why are you so sure about camp being good for me?"

He immediately blushed. Her dad's poker face was absolutely terrible.

"I may have done some research before I got home from work."

He stood up, left the room, and came back far too quickly with a mound of brochures. He dropped them on Sylvie's blanket-covered lap like some benevolent LARP king doling out a sack of gold upon completion of a quest.

There had to be at least thirty brochures. The one on the top of the pile featured a photo of a kid who looked enough like Dustin to make her relive the unpleasant memory of him ditching her all over again.

"Where . . . where did you get so many of these? So quickly?"

"A couple came in the mail. The rest I got from the library." He put his hands on his hips, clearly super proud to share this. "They have a whole trove of summer-fun brochures up at the front. Did you know that? I had no idea until Lara told me."

The cheese sandwich in Sylvie's gut bottomed out.

Lara. Of course Lara knew that.

Lara was her dad's friend from high school who owned the ice-cream shop next to the Evermore clock-tower. Ever since her dad had reconnected with Lara after

Sylvie's mom's death, it seemed like if there was one person who popped into Sylvie's life like an ever-present, nonplaying character, it was Lara.

Sylvie swallowed. She couldn't even be mad because she loved the library.

Her dad shifted his weight, and Sylvie knew this conversation was over before he confirmed it. "Welp, I'm about eighty-percent sawdust and twenty-percent sweat. I'm gonna take a shower, and while I do that, you're gonna take a look at those brochures." That didn't feel like a fair split. "Just have a look-see. It might make you feel better, Syl-Bear."

Sylvie had a hard time believing that.

CHAPTER 4

Monster Camp: A Place to Be Yourself

Her door newly shut and her dad rummaging around his room down the hall, Sylvie unfolded from her beanbag chair and dumped herself and the brochures onto her bed.

Magnus couldn't hop up on the bed himself—short-dog problems—and whined until Sylvie hoisted him up. Being a Cardigan corgi, he also couldn't curl into a ball because his spine just didn't bend like that, so he wound himself into a bread loaf, his nose pointed toward his toes at the foot of the bed.

Sylvie arranged herself cross-legged on the opposite end, her back propped against her pillow and the headboard, the brochures fanned out in front of her bare feet.

A shiny picture of a space shuttle caught her eye first. While it would've been cool to bum around in a simulation of zero gravity, Sylvie was sure that space camp would likely involve lots of math. Ew.

Next, she snagged on the survivalist-camp brochure that had been on top. It touted "real-life skills" and "high-adventure" and some sort of special "hunting expedition" for those taking some extra-long two-week course. The only combination of skills, adventure, and expedition Sylvie was interested in was the purely fictional sort.

On the far right of the rainbow of brochures, there was one covered in exaggerated-smiling-and-frowning theatre masks and a picture of a bunch of kids in silly costumes bowing on stage. Sylvie picked it up, examining their heavily painted faces and earnest expressions. With a sigh, she opened the trifold. Acting was a little like live-action role-play. Sort of. You got to play a character. To be somebody else for a while.

But . . . it was like comparing a chocolate chip cookie to an oatmeal raisin one. From afar, they looked similar, but in practice, they were completely different. And depending on your tastes, either could be a complete and total letdown. (Sylvie was team chocolate chip, for the record.)

Still, it might be fun. And perhaps she could get some ideas to flesh out her quests. Or something. Sylvie set that one on Magnus's tail to keep it separate from the others. It was a maybe.

As Sylvie settled back against the headboard, something black caught her eye. It'd been wedged under the drama one and some sort of "rodeo skills" extravaganza.

Her fingers brushed the paper, and she was surprised at the strangely silky texture.

Fully exposed to the light, Sylvie saw now that the brochure was upside down, the back facing her, labeled with her name and address written out in delicate, beautiful handwriting.

That was a surprise, indeed.

"Huh," Sylvie said to both no one and Magnus, who flicked an ear.

Just below the address label was a sticker, sealing it closed in a super good impression of berry-colored stamped wax. It was even raised and irregular and felt like candle drippings.

It looked like the letters MC.

Something about the fact that it was addressed to her—not her dad, nor "Current Resident"—made Sylvie's heart flutter. When she turned it over, it stopped beating altogether.

Because there, in pearly white type, glittering with the force of a hundred stars, were the words "Monster Camp."

With a high-pitched gasp, Sylvie's heart kicked back into motion, a new and steady drumbeat in her chest.

Fingers tingling, Sylvie scrambled for the seal. It fell away in an easy crumble, wax—real wax—scattering on her comforter. As the trifold unfurled in her hands, Sylvie's jaw dropped.

MONSTER CAMP: A PLACE TO BE YOURSELF

Her eyes flew over the text, the words jamming into her eyeballs faster than Sylvie could read them.

> *Spend a week with other monster*
> *friends . . .*
> *All monsters will experience adventure*
> *away from home . . .*
> *Sleep as a monster! Eat as a monster! Play*
> *as a monster! No humans allowed!*

Amid all the words were several small pictures of literal monsters doing literal camp things.

Hiking in the woods.

Crowding around a campfire.

Cheesy smiles on the side of a dock, feet dangling in a misty body of water.

Some kids wore full Frankenstein's-monster face paint; some bandages as mummies; a couple of witches huddled over a pottery wheel, clearly making little baby clay cauldrons together.

Under the photo of someone in a skeleton costume was a caption that read: *Our groundbreaking HURT program instructors will train, prepare, and role-play with all campers to ensure better experiences back home.*

Sylvie stared at the word "role-play."

As in live-action role-play?! At this camp she could LARP. For an entire week.

Goosebumps climbed Sylvie's arms. She suddenly straightened with a jolt.

If she was going to camp, this was it.

In the bottom right-hand corner was a neat listing of dates. According to the brochure, there were different weeks for various age groups, and the dates for rising seventh graders were . . . next week! Running Sunday through Sunday!

That was so quick, so soon . . . but there had to be a spot for her. There *had* to be.

This was meant to be!

Sylvie gripped the smooth black brochure tightly with both thumbs and forefingers, extremely concerned it would just—*POOF*—vanish from her grasp.

Without delay, while it was still whole and real in her hands, Sylvie staggered out of bed. Magnus lifted his head in question but let her go without a single yelp of "Help me down, Sylvie!" because even he knew it was crucial she show her dad this glorious piece of paper right away.

On shaking legs, Sylvie crossed her room. The entire hallway was heavy with shower steam and smelled of her dad's old-man soap, the bathroom door hanging open. His bedroom door was shut.

But then, because every single bit of this felt like it was meant to be, the door yawned open before Sylvie even raised a hand to knock.

"This one! I want to do this one! It starts Sunday. Can you call and make sure I have a spot? Or I could call! Maybe they want prospective campers to call?"

"Whoa, whoa, there." He brandished one placating hand while adjusting the hem of his shirt so it didn't crinkle weirdly out over the drawstring of his sweatpants. "Hold on, let me see."

Sylvie struggled to unclench her grip on the brochure so that her dad could read it. Taking the silky black paper, her dad flipped it around to inspect the description and pictures inside.

In real, excruciating time, Sylvie watched as his face sank from open and joyous to pinched and concerned. Suddenly, his whole expression was a flat line of trying not to show he was angry.

Which surprised Sylvie.

Finally, he said, "I'd remember this one. I didn't pick this up. Where'd you get this?"

His voice was all weird and controlled, and when Sylvie spoke again, so was hers. Like walking on eggshells and she didn't know why, exactly.

"It was in the pile. I didn't conjure it or anything." Sylvie flipped it over. "Dad, it has my name on it."

"Oh, so it does."

The way he said it, Sylvie had a feeling he'd seen it before—and hadn't expected to see it again.

"Syl-Bear, I'm sorry to get your hopes up, but a camp

where you pretend to be a monster all week is the exact opposite of why we're doing this." His gray eyes lifted to hers and there was a sigh heavy in the cut of his shoulders.

Those eggshells under her feet shattered anyway, and suddenly, Sylvie wasn't being careful anymore. She was being reckless.

"But Dad!" she whined. "It's *exactly* what I want to do. Look, it came to me! Maybe they found out about my LARPing site. I'm up to thirty-eight subscribers, you know."

"I do know because I get an email every time someone subscribes, so I can make sure they're not a creep." Her dad waved a hand. "The point is that I'm sorry to let you down, but you can go to any camp but that one, Syl."

"Why?"

His answer was immediate. Almost as if it had been rehearsed, even though her dad most definitely couldn't act to save his life.

"I want you to be yourself, Sylvie, I mean that from here to the moon and back—but you're also my little girl, Mom's little girl, and it's my job to protect you. Sylvie, you're a normal girl, with normal thoughts and feelings, and you need to get used to life as a boring old human." It was meant to be a balm, but it hurt. "The sooner you come to terms with the fact that you're not a vampire, no matter how much you pretend to be, the better your actual life will get, Syl. That's the tough truth of it."

To Sylvie's horror, her dad crumpled the beautiful silky paper into a ball and tossed it over his shoulder to the wastebasket by the desk he had wedged in his bedroom.

Sylvie gaped after the brochure.

"Dad!"

She tried to get past him, but he blocked the door and her view of the trash.

"Leave it, Sylvie."

She reared back, arms wound about her body, tears suddenly hot in her eyes at the indignity of it all. "Dad, that's not fair!"

Her voice was so high she was sure Magnus lifted his head.

"It might not be, but it's my rules." He thrust a blunt hand in the general direction of her bedroom. "There are two dozen good camps in there where you can make friends and focus all that creative energy toward something *real*."

His voice was fraught, and his eyes were big gray orbs of pleading. Which just made Sylvie's heart sink further, because why was he begging her? It was his idea! And she was the one with the right to beg. Because she didn't want to go!

After a tense pause, he said, "Just think about it."

Sylvie *had* thought about it.

Why couldn't he see that? She'd spelled it out for him.

But maybe he couldn't see it because he didn't *want* to.

Her dad took Sylvie's silence as contemplation. Unfortunately.

"I'll tell you what. How about I pick out the camp for you?"

"Dad."

"Or we can do a blind draw. Where's that old black witch hat you made Magnus wear last Halloween? Your closet?" His voice was lifting as he described the whole silly, stupid idea. "We can stuff the brochures inside and choose one. Fair and square."

"Dad."

He jabbed her with a finger, trying to lighten the mood. "Oooh, or we can fold them up into little paper planes and the one that travels the farthest down the hall wins."

"Dad." This time Sylvie said it with a sigh attached. He straightened accordingly, ready to listen to an actual sentence instead of a plea. "I'll pick the camp myself."

"From the brochures I got you."

Sylvie swallowed.

"From the brochures you got me."

Her dad seemed satisfied with that answer. He nodded and leaned forward from the doorway to palm her head like he used to do when Sylvie was much smaller and had bangs that fell into her eyes. Now the move just conveniently (for him) covered up her drawn-on widow's peak. "Great. I've got an early site call tomorrow, but I should be able to be home for a quick lunch. How about a decision then? That way, I can make sure you have a spot with time to spare?"

Rather reluctantly, Sylvie nodded into his palm.

"Good girl." He removed his hand. "Okay, how about something to eat? Dad's special dinner pancakes or Dad's special Pizza Tito's delivery?"

"Pancakes," Sylvie answered. It was more fang friendly, and Pizza Tito's always added extra garlic, much to a little vampire's dismay. Perhaps that was why her dad liked it so much.

The Way to
Monster Camp

Pancakes were yummy, but after enough maple syrup to call her plate both dinner and dessert, Sylvie's mind was racing. The finish line: finding a way to get to Monster Camp.

If there was anything that LARPing with Dustin had taught Sylvie, it was to not give up easily. If Dustin had his monster-slaying way, every single LARP she'd done with him would've been over in thirty seconds flat.

And so, hopped up on both gumption and grade A maple syrup, Sylvie decided that it wasn't time yet to give up on her Monster Camp dream.

Step one: retrieving the brochure.

Luckily, her dad ate his pancakes not with sugar-packed syrup but with a boatload of butter and nearly an entire package of turkey bacon, which meant that the meal had almost the same effect as a large Thanksgiving feast.

Add in the fact that he was totally zonked from a ten-hour construction shift in the new summer heat, and he was asleep on the couch before seven, sprawled out in front of some baseball game he'd wanted to watch. Which only reinforced Sylvie's belief that baseball was the most boring of all the sports.

But in that moment, she thanked the baseball gods for being so very boring, because on bare feet, she walked very silently into her dad's room and plucked the Monster Camp brochure out of his trash.

Of course, Magnus found this very interesting and wasn't quiet at all in trailing Sylvie, his nails click-clacking loudly on the scuffed wood floors. Worse, when she picked up the pace to her room, the dog thought it was a game and decided to both chase and bark after her.

"Shhhhhhhhhh," Sylvie commanded, finger to her lips, while herding her herding dog into her room. With one breathless glance down the turn of the stairs to the couch, she confirmed her dad was still a drooly pile of bones and sealed herself and Magnus into her room with the soft click of the big wooden door latching shut.

Happy to be with Sylvie, Magnus immediately gave up the chase and the cacophony that came with it and simply went to his favorite spot by the beanbag and lay down like the good boy he was. Which left Sylvie with an opening as long as her dad's evening catnap to investigate how to make Monster Camp happen.

Step two: mark down the dates and location of Monster Camp.

Step three: hide the brochure in her desk for safekeeping.

(Hopefully her dad didn't have a habit of riffling through his trash. Sylvie was pretty sure he was too busy to do that.)

The dates and location carefully noted, Sylvie next grabbed all the pamphlets from her bed and separated them into two piles. The ones with dates that corresponded with Monster Camp went to her right, the ones with dates that didn't overlap to her left. When she was done, only five camps were on her right.

Step four: find one nearby.

Sylvie's laptop was the kind that was pretty much only good for browsing the Internet, and she used it almost exclusively for her LARPing blog aka the one that her dad monitored with an iron fist and his email account.

Bringing up a new tab, she typed in the address for Monster Camp. According to Google, it was only five miles away! Just past the edge of the Evermore city limits, out toward the creek that divided Evermore from Frankensport, on an unmarked plot of land.

Next, Sylvie typed in each address for the remaining five camps on the right: drama camp, survivalist camp, engineering camp, basket-weaving camp, and robot-battle camp.

Drama camp: all the way on the other side of Evermore.

Survivalist camp: right next door to Monster Camp (of course).

Engineering camp: downtown, way too close to Lara's ice-cream shop.

Basket-weaving camp: in the park where Sylvie's worst day of summer had happened just hours ago.

Robot-battle camp: in the basement of the church down the street.

Sylvie stared at her results. With a long sigh, she picked up the survivalist-camp brochure. It didn't look any more appetizing than it had hours ago.

HUNT OR BE HUNTED! THE MIGHTY
SLAY TO WIN!

Most of the pictures were of oily kids in camo face paint and fatigues, holding things like crossbows and batons. But the worst were the ones of the same kids without face paint, posing with trout speared in a stream. Just smug triumph and panicked fish eyes staring out from the page.

Ew.

Even more disgusting to Sylvie was the list of activities, all of them slightly normal but then twisted with the same sort of *SLAY 3000* flourish Dustin would drone on about while hatching new ways to "kill" his vampire acquaintance.

Zip line into attack!

Shoot arrows with real points!

Camouflage and ambush techniques for

beginners to advanced SLAYers!

With a deep breath, Sylvie double-checked the dates. Yep, a beginner session started on Sunday. The same day as Monster Camp. And, according to a zoomed-in Google Earth snapshot, the only thing separating them was a small stretch of forest.

There was no denying it now. The way to Monster Camp was through the survivalist camp next door.

It wouldn't be that easy, of course. There was the matter of registration. And payment. And, well, the fact that she would be lying to her dad before coming clean with a bill and the truth at the end of the week.

But . . .

Sylvie touched her crescent-moon necklace.

Her mom would've let her go to Monster Camp. She would've understood. Her dad didn't understand now, but maybe he would afterward.

There was only one way to find out.

Sylvie's Monster Camp Plan: Phase 1

Sylvie's dad was pleased as punch.

Ecstatic.

Thrilled.

All the adjectives that Mr. Wooten encouraged them to use in sixth-grade English class—that not only had Sylvie picked a camp, but it would give her real live skills for her real live life.

Before Sylvie knew it, her dad was digging out the old duffel bag he used for his fishing trips "with the boys" before her mom died and gave Sylvie forty dollars cash to take to the grocery store for supplies.

Over the course of the next week, Sylvie very carefully packed the necessities for camp.

Stick-on fangs—check.

Trusty waterproof eyeliner pen—check.

Fruit-punch packets—check.

"You Suck" tumbler—check.

Three dog-eared LARPing manuals—check.

LARP binder—check.

Favorite vampire novels—check.

Backpack for camp activities—check.

Matching outfits of black jean shorts and black tank tops—check.

Bathing suit, towel, underwear, socks, umbrella, and all the other stuff—check.

She arranged all her vampire "contraband" along the bottom of the duffel and smothered it in clothes and jackets and the umbrella and everything else so that by the time her dad was shoving last-minute items (SPF 90! Bug spray! Band-Aids! Protein bars because, well, survivalist things!) at her, everything was perfectly covered.

Honestly, it was all so easy that Sylvie felt really, really guilty as her dad was helping her heave the bag into the car.

"What do you have in here?" he gritted out. "Magnus?"

The corgi barked helpfully right at that moment. He was perched precariously on the back of the couch, where he wasn't allowed, watching them load Sylvie's massive bag into the extended cab of her dad's pickup truck, parked in the street.

"Oh, I guess not," her dad said with a laugh and a shooing gesture at the dog, who absolutely did not get off the couch. But as they both buckled in, he sighed, Adam's apple bobbing as he tried to smile at her. It didn't reach his eyes. "I'm going to miss you, Syl-Bear."

That guilt of hers started to climb Sylvie's throat. Very quietly, her gaze pinned to her pale hands resting in her lap, she answered, "I'm going to miss you too, Dad."

And she would.

Though she was still going to go through with her plan.

Sylvie had never liked lying very much and most definitely didn't like lying to her dad. But in this case, it was the best for both of them. She was sure of it.

They rode in silence for much of the drive, listening to her dad's favorite classic-rock station as they made their way across town and toward the rolling hills by the river. Predictably, when the opening strains of Warren Zevon's "Werewolves of London" came on, Sylvie decided to talk over it. The world really needed more songs about vampires. Werewolves were just plainly inferior. Sylvie didn't want to hear Warren sing about werewolves meeting the Queen, and so she decided to strike up a conversation.

"So, what are you going to do until next Sunday?"

"Um, well, I thought I might get in a few extra shifts."

Not a huge surprise. If the weather was good and Sylvie was taken care of, he could make almost twice as much in a week as normal. Money didn't come as easily without two parents working. Not to mention her dad was picking up the tab for Sylvie's allowance (aka her fang money) and therapy visits for the anxiety that crept up in the years after her mom's sudden, accidental death.

"And," he continued, "I'm taking Lara to a play in Frankensport."

Sylvie froze.

"It's just one night—"

"Wait? Like, you won't be at home?"

"Well, yes, the play won't get out until late, and I thought it might be fun to stay at a nice hotel downtown. We've never done that before."

No. They certainly hadn't. Sylvie wrenched around and gaped at her dad, who was totally blushing. For real.

Every scant iota of guilt evaporated from Sylvie's body. Her dad was using her absence as an opportunity to take Lara, who was not even close to being nearly as cool as her mom, to a sleepover at a hotel. In another city! They probably weren't even going to a play. Her dad was somebody who thought Mr. Bean was high art.

"Don't be mad, Syl. It's a totally normal thing for adults to do. And Mr. Mortimer is already on board to check on Magnus, so he'll be fine."

The dog. Sylvie hadn't even thought about Magnus. Her dad was betraying both her and the dog. For *Lara*. The only good thing about Lara was the pints of free ice cream lining their Deepfreeze.

Dad either very much read Sylvie's anger correctly and tried to smooth things over or misjudged it entirely and plowed ahead. "See, we're both doing new things."

Sylvie wanted to scream.

Before she could, the pickup slowed, little bulbs of gravel flinging themselves against the undercarriage as they came to a turnoff. As Sylvie's dad bumped around the turn and pointed the truck down a well-treed drive, a large wooden sign with ridiculous camo-painted block letters came into view.

CAMP SLAY SURVIVAL TRAINING.

"Um, let me out here, please?"

"I can drive you up, Syl." He gestured with a big, calloused hand to a flagpole ahead. "That's got to be a quarter mile, and your bag weighs as much as you do. Don't be ridiculous."

But Sylvie was already unbuckling her seatbelt. He couldn't drop her up there, because then he'd insist on helping her check in or at least loiter long enough to see her get her paperwork and her cabin key and wave.

For emphasis, Sylvie rolled her eyes. "Dad, I can do it. This is survivalist camp. They'd probably see me as weak if you drop me off and lug my bag." The way he nodded without a second glance from the road made it seem like he was buying it. "I didn't pack what I couldn't carry. You wanted me to have this experience, and I want to start now."

In answer, he pulled in a U to face the opposite direction, back toward the main road, and parked along the side of the drive. The truck dipped sideways a little as it pulled half onto the grassy ditch that bled into the very same trees that separated the survivalist camp from Monster Camp.

They both got out, and Sylvie made a beeline for her massive bag, hauling it over her shoulder before her dad even got around the back bumper to offer.

She slammed the door shut and turned to him, and it might have been a trick of the trees waving in the afternoon light, but Sylvie was pretty sure she saw his eyes mist over a little bit. He tugged at his ball cap and then bent down and opened his big ol' arms for a big ol' hug.

Sylvie wrapped her arms around as much of his middle as she could manage. He wasn't a small guy. She buried her face in his shirt, the goopy film of SPF 90 he'd insisted upon sticking to the cotton of his worn T-shirt.

"I'm going to miss you, Syl-Bear," her dad said, his voice rumbling against the ear she had pressed to his barrel chest. "But this week will be good for you. And me, I think."

"Yeah." It wasn't the most elegant answer, but Sylvie couldn't find much more to say around the lump forming in her throat.

Her dad was the one to pull away first, but not before dropping a kiss onto her dark hair, and then placing his palm there like he did the night this started and meeting her eyes from an arm's length away.

"I love you, and I'll see you Sunday."

"Love you too, Dad."

He drew his keys from his pocket and backed away, around the truck. Sylvie adjusted the duffel strap, which was already cutting into the skin of her shoulder, and made sure he could glimpse her "happy camper" grin in the side mirror.

The pickup roared to life. Then, with a wave of a big hand out of a rolled-down window and a puff of exhaust, Sylvie's dad was gone.

CHAPTER 7

Sylvie's Monster Camp Plan: Phase 2

Sylvie was as prepared as she'd ever be for Monster Camp.

Fangs on—straight and sharp.

Widow's peak—defined and pointy.

Skin—extra pale thanks to the ghostly cast of the thick layer of sunscreen that her dad gooped on her face and arms before they'd even left the house.

She was crouched in the thin leg of forest that ran between the survivalist camp and her intended location. This place was full of shadows, slithering fog, and too many pine needles, but it gave Sylvie the time and space to become her monster self. Satisfied, Sylvie dropped the small compact she'd used to double-check her handiwork into her bag and took a deep breath to ease the annoying and persistent pang of guilt rising yet again in her gut.

With one more deep breath in, Sylvie wiped two

clammy palms on her black jean shorts, swallowed hard, and hoisted the duffel onto her shoulder. As she pulled herself out of her tight crouch behind her chosen tree, the massive bag thumped against her hip, the two dozen fruit-punch pouches swishing faintly from within. Whole lot of good the extra pillowcase she'd wrapped them in did in muffling the sloshing. Good thing she'd convinced her dad she could schlep all her own things independently.

As she moved in the direction of Monster Camp, a new mist of cold sweat seemed to replace what she'd just rubbed off her palms, and Sylvie placed a hand to her tummy in an effort to calm the rising panic there.

Her brain swirled with everything she didn't know.

What if they wouldn't let her in?

What if they frog-marched her over to Camp SLAY like a fugitive?

What if they called her dad?

With each step, panic soon replaced guilt, her muscles growing as cold as her hands. Her normally trusty Converse clipped rocks and roots as she failed to pick up her feet. Sylvie paused, closed her eyes, and scrabbled for her crescent-moon necklace. The moment her skin touched the metal, she felt steady enough to take in a deep breath.

Then, as her therapist had told her to do when the questions came, she answered them.

What if they wouldn't let her in? She wouldn't go in.

What if they frog-marched her over to Camp SLAY like

a fugitive? Then she would be at a camp where she was registered.

What if they called her dad? She would tell him the truth and ask him to pick her up.

None of it was ideal, but it also wasn't the end of the world. If Sylvie didn't get to be there, if she didn't want to be where she ended up, she could always go home.

Feeling a little stronger, if not still a little nervous, Sylvie dropped the pendant back against her throat and forced herself to march three big steps forward. The movement brought her through the trees and into the light of a driveway clearing on the other side.

Sylvie blinked hard, eyes adjusting. First, she spotted a big gate spanning the gravel. It was shut, even with the open drop-off time. Pivoting, she looked up the drive to a long, wooden Lincoln Logs structure. A big painted sign marked it as the administration building.

Hiking up her bag, Sylvie ignored the new pounding in her heart, tipped her chin up, and pointed herself in the direction of the administration building. As she got closer, she saw that there was a little folding table positioned out front, under the shade of a giant maple. Atop the table sat a smaller sign, like one would have at a lemonade stand: CHECK-IN.

And behind the table was . . . a skeleton?

Not like the kind that ran around at Halloween in sweat suits with bones painted on. Even at a distance, Sylvie could tell that it was a costume much, much better than that. It had to have been the skeleton she'd seen in the brochure.

She walked closer, trying not to stare. But . . . it was just super cool.

Sylvie was about ten feet away when the adult heard her approach, glancing up from the paperwork spread out neatly before them.

It had real human eyes behind its orbital bones, but . . . the rest of it was see-through. Literally all Sylvie could see was a skeleton. No hidden regular-person body beyond the bones. No, it camouflaged perfectly into the chair in some sort of costumed illusion that made this person, in this position, appear to be the kind of skeleton science teachers like Ms. Crouch hung up at the back of the class for display.

"Ah, hello!" they said, that skeletal face not smiling, exactly—the bones were just as rigid as regular bone would be, no muscles pulling the strings to make a smile—but friendly in look and tone, nonetheless. "Welcome to Monster Camp! I'm Amos."

A talking skeleton.

This had to be one of the coolest LARP costumes Sylvie had ever seen in person or in pictures. She knew adults LARPed, but this . . . this was another level. It was like staring into a 3D special effect but not at a movie theater.

When Sylvie's mouth dropped open at his greeting, and no sound came out, Amos tilted his head and prompted softly, "And what's your name, camper?"

"Um, Sylvie. Sylvie Shaw."

Amos immediately began to thumb through a stack of packets.

And Sylvie began to sweat.

She'd created a story for exactly this scenario—what she'd say when he couldn't find her name—yet it was all jumbled now as she watched his bony fingers dig through the remaining packets to the last half of the alphabet.

"Ah," he said, pinching a large manila folder from the pile. "Sylvie, we're glad you finally decided to join us this year."

What? That sounded like they'd *expected* her?

Confused, Sylvie just stared at her name as Amos flipped the packet around so it faced her. There, at the top, in beautiful shiny black were the words:

Sylvie Shaw, age eleven.

In her shock, Sylvie's mind launched into a sprint. Had they sent her brochures before but she'd missed them in years past? She'd thought they found her through her LARP blog, but she'd only launched that in computer class in January, so that couldn't be.

None of it made sense but . . .

But this is exactly what you want.

Before the packet could vanish, Sylvie snatched it up.

To her surprise, the skeleton laughed. It was a jolly sound and made his whole organless torso shake. "Well, I see you're eager to join us, Sylvie."

It occurred to Sylvie then to maybe use her words. She hugged the paperwork to her chest. "Yes, yes, I am."

Amos gave her yet another approximation of a grin. Grandma Marcy had always insisted a real smile was in the eyes, and Sylvie had never seen a better example than that very moment.

"And we're happy to have you, Sylvie. Now, inside that packet, you'll find your camper's guide, along with a lanyard and name tag. I'll also need to give you one of these. . . ." Amos held out something else: a little ring with a single key that looked like it was made of stone. Sylvie reached for it, but Amos pulled it back. Sylvie's heart pounded. Had he realized she wasn't signed up after all? "Wait a minute. Something's not right here."

Sylvie opened her mouth, ready to try whatever she needed to convince him to let her in. But before she could say anything, Amos continued, "You look to me like you're a vampire, correct?" Sylvie froze, then quickly shut her mouth and nodded. "Our mistake. You'll be needing this one instead!" He took back the stone key and offered a single old-fashioned key instead, the big kind with a long barrel and teeth. "You'll be in Cabin No. 7."

Heart singing, Sylvie accepted the key and slipped it into the pocket of her shorts.

"Do you need help with your bag?"

With the question, Amos half stood, allowing Sylvie to see straight through to his spine where his stomach should've been. It seemed like a really cruel thing to ask a full-grown adult wearing such an elaborate costume to haul around her heavy bag.

"Um, no. I've got it."

Sylvie added a nice smile with fangs, hoping he would understand that she was just feeling shy, not totally shell-shocked. Even though that's what she was. In the best way.

"Of course you do."

To her relief, Amos sank back into his chair. He pointed to a little path that branched out from behind his table and wound around the administration building. "Follow that path. You'll see signs to the cabins, but if you get lost, there's a map in your packet. Or ask anyone here. Everyone is friendly, even the ones with fangs. But I think you already know that."

Amos winked at her—well, as best he could. His pupil just kind of dipped and disappeared for a second. But it was definitely a wink.

CHAPTER 8

Welcome
to Monster Camp!

Sylvie Shaw, wannabe vampire, was in monster-LARP-nerd heaven.

Actually, she didn't know if vampires even believed in a life after second death. She'd have to add that to her character sheet. But whatever the answer, Monster Camp was *perfection*.

Clutching the orientation packet from Amos tightly to her chest, Sylvie stepped out from the creeping shadow of the administration building. The sight that sprawled out before her was so marvelous, her sneakers skidded to a complete halt, and she was quite sure her eyebrows were raised high enough to tap the point of her drawn-on widow's peak.

It was like she'd taken a right turn into a spooktacular utopia.

Though the sun was just as high and bright as a

moment before, everything under this sun on these grounds was like a modern Brothers Grimm tale on steroids.

To Sylvie's right was a gorgeous lake, obsidian and shimmering like spilled ink. Sharp rocks edged the water like crooked teeth, before both the rocks and the water disappeared into a shroud of mist so thick, it was practically sentient. Actually, it might have been sentient, because there was definitely some sort of shadowy movement going on over there.

Spread out front was a common area, nearly as large as the lake itself. Studded with games of all kinds—a chessboard with life-sized pieces; basketball courts with smiling skeleton heads where the lines and paint should be; sand volleyball and tennis courts rigged with spiderweb netting and super-sized, lifelike tarantulas weighing down the corners; soccer and softball fields with a thick layer of mist covering every inch of the ground save for the lines, goal boxes, and bases.

And studded across the common: kids.

Kids in the most amazing costumes Sylvie had ever seen.

Everywhere she turned were monsters her age—laughing and shrieking and just plain *playing* under the wide blue sky.

Sylvie's heart double-beat as it swelled to a new and bigger size.

It was all so overwhelming that Sylvie dropped her

duffel. She tried to compartmentalize, to use all the tricks her therapist had taught her for when the world was too much all at once. To focus on one small thing at a time and move on, methodical and logical, but instead, she just found herself gaping in awe.

A Frankenstein's monster was green and grinning while at home base on the softball field. He held what looked to be a taxidermic bat—as in the mammal in the shape of the wooden baseball thing—hitched at his shoulder, ready to swing but too busy cracking up enough to nearly bust his stitches with a fairy. She was on the pitcher's mound, as blue as the sky, dressed in a gown as glittery as the North Star, grinning in a way that totally made her teeth seem razor-sharp. She wound up to pitch but before she let go of the ball, some sort of mechanism shot water straight out of the sapphire fingertips of her free hand.

She wasn't a fairy—she was a water sprite.

The monster boy squealed and ducked too late, getting nailed square in the face with a blast of water. Giggling as rivulets ran from his sopping hair and into his eyes, he didn't even raise his bat as she pitched the ball right past him, a strike. Not only was the overall effect magnificent, but their makeup didn't smear or fade. Impressive application!

A new peal of laughter swung Sylvie's attention to the far left. There, three werewolves and three witches were playing sand volleyball in *full* costume.

The ball soared over the spiderweb netting, all six players shuttling about in the ash-gray, glittering sand. They leapt and dove and generally appeared not to give a single care in the world as to how long it would take to get all that sand out of paste-on hair (the werewolves were mighty hairy indeed) or other tight spots.

The single boy witch—warlock?—went to serve, hovering in the air for just long enough it almost looked like he was *flying*. The ball careened over the net at a nasty angle that forced a black-haired werewolf in a backward Seattle Kraken hat to rocket laterally to put a hand on it. He sent it back over without a pass to his teammates. The move surprised the witches, and the ball dropped to the court between them, earning him a point. The werewolves' side exploded in a round of high-fives and exclamations.

Sylvie's awe ballooned to joy.

For a whole week, Sylvie would quest, play-fight, improve her character skills, and hone attributes with real live monster-loving LARPers.

Monster Camp was a dream. *Her* dream.

And that made Sylvie's swollen heart tremble with a pang of nervousness, sudden and vicious. Her stomach knotted. Her exuberance shrunk back.

Would she fit in?

As impressed as Sylvie was, she was suddenly worried her stick-on fangs and lined widow's peak seemed a little underdone—though she was so thankful she'd taken the time to apply them in the woods on her hike over.

Clearly no one in here walked around out of character, even if they were all dressed for camp. The werewolves wore swooshy basketball shorts, tank tops, and sneakers. And two of them had what looked like matching(?) silver bracelets. The witches' costumes made Sylvie feel a bit less out of place. They weren't in robes, and they didn't have hats or pet toads or anything either. They simply wore just enough bracelets and beads to signal characterization. That flying trick didn't hurt either, of course.

But like being a witch, being a vampire wasn't about the costume: it was about the subtle touches and the characterization to back it all up.

And Sylvie had character in spades.

Wiping a spot of drool from her chin, Sylvie forced her hanging jaw closed and swallowed. Her fingers went to the silver crescent-moon necklace her mother had given her, rubbing her thumb repeatedly around the moon's inner curve.

Mom, you would've loved this.

Immediately feeling calmer and more confident, that internal monster of doubt slayed for the moment, Sylvie shouldered her bag once more and checked her cabin key. Number seven.

According to one of the *many* signs laddering up the Monster Camp flagpole in the middle of the commons, the camper cabins were in the extreme northwestern quadrant of the camp. Likely, Sylvie realized, the little buildings set in the distance that backed up to the grim-dark woods encircling the camp, past the rollicking game of sand volleyball.

Sylvie set off in that direction, deciding to cut across the common to sneak a better look at all the costumes. As she got closer, she couldn't tear her eyes away from the volleyball game. A petite witch with dark skin and pink hair was serving now and seemed to have rigged some sort of illusion that made the ball in her hands appear to be *on fire*.

It was a great trick . . . but not very effective, because the moment the flaming ball sailed over the net, the backward-cap werewolf whacked it right back over the net for a point. Same strategy, same result. Wow, maybe they should stop hitting it toward that guy—

THWACK.

Sylvie suddenly had a volleyball-shaped bull's-eye of pain radiating from her upper arm. Worse, a huge hairy body came sailing in after it.

SMACK.

With his attention pointed the opposite direction, one of the werewolf boys collided with Sylvie while batting the airborne ball back into the game.

"OOOF!"

Sylvie wasn't sure if she'd made the noise or if the werewolf had. Or maybe both of them together. All she knew was that the pair of them tumbled to the grass, falling in a tangled and graceless heap over her duffel, which had slipped off her shoulder with the first impact.

Sylvie logrolled away, heart pounding and chest heaving. When her vision cleared and she spotted him again, the werewolf was in a crouch, one arm propping him up in the grass as he balanced on the balls of his giant feet.

Forcing herself to stand, Sylvie glared at him, rubbing her arm furiously while waiting for an apology from the boy—er, werewolf. Up close, he had thick, dirt-brown sideburns that devoured the majority of his cheeks before running into hair styled as neatly as a thicket of black-berry brambles. He didn't look the least bit sorry for hitting her. And when he opened his mouth, he made it very clear he had no intention of apologizing.

"Watch it, bloodsucker."

Sylvie nearly stumbled back in surprise. "Watch what? You ran into me!"

The boy straightened to his full height now. He was a head taller than Sylvie and matted with enough stick-on hair to knit several very large, very boring brown sweaters. "I was just going after the ball. You got in the way of the game."

Sylvie thrust a hand at the clearly marked court. "The sand's over there. This is grass. I wasn't in the game, and you aren't either."

The werewolf boy flashed his teeth. He didn't have fangs, exactly, but he very clearly was proud that they were naturally pointy. "Stay out of my way, vamp, or you'll wish you died for real the first time."

With that, the boy literally *snarled* at her and ran back to the game.

Not just in costume, but in character, this werewolf. And totally rude.

Werewolves and vampires were traditionally enemies in everything from comic books to cartoons to LARPing. Sylvie wasn't sure exactly why this was, but she'd always thought it absurdly aggressive and stupid on the werewolves' part. It was never a smart idea for a living creature to attack a vampire for no good reason, because they were already dead and had no qualms about making sure you would be too.

Wolf boy was lucky the LARP wasn't active, or he'd totally be dead in two seconds. Everybody knew werewolves didn't have any special powers. They were just hairy, bitey, and loud. They couldn't even fly.

Sylvie shifted her bag to her nonthrobbing shoulder, straightened the orientation packet pressed against her chest, and headed toward the cabins. And that's when she realized that even though the werewolf boy meant to be a royal jerk, he'd actually paid her a huge compliment.

He knew she was a vampire. On sight. Without a telltale costume or even a glimpse at her character sheet. And maybe even before he'd confirmed it with her flash of fang, he'd recognized exactly what she was and played his part in response.

Live-action role-play, indeed.

Vera

Cabin No. 7 was unlike any cabin Sylvie had ever seen. She'd expected a Lincoln Log–style tiny house, all wood the same boring brown as that werewolf's hair. Maybe a little chimney or a porch if she were lucky. Instead, she rubbed her eyes in disbelief.

Rather than a cabin, Sylvie's officially assigned Monster Camp residence was . . . a miniature gothic castle?

Two stories high and packed with a mishmash of pointed arches, flying buttresses, and huge stained-glass windows set on either side of a massive wooden front door, it was built of big blocks of stone—like the kind used for grave markers. Twin spires rose toward the bright June sky, a pair of grinning gargoyles perched atop their highest points, like cherries decorating a stone ice-cream sundae.

Next door, No. 6 was clearly a witches' cabin, complete with "broom parking" out front, a potions shack out back, and a massive cauldron in full view of the window overlooking a garden choked with herbs. A little black cat sat on the stoop, glaring at Sylvie like she'd already gotten the down-low on her from Gunther and did not like what she knew about her vampire neighbor.

On the other side was the final cabin of eight, a black-painted, brick two-story that sure looked like one of the haunted houses Sylvie's dad never took her to at Halloween. The windows were all broken, and the door looked like it had been cemented shut by cobwebs. Sylvie was a little surprised by this; sure, the production value was impressive, but wasn't all that jagged glass danger-ous for kids? It must have been some special holographic effect or something.

Readjusting her duffel once more, Sylvie climbed the castle steps. The ornate metalwork lock set the keyhole between the gaping jaws of a bear. She inserted the key, and with a soft click, the door swung open.

Taking a deep breath, she stepped inside.

Sylvie blinked, adjusting from the bright light of the late afternoon to this filtered version, painted in a mosaic of blues and reds that glistened across a polished stone floor.

It was empty. Which gave Sylvie proper time to drink it all in.

The castle cabin wasn't two full stories but vaulted like an actual gothic castle or cathedral. It was wallpapered, which seemed like an odd choice for a castle or even a cabin, but the pattern consisted of black birds—crows, ravens, rooks, starlings, grackles—very goth, if not gothic. At the back, a door was situated under the head of a twelve-pointed white stag, and a metalwork staircase that matched the lock spiraled up, even though Sylvie couldn't see a landing anywhere above.

And atop a roaring, black bearskin rug lay two coffins, side by side. They were polished to a high onyx shine, gold accents running around the rims and a pair of handles at the top and bottom of each. Sylvie bent to run a hand along the closest coffin. Her fingers curled around the gleaming handle, lifting it to find a soft, velvet interior fitted with a pillow and a blanket.

Sylvie swooned. *The coolest beds in the coolest cabin at the coolest camp—*

"Hi, I'm Vera."

"Argh!" Sylvie dropped her bag, her packet, and her train of thought all in that order.

It wasn't very dignified for a vampire to yelp, but she'd thought she'd been alone.

Yet there, in the middle of a room that had been empty when she'd previously inspected it, was a slip of a girl, looking like she wanted to fade into the wallpaper.

Tall and thin like a beanstalk, she had a bright shock of thick bloodred hair and skin somehow paler than Sylvie's, even with her current sunscreen mask. The girl's dark eyes were abnormally large and flared with surprise as she smiled sheepishly at Sylvie, tight-lipped and small, like she was afraid to show her teeth. "I didn't mean to scare you," the girl—Vera—said, her voice so soft it was like a wisp of smoke.

"Um, no! Sorry, you didn't. My name is Sylvie, and I don't scare." She tried to recover, but she hadn't even realized she'd thrown her arms up about her face as protection. Sylvie lowered them, her cheeks flaming in a way she couldn't disguise. With a toss of her dark hair, she purposefully flashed her fangs with a confident tip of her chin. "It's not you; I was just surprised because I was distracted . . . I just—did you know there's a mouthy werewolf out there?"

Vera didn't hesitate or ask which werewolf Sylvie had seen. Instead, she let a little tick of anger creep into her soft voice. "That's Chad."

Of course his name was Chad.

Sylvie grimaced and flopped onto the top of her coffin. It was surprisingly comfortable for polished wood. "He's decided to lean into the whole 'vampires and werewolves are mortal enemies' trope before we've even started."

"Sounds like Chad." Vera shrugged. "He was like that last year too."

Vera sank onto her own coffin lid, her butt balanced on the very edge so her bony knees came up high, and she folded her elbows on top of her kneecaps. She'd made origami out of herself, all tucks and angles. This girl seemed to have more ways of disappearing than the Invisible

Man. Maybe she needed some encouragement. "That's so cool that you've been here before. It's my first time."

Vera bit her lip. "It *is* cool . . . well, except for Chad."

Sylvie was pretty sure she could handle Chad. She'd had plenty of practice with bullies at school, of course, though she couldn't deny she was disappointed to encounter one here. And where was the game master on all this? There were rules against player-on-player abuse.

But then Vera's eyes brightened. They were the color of ash. "Maybe it'll be easier with two of us."

Sylvie smiled wide enough that there was no mistaking her expertly placed fangs. "You're a vampire too."

Vera nodded, then blushed. Even with the milk white of her skin, the color was muted and dusty. "Half vampire, actually. My dad is, but my mom's human."

Oooh, sweet backstory.

Sylvie was just about to serve up that exact compliment when she realized Vera had only paused and was still going. "Chad and some of the other kids don't like that I'm not all monster . . . and it doesn't help that my fangs haven't come in yet."

Vera presented her teeth to Sylvie. They looked just like any regular kid's. Maybe that was the problem—and a really cool solution to save money on stick-on fangs.

"Yours look amazing, by the way." Now Sylvie was the one blushing. Maybe Vera couldn't afford good fangs? The realistic ones were a little expensive after all. "I hope mine look like that."

"I'm sure they will. Mine looked like yours," Sylvie assured her, stepping into true role-playing now. "You know, before."

"My parents—well, my dad," Vera went on, softly still, "hopes that maybe just by being here, around others like us, that my monster DNA will snap to attention or something."

"You're about to get a whole week of close contact with a full-blooded vampire outside of your family," Sylvie said, latching on to Vera's personal world-building and improvising. "Surely that'll help nudge that transformation along."

Her roommate beamed. Sylvie began mentally counting the number of stick-on pairs she'd packed to see if she might be able to share some with Vera—maybe halfway through the week she could suddenly sprout fangs overnight.

"Um," Vera started, "so, can you be outside for long periods? No issues?"

The sunlight. Of course. Vera had an excuse, being half human and all, but Sylvie had already told her she was a full vampire. This was where the lore got a little fuzzy. Things would be much easier if their world-building meshed. "I'm okay with a bunch of sunscreen." She gestured at her extra pasty face. "We're far enough north."

That answer must have been good enough for Vera. "In that case, do you want to see something?"

"Sure."

Vera popped up energetically and made a beeline for the wrought-iron staircase that spiraled around the circular castle walls. Sylvie craned her neck into the shadows above, but still couldn't see another floor, even as they mounted the first step with a hollow clang and began to climb.

As the stairs creaked under their collective weight, it really did look like they were literally going nowhere, but then on the third step from the top, Vera raised her spindly arms overhead and, with a mighty shove, revealed a square of the sky above.

A trapdoor.

"This is my favorite part," Vera whispered with a quick look back that included a real, true grin, before taking the final steps in one long lunge and disappearing onto the rooftop above.

Sylvie hauled herself through the square hole, squinting hard in the fresh light. She blinked. The roof was fitted with flat black Astroturf, a wilted-rose-topped bistro table with twin chairs, and a protective parapet capped by the gargoyle-topped spires that could be seen from below.

As Sylvie pushed herself to her feet, Vera rubbed the head of each gargoyle.

"This here's George," she said with a tip of her hand to the one on the left. "And this is Ringo."

Vera had definitely warmed up.

"Like The Beatles?"

"Yeah. John and Paul used to be over there," Vera pointed to two nubs on the back side of the castle roof, which had matching spires Sylvie hadn't seen from below. "Before they broke up."

Sylvie laughed—*broke up*—and gave Ringo a gentle hello. "I can see why that's your favorite part."

"Oh, the head rubbing? No, that's just for good luck. My favorite part is this." Vera threw her thin arms wide and looked out before her. Sylvie looked out too.

The view was incredible. A 360-degree, undisturbed panorama of the camp. From the haunted-looking mist around the lake to the expansive, monster-dotted lawn to the wild stretch of spindly-treed forest hugging the property like warm hands around a mug of tea.

Somehow, the elevated view doubled the magic of the place. Here it was, spread out before them, this world that was theirs for a full week. Down to each blade of grass and grain of sand, it was a stage for their imagination, and even with defined boundaries, the possibilities for role-play were endless.

"Wow," Sylvie sighed. She could spend all night up here once they had their official LARP information, daydreaming about the next day's course of action. Her LARP brain was already moving a mile a minute and doubling back on herself, because something Vera'd said made her wonder if it was normal to destroy property mid-LARP.

"Wait, so what happened to John and Paul? Did they get wrapped up in some sort of adventure?"

Vera shrugged. "They ended up in the bottom of the lake on a dare a few years ago, and Nessie refuses to bring them up. I guess they remind her of home."

"Wait? Nessie?" Sylvie's brain pinged on the movement she'd seen in the misty lake water. "Like, *Loch Ness Nessie*?"

"Yep. Relocated stateside with Master Gert. Tourists were giving her panic attacks. She's much happier here. And not a bad lifeguard."

Sylvie couldn't tell if Vera was kidding, but the idea of a big old mechanical Loch Ness monster manning the lake was pretty hilarious, even if Sylvie half hoped the adults still watched the water as actual lifeguards—swimming wasn't exactly Sylvie's best skill. "So, um—"

"CAW-CAW!"

Sylvie dropped and immediately ducked, hands over her head, spine pressed against the spire topped by Ringo the gargoyle. From her tight little ball shape, she was sure that at any moment, the sharp talons of one of the birds detailed in their cabin wallpaper would clasp her about the wrists and carry her into the forest for Sylvie-shaped supper.

To her surprise, through the muffled thickness of her arms and knees, Sylvie heard the faint sound of Vera laughing.

"It's loud, I know."

"What—what was that?" Sylvie peered up at Vera.

But Vera was smiling that tight smile and pointing

across the common to the flagpole. Balanced atop it sat the largest bird Sylvie had ever seen. It might have been one of the black birds etched on the walls below, but it was also the size of a baby pterodactyl. Sylvie slowly unfurled from her crouch and raised herself to her full height, her attention never leaving the giant bird as it spread its massive wings and let out another earth-shattering "CAW-CAW!"

"That," Vera said, "is Rupert. He keeps us on task."

Sylvie kept one eye on the bird as he flapped about and hopped from one balancing, talon-marked foot to the other. She asked, "And what task is Rupert expecting us to do right now?"

"Attend the opening ceremonies, of course! You haven't had time to read your orientation packet, I assume?" Sylvie shook her head and Vera moved to drop through the door and back onto the stairs. "Hurry up, we won't want to be up here when he takes off. He likes to poop on liftoff, and we're in the flight path back to his nest."

Opening Ceremonies

These are my people.

That thought clocked Sylvie hard enough to shake her fangs as she and Vera snaked through the final turn of a path leading from the row of increasingly eccentric cabins.

There were eight in total: a skull with nostril entry; a creepy, dead-eyed gnome (complete with beard and hat); a giant high-heeled shoe with a witch's striped stocking rising out of it toward the sky; a legitimate cave with a boulder rolled over the "door"; and a "cabin" that looked to Sylvie like a super-sized koi pond with the same mist that enveloped Nessie's lake. Plus, of course, the haunted house and witch's quarters that sandwiched their castle.

Past the watery depths of Cabin No. 1, Sylvie and Vera turned down a path toward a wide, round campsite carved into the closest edge of the sprawling, spindly woods.

The summer sun wasn't anywhere near the horizon

just yet, but the tightly-knit trees around two-thirds of the campsite made for a heavy wave of shadow, buffeted by a fog that rolled out of the deeper forest in big, ghostly tufts. The fog seemed to find any space that shadow touched.

A snapping fire leapt hot and hungry in the center, surrounded at a safe distance by downed logs, flattened with age and wear. The seating was arranged in a pentagon, the points of each log forming a side. Several of the logs were already filled with campers, slotted together like beads on a friendship bracelet.

All the kids Sylvie saw earlier were in attendance, plus more. Now there were two ghosts, a chartreuse-skinned girl goblin, and . . . a girl with hair so long it wrapped her body like a full-length cape. Maybe another witch? Or a siren? Something else? Sylvie wasn't sure. But just as before, their costumes were the best she'd ever seen. Even this close. And every single monster seemed to be in character. Not just waiting for an interaction, backstory in hand, but they were *role-playing* like monsters at camp would.

The pair of ghosts were unreal in the same way Amos's skeleton was mind-boggling. They sat together on the far side of the fire; their costumes constructed from some sort of fabric that made it look like they were as gaseous as smoke. From Sylvie's angle, they seemed huddled so closely that they overlapped as they whispered in each other's ears like their secrets meant life or a second death.

The Frankenstein's monster was seated with the water sprite, goblin, and long-haired girl, his patchwork of stitches stretched taut as he grinned in green delight at the goblin, who was contorting her very long, very blue(!) tongue into something that looked like a five-petaled daisy bursting out of her mouth. The water sprite frowned with a flip of her black hair.

Chad the werewolf sat, aggressively waving his hairy hands as he told some story, on another log. The black-haired werewolf nodded along and adjusted his hat while the other bespectacled werewolf boy seemed bored and kept fiddling with his bracelet.

The witches were shoulder to shoulder a log away, knees knocking, as the pale girl in the middle held a leaf that appeared to be riding its own gust of air. The leaf danced and spun in the girl's palm, and the force was enough to blow tendrils of brown hair around her round face. Even at this distance it looked so real that Sylvie's mind raced to solve the trick. An air compressor in her sleeve? No, it was eighty-five degrees, and she didn't have sleeves. Maybe—

"Do you want to take a seat?" Vera asked, gesturing toward an unoccupied log. It would put their backs toward the rest of the camp, facing inward toward the trees. It also meant they were basically as far away from Chad the werewolf as possible.

Probably a good move.

Sylvie sat down, and her heart rate sped up. Opening ceremonies had to be when they'd learn the week's LARPing theme, the plan, the rules. All of it. Swallowing hard, Sylvie wiped her sweaty palms on her shorts, her excitement eclipsing her nerves.

A hush descended as two figures appeared from the forest and stepped into the inner circle. One was Amos, just as see-through as before, bony forearms crossed over his sternum. He was in close conversation with the tallest person Sylvie had ever seen in real life. Rupert the enormous black bird sat upon this person's shoulder, looking like a ridiculously large but perfect accessory to their choice of costume: all black, with short, asymmetrical raven hair and a glorious cloak—no, cape.

That cape was so shiny and rippling, it seemed as alive as the night sky as the person stepped forward, a welcoming smile spread across a long, thin face.

"Hello, and welcome to this year's section of Monster Camp for rising seventh graders," they said in a full and friendly voice, arms thrown wide with a dramatic arch of their spine. Their voice was British and musical, which made the performance extra theatrical. Sylvie wondered if they were doing an accent or if they talked like that all the time, even when camp wasn't in session. "As many of you know, I am the camp director, Master Gert."

Every proper LARP had a game master. It was only fitting that the camp director would be the game master for all players here. They'd make the rules, enforce them, and settle disputes.

"While you are at Monster Camp, you are in my care. My door is always open to you, anytime, day or night." They extended an arm to the skeleton. "You should have received a welcome packet from Counselor Amos, my right-hand man, and our human-anatomy instructor." Amos gave a little wave. "I know the first thing all of you did was hunker down in your cabins and read all seventy-seven pages of material. . . ."

It was obvious from the nervous glances around the fire that no one had done that.

"*But* I hope you'll bear with me as I go over a few basics of Monster Camp." No one objected. "Before we get started, if you could excuse me, Rupert, I have a good amount of gesticulating to do."

The massive black bird gave a warble of disapproval, but took the hint, lifting off from Gert's shoulder and sailing to a dead pine that marked where the campsite ended and the forest began. Gert rolled their shoulders and smoothed the talon-shaped wrinkles from their cape.

"There," Gert said, and again spread their hands wide. "First of all, we've divided you into two groups—Fang and Fester. You'll find your group identification on your lanyards."

There was some shuffling as campers shifted and conferred. Vera had given Sylvie a heads-up on this one. To Sylvie's delight, she and Vera were in the same group—Fang.

Master Gert waited until the crowd settled, the lanyards back in place.

"Both groups will have the same camp experience, but your activities will be mirrored. For example, Group Fang will start each morning promptly after breakfast with Human Understanding and Resources Training. HURT is part engagement skills, part survivalist training, and part cultural education about humans. It is core to your camp experience and will provide you with a wide range of valuable skills that you can integrate into your everyday life to not only survive out there but thrive to the best of your abilities."

A whole week pretending to address humans as your monster self? An interesting way to set up a LARP. Sylvie wondered a little bit why half the week's focus would be on nonmonsters instead of, well, the fun they were bound to have as monsters. But maybe everyone here—even Chad—had bullies at home. And bullies were the worst nonmonster monsters around.

"After lunch," the director continued, "you will move on to recreational camp activities."

Everyone nodded. Huh. Sylvie had assumed the whole camp would be focused on LARPing. But stuff like horseback riding and crafts would still be fun and might be a good way to get to know these kids outside of the LARP. Maybe they'd even get close enough to stay in touch after camp was over.

"Group Fester," Master Gert continued, "will begin

with recreational activities and spend afternoons on the day's survivalist lesson. Free time starts each day at four. Dinner is at six. Scary human stories at seven. Cabin curfew at nine. Lights out at ten."

"Nessie totally tattles if we're loud after curfew. If she can hear it from the lake, it's too loud, and she doesn't care who gets in trouble." Though Vera was solemn and serious, Sylvie grinned. The world-building around the camp regulars was amazing. Nessie's grumpiness added yet another layer onto the characterization Vera had hinted at with the gargoyles. So cool.

Master Gert's voice cut through Sylvie's thoughts.

"Now, tonight is a little less structured than the rest. We know you're equally tired and wired, and we want you to sleep up for an excellent morning. Therefore, there will be no scary human stories tonight nor a formal dinner. Instead, the mess hall is open for grab-and-go until eight. Feel free to relax in your cabins or explore the grounds until curfew. But"—the director held up their hands again, stopping another round of fidgeting before it had the chance to start—"before I dismiss you, I'd like to introduce you to our camp leaders and address ground rules."

Master Gert grabbed a fistful of their cape and made a motion. Amos signaled from his clipboard to the woods.

"First up, I'd like to introduce you to our HURT instructor, our magnificent survivalist expert, Yeti."

On cue, a monster as white as snow emerged from the shadows beyond Amos and stomped heavily to Gert's side. The master was tall, but this yeti's costume was a head above them—eight feet at least. His face widened in a massive, toothy grin, huge hands clasped in front of its body as it rocked on its feet, toes the size of tennis balls, lifting and wiggling. Like Amos, he waved.

This costume was even more epic than Amos's skeleton.

And yet even the yeti had peers, because a moment later, two of the most magnificently-designed monsters Sylvie had ever seen stepped out of the forest cover and into the clearing.

"Next, I want to introduce you to two masterful monsters who wear more than one Monster Camp hat. First, Mummy G, our head chef, mess-hall manager, and potions instructor."

Master Gert flicked a smile and a gesturing hand toward a classic bandage-style mummy who had ambled out of the woods. The wrapping of the bandages was thorough, leaving just a dark slit where her eyes were. She waved.

"And Scott, our lead groundskeeper and recreational instructor."

A manticore rumbled into the firelight, and Sylvie's heart nearly lurched from her chest. Head of a man, body of a lion, tail of a scorpion. Like the yeti, he wasn't human-sized. And for the first time, a hint of shock crowded out the awe she felt in watching this parade.

No mere costume could replicate what was standing

in front of Sylvie, smiling with too many teeth.

Epic no longer described what this was. It was SO REAL.

Then, Sylvie noticed what was trailing this big, smiling, friendly manticore: a zombie. He was ratty, gray-faced, and appeared to be chained to Scott's belt. The man wore a workman's jumper with the words "Do Not Taunt: Zombie at Work" emblazoned across both the front and the back. The zombie didn't wave.

"Scott's crew is fully zombified, but don't worry, they are very tightly spelled and won't try to gnaw on your limbs." Gert winked at Sylvie. "We haven't lost a camper yet to zombification."

This was just out of this world.

Sylvie's mind whirred. Were all these staffers and their magnificent costumes part of the narrative?

"Now," Master Gert began as Amos returned to their side, "before I let you go, I promised a discussion of the rules. They are very simple, short, and to the point, but I do want you to listen carefully."

Sylvie waited in that pause, wishing she had something to write with to jot them down. The rules were crucial to a good LARP. She'd need to follow them closely for this week to go as well as she hoped.

"Here at Monster Camp, there are only two overarching rules that we expect our campers to commit to at all times." Sylvie held her breath. Master Gert smiled beatifically. "Be kind and be yourself."

That . . . was it? Sylvie was somewhat shocked, considering the dog-eared manuals she had stuffed in her duffel detailing common criteria for long-form LARPing. These rules were so simple, there had to be a catch.

"Though you will have daily instruction on the art of human interaction, I assure you that no humans are able to encroach on our camp. Our human shields are sound, and our other layers of protections are carefully and steadfastly in place."

A nasty little laugh trickled into the warm air from Chad's general direction. "There must be a leak."

The werewolf made no secret of what he was implying, his cold stare set on Vera: they'd let in a half human.

It was suddenly very obvious to Sylvie that, despite its advantages, there was a real burden of Vera's partial-human backstory when mixed with the camp's own characterization and world-building.

Vera's cheeks blushed furiously as her large eyes darted down to the fingers clasped in her lap. Sylvie's hand fell to Vera's cool wrist, a retort building on her lips about how her roommate's fangs were totally going to come in this week—because Sylvie could make that happen—when a shout stopped her plans cold.

"Watch it, hair ball!"

Sylvie's head whipped up at the words, just in time to see that the pink-haired witch was standing, both hands out and pointing furiously at Chad. A burst of energy ripped from her bubblegum-painted nails, invisible save for the way it sawed the leaping flames of the campfire right in half, and then—

Chad was no longer Chad.

Where a hairy boy had been sneering upon his log now sat a . . . dog.

Not a werewolf—that would've made sense. No, a tiny, floofy thing no bigger than a bowling ball and mostly hair. Its little face was immediately screwed up with agitation as it yipped short, angry barks from where Chad had previously been seated between the other werewolves.

Sylvie gasped, staring as the girl lowered her arms, a smug smile on her face. Her witchy friends glanced around nervously. Yet they didn't seem to be surprised.

In fact, no one seemed to be surprised.

Not Vera, not Chad's neighbors, not even Master Gert, who simply wound their arms about their chest, tilted their head, and spun a repressed grin as they issued a reprimand. "Now, there'll be none of that, Freya."

"He deserved it!" the girl argued, voice high and angry. Her brown cheeks flushed in the firelight. "Witches are human-adjacent, and he knows it."

Sylvie's mouth went dry. Gooseflesh prickled at her arms. She blinked at the girl, the dog, Master Gert.

That strange lurch she'd felt at Scott's introduction was now a furious twist in her gut.

No. It can't be.

With ease, Master Gert pointed one slim finger at

the yipping dog—a Pomeranian, Sylvie's mind finally supplied—and muttered something too muffled to hear. Suddenly, the snarling butterscotch puffball became Chad again.

Just *POOF*, and Chad was Chad, angry-eyed and panting.

The Frankenstein's monster clapped with enchantment, the backward-cap werewolf ruffled Chad's mess of hair, and Freya scrunched up her nose in an instant sulk, her hard work undone.

Sylvie couldn't breathe.

If that was magic. Actual magic and not a trick . . . then . . . then . . .

"As previous camp attendees, I would hope that you both were merely demonstrating what is *not* tolerated for our new campers." Gert's attention swiveled between Chad and Freya. "There will be no name-calling and no magical manipulation, please and thank you. We deal with enough vitriol outside these grounds from *humans*."

The need for oxygen was building in Sylvie's lungs. Her hands started shaking in her lap. Spots appeared before her eyes.

Master Gert's cape fluttered as they addressed the campers in a sweeping arc. "Any such demonstrations will not be tolerated and may be cause for your removal from camp, understood?"

Everyone, even Chad, nodded. Well, everyone but Sylvie, who was still as stone.

Gert gave a tight smile. "At Monster Camp, you are free to be as monstrous as you want to be as long as you aren't monstrous to one another."

This wasn't a camp for role-playing monsters.

Monster Camp was a camp for *real live* monsters.

And Sylvie Shaw, wannabe vampire but total human, was stuck inside for an entire week.

CHAPTER II

Monsters.
Real. Monsters.

Sylvie ran from the campfire like a bat out of H-E-Double Hockey Sticks.

Or, well, an eleven-year-old girl stumbling forward, trying very hard not to appear to be escaping with actual monsters on her heels.

"This can't be happening," she muttered once, twice, three times before stopping herself.

Monsters probably had really good hearing. To go along with real fangs, real magic, real hatred of humans.

Humans like her.

How long had Sylvie wished for a world with monsters?

For the things that went bump in the night to blink back? For fangs and claws and spectral apparitions? For magic spells and beasts in the wood and full-moon shape-shifting?

Now her imagination was outside of her mind.

Clomping around the grounds of camp with hooves and talons and a lust for the very blood that ran inside her body.

What if they found out about her? Would they kill her? No—they'd let her in. Surely they'd admit their mistake.

But they wouldn't let her go.

Maybe Freya would be allowed to turn Sylvie into a dog, trapping her in that little furry body with no way to ever tell anyone what she'd seen.

Or what if they decided Sylvie had to become a monster too? If Chad bit her, could she become a werewolf? Was that really how it happened?

What if Vera's monster DNA came in, she sprouted fangs, and the first thing she did was—

"Sylvie?"

Louder than she'd ever heard, Vera's voice rang out into the quiet of their little castle.

Her mind a muddled mess and panic attack flaring, Sylvie hadn't truly tried to escape. What was the point if there was a human shield thing? Somehow it let her in, but it surely wouldn't let her out.

So instead, she'd run through shadows and fog *much* thicker than before straight to their cabin, jumped into her coffin bed, banged the lid shut, and tried to make it all disappear.

It didn't work.

"Sylvie?" Vera tried again.

Clutching her mother's necklace between both hands now, Sylvie screwed her eyes closed and tried to make her voice light and normal. "In here."

Sylvie didn't open the coffin lid, and, to her relief, neither did Vera. Instead, Sylvie heard a few soft footsteps and then the sigh of the other coffin as Vera perched on its edge. "Um, you left kind of quickly. Are you okay?"

"Okay" was the last word Sylvie would use to describe her mental state.

But she couldn't let Vera know that. Sylvie knew everything there was to know about vampires. They were lightning quick, and their strength rivaled any comic-book superhero. Even a half vampire had to be faster and stronger than a normal human. Sylvie wasn't about to underestimate Vera.

With a deep breath, Sylvie opened the coffin and sat up. She tried very hard to look normal and not like she was hiding. "Oh no, um, I'm fine."

"Are you sure? You look a little . . . red."

The blood roaring in her ears was so loud, Sylvie couldn't even hear her own heartbeat. She reached for the nearest excuse. "Just a little hungry."

Vera peered at her. "The mess is self-serve, tonight." Yes, that's what Master Gert had said. "I know eating away from home can be weird, but don't worry, the blood they have on tap is good. Promise."

Oh. No.

"Mummy G has years of practice." Vera's tight smile was back. "Gets it right to 98.6; she knows scalded blood is a waste."

Sylvie gagged. She tried to cover, but her roommate didn't miss it. "Yeah, burnt blood is nasty. I know." Vera raised her eyebrows hopefully. "So, do you want to go by the mess, or . . . ?"

Sylvie's stomach lurched. She really was hungry, but if she went to the mess hall, she couldn't grab any of the available food—she'd be served body-temperature blood and have to drink it. Or pretend. But Vera knew how a real vampire drank blood—she'd catch Sylvie in an instant. If only she'd been smart enough to use Vera's backstory, er, *background,* and announced herself half human too.

"No, you go ahead." Then, because Sylvie both wanted to know and it seemed like the type of question a real vampire might ask, she swallowed down the bile and said, "Do you, um, eat human food too?"

Sylvie twisted the crescent-moon necklace at her throat.

Vera nodded her head and swept a lock of long red hair behind her ear. "I go to human school, so it's all French fries and cheeseburgers most days. And then dinner is normal—even Dad eats with us. Sorry, I know that's probably gross, but it doesn't hurt his stomach too bad—"

"Not gross at all," Sylvie rushed out. The idea that vampires *could* eat food, just typically *wouldn't,* was going to be a lifesaver if she was understanding this right. So she said, "I go to human school. I'm one with the cheeseburgers when I have to be. Iron stomach."

To her relief, Vera nodded. "Yeah. So you get it. I

know some vamps don't—Dad's family usually sits on the porch when they visit, and Mom makes dinner. They act like she's roasting a skunk or something. Very dramatic."

"They'd seriously benefit from time in the middle-school cafeteria."

"Right? Wimps." Vera smiled with teeth this time. "Anyway, we have a mug of blood together after dinner. Just Dad and me. It's our little thing."

"That's cool."

They were quiet for a second, and in that pause, Sylvie's tummy rumbled so loudly that Vera's eyes skipped to her belly and then away. Did vampires' stomachs rumble? That wasn't something Sylvie had ever learned from her books and movies.

"Um, so, do you want me to bring you a to-go cup? I don't mind." Vera's brows pinched together, confusion and disappointment on her face, whatever vision she had of the two of them clinking their mugs of blood together dying a quick death in her big eyes.

Vera was so kind.

It was on the tip of Sylvie's tongue to tell Vera the truth.

That this was the biggest mix-up in history. That she was a human pretending to be a vampire.

Would Vera hide her secret? Or would she out Sylvie in an instant?

Sylvie's train of thought crashed in the pit of her rumbling stomach.

If she was going to survive this week, no one could know. Not even Vera. Sylvie was going to have to do exactly what she did best: pretend to be a vampire.

Sylvie could do this. She *had* to do this. Or she'd be fed to the literal wolves—er, werewolves.

And Sylvie wasn't going to be a snack for Chad or anyone else.

Determination stilling her shaking fingers and quivering gut, Sylvie swallowed, gave Vera her best sheepish grin, and added to her backstory in the safest way she knew how. "This is really embarrassing, but I'm on a special diet. I brought my blood from home."

Sylvie waited, struggling not to hold her breath.

"Oh no, don't be embarrassed! My uncle has to be careful like that too. Gluten gives him hives." Sylvie exhaled, and Vera's lips turned up in her tight, little smile. "Your secret's safe with me."

Sylvie forced herself to return the grin. Show her fangs, tip her chin, and play her role to the very best of her ability. "Thanks, Vera. I'm so glad you get me."

The disappointment on Vera's face cleared. "I'm glad you get me too." She stood, and Sylvie's heart began to slow to its normal rhythm. "It's seven thirty . . . um, I need to get going if I'm going to get dinner or blood."

Despite her growling stomach, Sylvie felt a little too nervous to eat anything—but now that she knew she didn't have to subsist on protein bars and fruit punch all week, she decided maybe she should repay Vera's kindness and learn something in the process. "Actually, you know what, can I still come with you? Just to see more of the camp—or, at least, where the mess is?"

"Yeah, of course." Vera brightened further. "But don't worry. You don't have to act like you're into the food—even the blood, if you can't have it. Master Gert means it when they say we're just supposed to be ourselves. A whole week to be monsters just as we are—no pretending."

Vera opened the door, and before they ducked into the night, Sylvie took a deep, steadying breath, looked her real-live-monster roommate directly in the eye, and answered, "No pretending. I like that."

Sylvie's Monster Camp Plan 2.0: Survive

Pretending was the only thing Sylvie had in mind as she strapped on her backpack for her first full day at Monster Camp.

She'd gotten up before the sun to carefully apply her fangs and widow's peak, scarf down a protein bar, pour a pouch of fruit punch into her "You Suck" tumbler, and bury the evidence deep in her duffel bag. She saved slopping on a thick layer of sunscreen for when Vera was up, because it seemed like a good, nonsuspicious vampiric activity.

This was very soon confirmed by her half-vampire roommate.

"Can I try some?" Vera asked as Sylvie finished rubbing a thick film of the stuff across her bare legs and took a big sip of "blood" from her cup. "That must be good stuff if you're a full vampire and can wear tank tops and shorts."

Sylvie gagged, fruit punch nearly spraying out of her nose. She coughed into her elbow, shaking her head as Vera shoved the remains of her to-go bagel into her mouth and thrust a napkin at her to help. Sylvie accepted it but didn't use it, fearful that any dab of red wouldn't smell like blood or even look like it—the punch's consistency was all wrong up close and Vera would *definitely* notice.

"Yeah," she wheeze-coughed in answer after swallowing. "It's good. Give it a try—I have plenty."

After Vera was covered in her own thick coat, Sylvie dropped the sunscreen bottle in her backpack, now knowing that she had to reapply every few hours or suspicion would definitely set in. Her dad would be pleased with the effort if he only knew.

At eight strikes of the bell, facilitated by Rupert, who personally wrapped his massive talons around a large bell hanging from the administration building with an opening and closing "CAW-CAW," Sylvie arrived at the sign-covered flagpole with Vera.

Master Gert and Amos stood on either side of the pole. There weren't labels indicating the groups or anything, but Sylvie recalled that Group Fang would start its day with HURT, which meant with Yeti, who was next to Amos. The massive yeti was sipping something hot from a travel mug as they nodded over paperwork together.

Before drifting toward Yeti, Sylvie glanced over to double-check with Vera. Her roommate wasn't only stopped but staring. The slim fingers hooked into her backpack straps were bone white. Turning very slowly on her heel, Sylvie followed Vera's line of sight—straight to Chad, next to Yeti.

"Seriously?" Sylvie asked under her breath. "Werewolves have fangs, but I didn't think our groups were, like, *literal.*"

That was a major bummer.

"It's not exactly literal," Vera whispered, her hangdog face pointed toward the grass Scott and his zombie team maintained so beautifully. "But we need an even split for the camp curriculum, and Master Gert is all about us working out our differences through shared experience and understanding."

All those words sounded way too grown-up. "Is that from the paperwork they gave us?" Sylvie had started the seventy-seven-page opus but hadn't made it far.

"No, it's from my memory."

Vera leaned in, her whisper going featherlight, her breath cool and close. "Last year, Chad and Milo were in my group too." She gestured at the bespectacled werewolf. "Milo is fine but can't say no to Chad, which means if Chad wants to pick on you, it's always two against one."

Sylvie wondered why the third, black-haired werewolf wasn't included but focused on Milo.

"Uh, are we sure Milo is 'fine'?" Sylvie asked, working hard to publicly commit to air quotes while side-eyeing the other werewolf. His hair was closer to blond than brown, and he wore glasses, but in almost every other way he was basically a carbon copy of Chad, down to their silver dude bracelets. Their tank tops, shorts, and shoes were even the same brands. At least the kid with long black hair wore a hat.

"I went to Master Gert after two days last year, and they gave me the rigamarole I just regurgitated to you." The cords of Vera's throat tightened with a deep breath. "I tried to just stay out of his way. But when you're the target, it's hard to hide. He'd literally ask to be paired with me, knowing he could be a jerk and get away with it." Ugh, that was a Fisher Loggins move. "Sometimes, Milo would beat him to it and choose Chad as a partner. I think he knows Chad is a turd . . . but they're cousins, so he doesn't really do anything to stop him, but just, like, negate him."

Oh. So that's why the black-haired one wasn't grouped with Chad and Milo.

"Well, like you said yesterday, it'll be easier with two of us," Sylvie said, trying to convince herself too. She and Vera were a package deal, even if Sylvie shared the opposite half of Vera's gene pool than what her roommate thought.

Everybody else in Group Fang was slightly less worrisome. The black-haired werewolf was there, plus the Frankenstein's monster, the water sprite . . . and Freya. It seemed all too convenient that after their tiff yesterday, Chad and Freya were in the same group.

Maybe a little purposefully, Sylvie and Vera clumped themselves closer to the witch, who was busy making sorrowful eyes at her coven friends—clustered over with Group Fester. The ghosts were over there too, plus the goblin girl and the one with long hair. Sylvie still had no clue what type of monster this girl was, but considering she didn't know monsters were truly real until twelve hours ago, there was likely a lot she didn't know about *actual* monsters.

By Sylvie's count, there were eight campers in Fang and six in Fester. That seemed a little odd not to have it seven and seven, especially given what Vera had said about having groups of equal size. Maybe this year they could vote Chad off the island and send him to Fester and—

"How are we doing this morning, Sylvie?" A long, thin hand landed on Sylvie's shoulder.

Sylvie's mouth dropped open as her eyes combed from the hand, up the arm, and to the pointed face of Master Gert. The director smiled and blinked at Sylvie as the girl's mind whirred. Why were they asking? Vera was right next to her, why not include her? Why zero in on Sylvie?

"Um. Good."

"Excellent. I wanted to introduce myself last night, but I turned around and—*POOF!*—you were gone."

Oh. Yes. Of course. She'd met Amos but not officially Master Gert. Of course, the director would want to meet one-on-one with new campers. And she'd literally ran from the campfire the second they'd adjourned.

Should she make a bat joke? About how she—POOFed into one? Did real vampires actually turn into bats?

Master Gert's fingers squeezed Sylvie's shoulder as their dark eyes seemed to take in every inch of Sylvie's costume—Converse All Stars, black jean shorts, black tank top, widow's peak. A spike of fear crackled across Sylvie's chest, and she forced herself to smile with fangs visible, hoping that this close, Master Gert couldn't smell the human under the vampire gear. She suddenly snapped her lips shut, worried the fangs looked fake in broad daylight at point-blank range.

"And then when I stopped by your cabin, it was empty."

Sylvie was starting to sweat. Then things got worse—Rupert landed on the director's shoulder, his beady bird eyes immediately boring into Sylvie's skin like an exact replica of his master. Was that suspicious? Was Master Gert supposed to know where she was at all times?

"We were at the mess," Vera supplied when Sylvie didn't. "Super hungry."

"Oh, yes. Of course. Low blood sugar is a terrible thing." Wait, was that a joke? About vampires? Or a test? Sylvie clutched her moon pendant. Master Gert tipped their pointy chin at Vera and nodded. "Well, Sylvie, please know that we're happy you've finally joined us this year, and we hope you have a splendid week, right, Rupert?"

The bird nodded.

"If you need me, my office is in the administration building. And if you're not sure, just signal Rupert. He always knows where I am, and he'll keep a bird's-eye view on you this week."

Oh. Oh, no. The last thing Sylvie needed was a massive avian tattletale following her wherever she went.

"Um, no, I'm good. He doesn't have to do that. It's—"

"It's his job to make sure all campers at Monster Camp are having a scary good time. Anytime you see Rupert, know I'm there with you in spirit. He's my eyes in the sky."

With that, Master Gert winked, turned, and clapped their hands together for everyone's attention. Rupert, though, kept his unblinking gaze on Sylvie, his whole body rotated to watch her from the director's shoulder.

Gulp.

"Good morning, everyone! I see most of you have yourselves arranged, but just to confirm, Group Fang is over by Yeti, and Group Fester is here, next to me." There was some jostling, and Master Gert waited patiently. In the morning light, their eyes were a startling black, the irises blending into the pupils with exactly zero delineation. "Excellent. Counselor Amos will lead roll call."

The skeleton stepped forward and first ran through Group Fang.

Sylvie, Vera, Freya, plus Chad and Milo. The other werewolf was Lenny, the Frankenstein's monster was Francis, and the water sprite Bebe.

Next, Group Fester. The two ghosts were named

Zephyr and Norah, the two remaining witches were Benedict and Annika, the goblin girl was Tatiana, and the long-haired girl was Vivian.

After Vivian's very operatic "HERE!" rang out—maybe she was a siren?—Master Gert's thin, dark eyebrows pulled together. They let out a big sigh. "Fade? Has anyone seen Fade?"

Tatiana and Vivian burst into high-pitched chuckling. "Good one, Master Gert," Tatiana called out, the sun glinting off her bald, chartreuse head as she threw it back in laughter. Sylvie noticed now that the goblin's teeth were as razor-sharp as Bebe's. Like a shark's but shrunk down into a child-sized mouth. Her skin prickled with goose bumps at the thought of what either one of them could do to normal human skin like hers.

Sylvie furrowed her brow at Vera, who immediately understood her confusion and whispered, "You know 'The Invisible Man'?" Sylvie was familiar with H. G. Wells. She nodded. "Fade's an invisible boy. And he thinks sneaking around is soooo hilarious."

Master Gert very obviously did not think it was funny. They spun toward the campers, hands on the hips of their trousers. Today they wore yet another magnificent cape that sprayed rainbows over its high-shine fabric as they twisted in the sunlight.

"Francis?" They tipped their chin toward the Frankenstein's monster. "Benedict?" This time their chin swung to the witch. "Did he leave the cabin with you all?"

Both of Fade's roommates nodded. "He was with us in the mess hall—"

"Found his name tag!" the water sprite announced, plucking a lanyard from Francis's back pocket.

The Frankenstein's monster shrugged his shoulders all the way up to the bolts in his neck. "I didn't know he put that there."

Master Gert addressed the crowd at large, slightly perturbed but also seemingly not surprised. "Fade, please announce yourself and put on your lanyard, or I'm going to have to bring out the big guns."

A little snickering came from somewhere. Everyone's heads swiveled around.

Sylvie leaned into Vera. "Um, I'm afraid to ask, but what are the big guns?"

"Not actual guns. Don't worry."

Before Sylvie could press harder, Master Gert waved a hand. "Bebe, let it rip."

The sprite thrust her blue hands outward and sprayed the entire perimeter around the flagpole with water.

Sylvie barely had time to squeeze her eyes shut, let alone get her hands up, before the ten sweeping-fingertip jets nailed her. When her eyes blinked open, water droplets clung to her eyelashes, and everyone was dripping from head to toe, including all the adults.

Yet there, in a small void between both ghosts, was the very watery outline of a boy. He stood, dripping and completely, amazingly invisible.

Master Gert pursed their lips. "Fade, let's have that be the only time we pull that trick this week, or I will enlist our Scott and his zombies with the very important task of spraying you with superglue and crusting your entire body in glitter."

"Ah, man." Fade's voice was much richer than Sylvie would've expected. "Did Mom give you that idea?"

"Your mother gave me *lots* of ideas, because she very much wants you to participate in this camp and not spend the week as a spectator." Fade had nothing to say to that, and his waterlogged shoulders seemed to droop. "Now, please go collect your lanyard and stand with Group Fester."

Fade did so, and to Sylvie's surprise, the lanyard looped around his neck and stayed put like everyone else's. That meant even when he dried off, as long as he wore it, everyone could at least know he was around. She wondered absently if he wore clothes or even shoes and if she just couldn't see them, because the ghosts were definitely wearing equally spectral hiking gear.

Speaking of clothing, Sylvie pawed at her soaked tank top, trying to wring out the fabric. She failed.

"That was simply refreshing, wasn't it? Thank you, Bebe," Master Gert said, rubbing the back of their hand over their sopping face. The water sprite beamed. "Now that we have everyone, it's 8:01, which means it's time to begin the morning session. And, though I know all of you were listening closely when I described your typical day last night, this year we're doing things a little differently."

"Different" couldn't be a good thing from Sylvie's point of view.

"This year, day one is going to be spent on working together!" Clearly this really was different, because there was a collective ripple of confusion among the Monster Campers. Master Gert didn't waver in their proud grin, though. "This morning, we're going to have a joint Fang-and-Fester HURT session, and after lunch, we're going to do a special team-building activity!"

That . . . did not sound good. Team building sounded like a chance for everyone to be looking at Sylvie a little too closely, not a chance to disappear into the shadows.

Apparently, Vera had the same thought. "If 'activity' means 'competition,' Chad's going to figure out a way to make sure it's my fault if we lose."

Sylvie didn't know what to say to that, because Vera was probably right, and false hope didn't help anybody.

"Okay, friends!" Yeti faced the dripping campers with a big, watery smile. "I know we're a bit wet, but don't you worry! Today's joint HURT lesson starts with a hike, and that'll dry us off very nicely, I'm sure. This way, campers!"

And with that, the giant yeti pointed the sodden mish-mash of kids toward the claustrophobic pines surrounding the camp common.

As the squiggle of bodies stretched into a line trailing Yeti into the woods, Sylvie's nerves jumped. She spun a little but noticed Amos and Master Gert waiting and watching to make sure no one vanished like Fade had before roll call. Master Gert met Sylvie's eyes over their to-go cup and smiled. On their shoulder, Rupert simply stared unblinking at Sylvie. Ugh. Sylvie forced herself to grin back at the both of them. Next to her, Vera fell into line and started moving.

Clutching her mother's necklace in her clammy fist, Sylvie put one Converse in front of the other and followed more than a dozen real live monsters into the dark woods.

Into the Woods

Sylvie was gripping her backpack straps so tightly that her fingers had gone numb.

They were about a mile up the trail into the forest now, the trees so tightly clustered, their branches crowded out the sun. The shadows were thick and creeping, snaking along the forest floor, threatening to snatch at Sylvie's ankles and drag her into the foggy dark.

Yeti was leading the group at a good clip, but not so fast that the monsters up front weren't laughing, singing, constantly talking. They were a riot of happy sounds, wafting toward where Sylvie and Vera trudged forward in silence at the end of the camper line. It was probably her fear snagging hold of her imagination and tugging hard, but Sylvie was sure the forest's vines crept closer as she and Vera navigated the trail.

Still, even though it was impossible, the whole combination was enough that Sylvie's heart slammed against her rib cage as if she were running. A sheen of cold sweat clung to her skin, smothered by her thick coating of sunscreen. Her muscles were jittery, and her stride stuttered. Several times, she caught the toe of her shoe on a rock, root, or one of those moving vines and stumbled forward on shaky legs. More than once, Sylvie had glanced over her shoulder, back the way they'd come. She saw nothing but Amos and Master Gert blocking the thin ribbon of trail.

No way out.

Except maybe through the trees. Straight through to the camp next door? Perhaps. Though she couldn't see the sun and had no idea what direction they'd gone. And then there was the matter of the human shield. She'd gotten lucky somehow upon arrival, but considering how unlucky she was to find herself in the middle of a group of human-hating monsters, Sylvie wasn't confident her luck would help her much now.

If she bolted without some other helpful distraction, she'd be caught in two seconds.

Sylvie could not be caught.

Fear skittering every pulse point, Sylvie ran through her therapist's suggestions to ward off panic attacks.

Breathing through it—easier said than done while hiking. Progressive relaxation—tensing her muscles one at a time and then releasing them—which was, again, difficult to do while hiking. In fact, the best thing she thought to do was to try to keep her mind in the present, which equated to basically playing "Slug Bug" with her surroundings.

Unfortunately, every answer made her more aware that she was stuck in the woods with a gaggle of monsters.

Counting five things she could see around her. A walking skeleton, Yeti, three werewolves.

Four things she could touch. Her clammy skin, sweaty clothes, half-dead roommate's shoulder, the suffocating trees.

Three things she could hear. Chad's terrible laugh, Lenny's much nicer one, the swish of Master Gert's cape.

Two things she could smell. Her sunscreen and the fruit punch that in no way smelled like the to-go blood in Vera's mug.

One thing she could taste. Bile lapping at the back of her throat.

Sylvie swallowed thickly and peeled one set of fingers off her backpack strap. They numbly clawed at her necklace, clamping down, all tingly on the familiar crescent-moon shape. Her thumb prickled with returning feeling as she ran it along the edge.

Hopeless, Sylvie tried the only other thing she knew how to do. Talk.

"So, um, do you hike much?" she asked Vera. Those were the first words Sylvie had said in probably thirty minutes. They sounded as numb as her hands felt.

"Um, sometimes," Vera answered, that little smile back as she glanced over her shoulder. Her fingertips skimmed a tree for balance. "On cloudy days. Or at dusk. Makes it easier for Dad."

"Um, yeah, that's what we do too," Sylvie said, immediately wishing she hadn't decided to make small talk this way. Then, because it's much easier if there's a little truth to a lie, she added, "Though usually we only hike somewhere to climb."

"Like rock climb? With ropes and carabiners and stuff?"

"Yep. Mostly we do it inside, but, um, if the weather's right, we'll do it outside."

None of that was a lie. Her dad did like to rock climb, and it was something that he'd been teaching Sylvie the last couple years. It'd been a suggestion from her therapist. A literal metaphor for self-reliance. But it'd been her dad who really took to it, piling gear and indoor lessons at the local climbing gym onto his credit card.

"That's cool."

Sylvie was relieved when the muffled clapping of furry paws finished off Vera's reply.

"All right, Monster Campers! We're here!" Yeti yelled from up front.

The massive monster had stopped at the mouth of a clearing and, with a sweeping motion of his huge, furry arms, began gesturing the campers forward to their destination.

As Sylvie and Vera inched forward, the site that came into view was—well, it couldn't be right.

They hadn't arrived at yet another campsite or outdoor amphitheater or anything else that made sense for a camp-appropriate classroom.

No.

It was a structure so old and so dilapidated it looked like it was glued together by ghosts.

The building—if you could call it that—leaned to one side, a rectangle gone trapezoid with time and disuse. The wood was unpainted, rotten, and peppered with so many holes, it could've been made of moldy, brownish Swiss cheese. The roof bowed like the back of an ancient cow, every single window was shattered, and where a door should've been was a gaping mouth. At the sturdiest end was a big paddle wheel, similar to what Sylvie had seen on a picture of a steamboat. But there wasn't water near it, just a huge mud slick.

"A . . . mill?" Sylvie whispered to Vera.

"An abandoned mill," Vera confirmed.

Sylvie was pretty sure it was haunted. She was also pretty sure she shouldn't say that within earshot of two actual ghosts. Zephyr and Norah probably wouldn't appreciate that very much. Or her observation that the moldy wooden planks were glued together by their species.

"We're having class in *there*?"

Vera shrugged, unconcerned.

In fact, now that Sylvie was looking around . . . no one seemed concerned.

All three witches entered the lilting building on Yeti's

heels; Francis and Lenny were slinging mud at each other by the wheel; Zephyr, Norah, and Bebe used their ability to fly to survey the roof; Tatiana and Vivian were prodding at what looked like a big ol' mine shaft with a chain slung across it and the words DANGER, KEEP OUT in big, bold letters; and the werewolf cousins—

"Hey, hey, hey, no you don't," Master Gert bellowed, streaming past Sylvie and Vera. "It's a building, not a jungle gym! Get down."

"Aw, man." Sylvie knew that voice—Chad's. It'd come from the paddle wheel, his furry head poking over the top. Master Gert was tall, but they craned their neck to stare up at him, hands on hips. "But they're up there!"

Chad thrust a hairy arm out toward the general direction of the three flying monsters.

"Yes, disturbing nothing but the breeze," Master Gert said, and Sylvie had to admit, she was pleased Chad wasn't infallible. "Milo, you too."

Milo poked his head out from behind the wheel as Chad climbed down. He didn't seem to be actively climbing the rickety wheel, but his cheeks pinked heavily under his glasses. "Um, sorry, Master Gert."

The director nodded. "Apology accepted, Milo. Everyone inside. Francis, Lenny, wipe your feet. Fade, don't think I can't see that wheel moving. You're on top of it. Get down."

Two seconds later, there was a new set of footprints in the mud below the mill wheel. "And wipe your feet too, please," Master Gert directed without so much as looking over their shoulder. "Have some respect."

"Um, why are we respecting the abandoned mill?" Sylvie whispered to Vera, half-certain now that the building was a monster itself, sentient somehow. The way it creaked with the breeze, it actually did look like it was breathing, its rotting body expanding. Not only did it look like moldy Swiss cheese, it *smelled* like it.

"This was Yeti's home for about fifty years."

"You're kidding?!" Sylvie was flabbergasted.

"What better place to hide than an abandoned mill?" Vera answered. "Master Gert founded Monster Camp, but they did it with the legal purchase of Yeti's old homestead. Yeti's been here literally since the beginning. It's mutually beneficial and stuff."

Inside the mill, the floorboards sighed under Sylvie's weight, each dusty plank speckled with daylight from the rotten walls, saw-toothed panes of remaining glass in each window, and the snatches of roof that had fully given out.

None of this was safe. None of it was normal. Sylvie was not fine.

"Welcome to my old stomping grounds, Monster Campers!" Yeti announced from up front, his white fur stark in the creeping shadows and arrows of light. "Everyone get cozy, it's time to get HURT!"

CHAPTER 14

Humans HURT

Sylvie was totally going to die in here.

She was sure of it. This was a trap. The real monsters had her all figured out, and day one of Human Understanding and Resources Training was going to kick off with the ambush and subsequent capture of Sylvie, before moving on to cooking her on a spit and playing Operation on her insides.

"Where do you want to sit?" Vera asked. Her words were soft, but Sylvie flinched before she could cover it. She rubbed at her arm as if she'd meant to do that.

"Um . . ."

The groups had basically divided into Fang and Fester, save for the witches, who made up the first row, three across. Behind them, their respective groups fanned out in clumps, cleaved in half by a thin line of space under one of the natural skylights. Yeti stood up front,

Master Gert and Amos joining him off to the Fester side.

On shaky, stuttering legs, Sylvie very carefully arranged herself at the intersection of where she could see the sky (and therefore be assured the roof wouldn't cave in), where the floorboards looked sturdy enough to hold her weight, and where the door was literally two strides away.

This put her off to the extreme far side of the Fang cluster. Like, not just in the back, but in another zip code.

If Vera noticed, she didn't say anything, plopping down next to Sylvie, crossing her legs, and shifting her backpack into her lap. Sylvie kept her backpack on and pulled her knees to her chest.

Ready to run.

From her spot, Sylvie scoped out all possible exits. The door, of course, but also the exit to the mill wheel and the blown-out windows with the fewest shards of glass clinging to their frames. Once outside, she knew the trail was probably her best bet, but if that was blocked, she'd follow the mud down the path where the river used to run through the forest, or, if she couldn't reasonably get away, Sylvie was sure she could climb a tree or even slip in the mine shaft to hide—if she had to.

Door. Wheel. Windows. Trail. River. Mine.

Sylvie's mind chanted the possibilities as she hugged her knees so tightly, her rabbiting heart thumping against the thighs of her black jean shorts.

Yeti clapped his paws together, obviously trying to get their attention.

"Happy Monday morning, campers, and welcome to your first session of HURT!" Yeti crowed cheerfully. "It is my goal with our HURT course of study that each year, you gain valuable knowledge in understanding our human counterparts and that I give you as many resources as possible to navigate the same space with them."

"Hey, isn't that the exact wording printed in the brochure?" Freya asked with a very teenager-like arch of her eyebrow.

That was when Sylvie learned it was possible for a yeti to blush.

"Yes, that's the official parental-level jargon I wrote myself to sell it to your guardians."

Sylvie had memorized her brochure but only recalled the HURT program mentioned in the caption of one of the photos. She didn't recognize this particular jargon. Had she gotten a different brochure than everyone else?

If so, that . . . was not a good thing.

Her hands were still tingling, and between that and her racing heart, Sylvie realized she now had two of the three symptoms that usually indicated a panic attack. If nausea swept in, she'd have to get out of here, no matter what. Sylvie started to sweat anew, a flush of wetness building in the hollows under her eyes.

Yeti clapped his hands again and smiled with too many teeth.

"Now that we have the official description out of the way, I want you all to humor me with what you know.

Most of you have been here before, so can you just shout out what HURT stands for? Ready? Go!"

A big furry hand came up over his head in the same movement Mrs. Didius used when directing Sylvie's orchestra class through a musical piece. Sylvie played the cello, and right now her gut was vibrating like a poorly-tuned instrument.

"Human Understanding and Resources Training!" they shouted out in semiunison. The old mill seemed to sway with the sudden sound. Sylvie's breath caught for the exact length of time it took her to be sure the remaining roof wasn't going to avalanche in.

Yeti squeezed his eyes shut and did a little squat of appreciation.

"Very good!" His eyes sprang open, and that's when Sylvie realized they were a lovely cool brown. She'd thought they were gray. "It's important to remember the whole acronym, but if you remember anything, remember those middle words, because they're the literal heart of what we're trying to accomplish—understanding and resources."

Sylvie was pretty sure there was a metaphor in that middle part somewhere, quite literally, but didn't say anything.

Chad craned around and sneered to Milo and Lenny, "I understand humans fine—they're all just big, uninteresting meat sacks with no powers."

As if on cue, the other boys laughed.

"Now, Chad, I know you're just trying to be funny," Yeti said, though Sylvie thought that a rather generous assessment of what Chad was attempting to do, "but this is where the understanding portion comes in. Humans are a lot of things, and the more you know about them, the easier your life will be."

And now Chad laughed.

"Aw, come on, Yeti, give me a break. There's a reason humans think you're a myth—because they never actually have a conversation with you. They just run away screaming, wusses that they are."

"Humans are sensitive to the idea of monsterkind, but that doesn't mean we shouldn't learn all we can about them," Yeti answered sagely, completely ignoring Chad's assertion. The werewolf didn't press, but instead made ridiculous faces at Milo and Lenny, who obviously agreed with him. To Sylvie, that was almost worse. "Understanding is the first step toward respecting one another. And the resources you'll learn here will help you get to a place of understanding by the end of the week."

That made sense to Sylvie, though more than anything, she was telling herself that she needed to be very careful not to show she knew too much about being human. Playing the quiet game during any mention of humanity seemed like the best possible course of action.

"But they don't know anything about us on purpose," Milo piped up. He was much calmer than Chad, but it didn't escape Sylvie that he'd also spoken out of turn. His hand wasn't even raised. "If understanding is the best way to bridge humankind and monsterkind, why aren't we out there, hitting the pavement with a decent PR campaign?"

When Yeti didn't immediately answer, Milo blinked expectantly at Master Gert and Amos. After a moment, the director stepped forward.

"As the oldest monster at Monster Camp, perhaps I should be the one to explain," they said to Yeti.

The massive monster swept his arms forward to a spot near the front in invitation before receding against the wall. To Sylvie's relief, he didn't lean on it.

"First, I want to acknowledge that every monster here is from a different background," Master Gert said. "Some of the information I'm about to cover may be something you already know from elders in your individual communities. However, please be mindful of the fact that not every monster group is as forthcoming with historical information. Some of your fellow campers may not know what I'm about to explain, and please do not shame them for their ignorance; it is not their fault. Remember the first of our two rules—be kind."

Master Gert waited several beats for that to sink in, making eye contact with several campers before continuing. Perhaps it was because she was already on edge, but Sylvie convinced herself that Master Gert held her gaze longer than anyone else's.

Sylvie glanced down, staring hard at the rotten floorboard directly in front of her. The director continued.

"Thousands of years ago, monsters lived in the open. Many didn't seek out human contact, but they didn't hide—not like today. In fact, some forged cooperative relationships with humans, myself included."

They smiled gently here, and, not for the first time, Sylvie wondered what kind of monster Master Gert was.

"But," they went on, vertically brandishing one long index finger, "about a thousand years ago, that relationship shifted. Humans were more connected than ever, and with that unprecedented connection, worldwide opinion about monsters began to change. In a very short time, monsterkind became something to fear."

At the drop of the final word, a heavy silence descended on the classroom space, and something equally weighty plunked in Sylvie's gut. It wasn't the nausea she'd been dreading—it was guilt.

Sylvie *did* fear them. The moment she knew they were real, everything she'd ever loved about monsters evaporated.

"But they *should* fear us," Lenny said, and raised both his arms high, his thumbs pointing at his immensely shaggy head and ever-present Kraken hat. "We're awesome."

Titters of laughter passed through the campers at Lenny's proclamation. Master Gert's mouth kicked up to one side in a little smile. "Yes, we are. But often awe-inspiring people and actions can be misunderstood, which only adds to fear. First, the monsters who were not human-adjacent had to withdraw—as some of you know well, when it's impossible to hide your true nature, every interaction with a human could be a death sentence."

Lenny's arms sank back to his sides. He had nothing to say to that.

"For the next few hundred years, non-human-adjacent monsters secluded themselves in places that were hard for humans to inhabit. The north and south poles, the hottest deserts, the deepest caves, the highest mountains. And, unfortunately, those extremes, the change in diet, and the general stress of being found caused numbers to dwindle and some monster species to become extinct."

"RIP dragons," Vera whispered next to Sylvie.

Completely stunned—*DRAGONS?!*—Sylvie's lips dropped open before she could stop them. She tried to school the rest of her expression, maybe act like she was going to say something thoughtful, but before she could come up with something that wouldn't sound completely uneducated, Master Gert swept their cape around to continue their lesson while pacing across the groaning floorboards.

"For some time, human-adjacent monsters were able to live among the masses without immediate threat of persecution. Of course, that changed when magic became something to fear and witch hysteria bloomed into a worldwide phenomenon."

Master Gert inclined their head toward the trio of witches up front. "The years of witch hysteria weren't just bad for witches, but for humankind as well. About half the women and men tried and executed as witches were just basic humans."

"But it wasn't just witches and humans affected."

It took Sylvie a long moment to realize the soft voice was Vivian's. She was twisting her long hair absently between her fingers.

"Yes, banshees, vampires"—here, Master Gert nodded to Sylvie and Vera—"and other human-passing monsters were also sadly lumped in and murdered."

Ah—*Vivian was a banshee.* As Sylvie wracked her brain, trying to think of what a banshee's special qualities were other than, well, wailing, Chad whispered something to Lenny and Milo and they sniggered, shoulders quaking. Clearly they didn't think this was a sad thing.

But Sylvie had to admit, for as terrified as she'd been for the past several hours . . . it was sad. Truly sad.

"Fast-forward to today. Now the world is so populated that even our most reliable hiding places are studded with humans. Cameras are everywhere, drones fly overhead, and we're so connected, it's impossible to sneeze without someone—or something—hearing it."

There was a lot of nodding.

"These days monsters live in the shadows. Our numbers are small, which, as we all know, helps very much with the business of hiding. Every few years, there's a sighting that puts an entire generation of monsters in danger. Yeti, Scott, and Nessie all live at this camp because of the intense scrutiny that happens after each sighting."

How many times had Sylvie watched that documentary about yetis and Sasquatch? How many times had she read those blogs insisting some farmer in Sweden had located a mass burial of manticore bones? And Nessie? Sylvie had a T-shirt with the famous grainy photo of the monster's head peeking out of the water. Until about fifteen hours ago, Loch Ness had been near the top of monstrous places Sylvie wanted to tour as an adult.

"And though technology has helped immensely in keeping monsterkind more secure, the number of safe havens has only gotten smaller since the turn of the last century. Technology helps as much as it hurts." Master Gert smiled tightly. "Of course, some monsters are able to pass as humans and walk and work among them with protocols in place. And some who can't still do work with humans in a shadow capacity—"

"My parents work for the CIA," blurted the disembodied voice of Fade.

"Yes, that exactly, which is wonderful." Master Gert gestured with a long hand toward where Fade's lanyard hovered at chest height next to Benedict. "But that being said, the truth is that I asked Yeti to develop our HURT criteria to help you all cope in a world that is increasingly less friendly to monsters with each passing day."

Something cold was rising in Sylvie now. Her skin itched. Her chest tightened as her heartbeat slowed to an occasional, sluggish thump.

"I won't sugarcoat it, plasma-coat it, beetle-coat it—no matter your monster makeup, you are part of a generation that faces the largest hardships toward all of monsterkind in centuries. Between technological advances, a human population that is becoming more willfully ignorant to anyone unlike them, and irrepairable damage to the environment that puts our monster refuge in danger, there will be innumerable challenges in the coming years."

That heavy silence was back. The wind whipped through the clearing outside, rattling the barely clinging shingles and whistling through the cracks and holes in the walls. But even the breeze couldn't budge the weight that covered them like a blanket of wet snow.

"We'll have plenty of fun and games here this week. You'll have as many happy memories as you've had in years past. But now that all of you are older, Monster Camp isn't just about being a place to be yourself and have fun; it's a place to be yourself, have fun, and learn everything you can to ensure that not only do you survive as you grow into adulthood, you thrive."

Behind Master Gert, Yeti and Amos were nodding.

"Be kind and be yourself are our rules in this camp because we believe those should be your rules for a good life. By some estimates, there are less than a thousand full-blooded monsters living within the United States today."

Sylvie's breath caught. *A thousand?* There were a thousand people in her middle school on any given day between the students and the staff.

"Though those numbers are only an estimation, because any sort of official monster registry would be extremely dangerous," Master Gert continued, "they are likely only off by a few percentage points. We are a small group no matter how you cut it. Which is why being kind and being yourself are crucial. There are very few of us left. We shouldn't shortchange ourselves or our kind with self-loathing, petty disagreements, or any other harmful behavior."

Chad suddenly seemed to find his shoelaces very interesting.

"Now," Master Gert said, with a Yeti-like clap of their hands, "I did promise I would answer Milo's question, and I'm afraid I've gone the long way around. Milo, to be frank, it would not benefit us to blast out a public relations campaign about how cool monsters are, because the risk is far too great. Humans outnumber us millions to one. If we reveal ourselves and they like us? That would be a true watershed moment. If we reveal ourselves and they don't like us? Or even a fraction of them don't like us? We're as good as extinct. All of us."

"But that could change in our lifetimes, right?" This question was from Tatiana, hope in her big goblin eyes.

"My dear, I'm one thousand two hundred two at Samhain." Sylvie was floored. They looked younger than her dad! Maybe Master Gert's monster genes meant they didn't visibly age. "I haven't seen an opportunity in my lifetime for a safe collective reveal."

"But . . . but you used to live among the humans," Vivian said softly. "They trusted you with their kids, didn't they?"

Master Gert kicked up a brow, the corner of their mouth going up with it in a smirk. "Yes. But they didn't believe I was a monster. If they had thought I was one, well, I most likely wouldn't be standing before you today."

No one seemed to have anything to say to that, though Sylvie's mind was racing now, wondering just what people thought Master Gert was. Not a vampire or they would've said something to Sylvie, surely. A witch? That didn't seem right. Maybe a banshee like Vivian? Did banshees live with humans?

"Okay, on that note, I'll turn things back over to Yeti, who will give you an overview of what to expect from your HURT session each day this week, and then we'll head back at the sound of Rupert's alarm to what is sure to be a scrumptious lunch from Mummy G."

Yeti stepped forward, and Amos began distributing flyers with information about the week's Human Understanding and Resources Training lessons. Sylvie accepted hers with fingers that, like the rest of her, suddenly felt too much.

She wasn't numb anymore, anywhere. Instead, she could feel every beat of her heart, every breath, every blink and twitch, and the splintered wood digging into the back side of her shorts.

Guilt filled her to the brim, cold and thick. She kept

swallowing to no avail. She blinked at the paper in front of her but couldn't focus on any word but one.

Human.

It swam in her vision, tumbled through her mind, sharp and mean against everything she'd just learned about monsters. About the people in this room.

Terror still lingered in Sylvie's gut, her fingers trembling and her heart too fast, but the feeling was less now, because now she knew every single person here had far more reason to fear her than she had to fear them.

CHAPTER 15

Dine and Dash
(Away from Chad, OMG)

Walking back to the main camp, Yeti took a different trail, which popped the group back out of the woods by what had to be the camp staff quarters.

The cabins were larger and less whimsical than the camper lodging, perhaps a remnant of whatever had been here before Monster Camp. These looked like the little log-cabin-style buildings Sylvie had expected upon her arrival. But they were decorated in the way of permanent residency. With TV antennas and wind chimes and doors that occasionally weren't the same utilitarian brown of their bodies.

Vera nodded toward one with baby-pink shutters and a matching door. "That one's Yeti's. Definitely a step up from the old mill. More watertight."

"A hundred percent."

Sylvie's heart lurched at the sight of the cheery little

cabin. It had window boxes with purple flowers, a wind chime jingling merrily next to a hummingbird feeder. As large as Yeti was, he'd have to duck to enter his own home, but after fifty years in that crumbling old mill, that little cabin had to have felt like a dream.

Not having to hide out in the open probably felt just as good to Yeti.

Sylvie suddenly wondered if he had a family . . . or if he was the last of his kind. Actually, she wondered that about all the adults. To be totally alone . . . no one—monster or human—should have to feel like that.

At least Monster Camp gave them, as the brochure said, a place to be themselves.

As Sylvie's thoughts churned forward, guilt pressing against the base of her throat, she followed Vera as the line popped out into the main lawn, the flagpole and all its many signs right in front of them, the lake to their left, and the general common area mostly ahead.

They wound across the grounds, and for the first time, Sylvie noticed the zombified crew working under the direction of Scott. The massive manticore was currently tending to a two-man zombie team in their matching jumpsuits as they carefully raked the sand-volleyball court, erasing yesterday's added blades of grass and grit. Scott stood in the center of the court in a specially-sized ball cap that read "GROUNDS LEADER" and petting the giant spider that lived in the web . . . one Sylvie now suspected wasn't animatronic. He waved.

"Lunch! Finally," Chad whined up front as Yeti led them to the long, low building that was the mess hall. "I could eat a whole heifer."

"You probably will," Lenny joked.

"If that's a dare, I'm taking it."

"Gross," Freya sniffed.

Sylvie wasn't sure what to make of any of this. Was it a joke? Or truly a dare?

Last night, she'd walked with Vera to the mess hall, but she'd stayed outside when Vera went inside for her brown-bag dinner and to-go cup of blood. Sylvie was so out of sorts that she didn't trust her stomach not to betray her if she got within ten feet of food. That morning, she'd chickened out again and just made a "cheers" motion toward Vera with her "You Suck" tumbler as her roommate went inside to collect her bagel.

But now, Sylvie was finally ready to eat something besides a protein bar. Maybe. She honestly wasn't sure what to expect. Vera's brown-bag dinner the night before looked normal—a sandwich, chips, fruit—but Sylvie had been pretty distracted by the fact that she was washing it down with actual 98.6-degree *blood*.

The boys rushed into the building first, because of course. Vera halted under the shade of a big tree beside the door, and Sylvie ended up doing the same, letting the rest of the kids from both groups in first. Once the ghosts slipped past and they were the only ones left outside, Sylvie followed Vera inside.

It took a few seconds for her eyes to adjust, but when they did . . . Sylvie was flabbergasted.

Chad did have a side of cow on his plate.

Or, well, the chopped-up equivalent.

Piled high were raw cuts of pink steak marbled with fat and glistening with condensation, a few chunks of ice melting beside the bottom layer. Chad had already stuffed a T-bone into his mouth, his slightly pointed teeth gnashing furiously. Like he was tearing into a face-sized slice of pizza and not raw meat.

Across a picnic-style table, Milo's plate matched Chad's, though his manners didn't. The blond werewolf was polite enough to use a knife and a fork. Meanwhile, Lenny was next to Milo, motoring through an entire plate of vacant-eyed sardines. He had a second plate that housed discarded baby-fish skeletons, their bones threading together, sharp and white.

Sylvie's stomach ping-ponged around her gut like the meanest kid in the bounce house. Fruit punch wafted into her nostrils, fed by acid that licked at the back of her throat.

"What are you looking at, vamp?" Chad snarled. His lips glistened with grease. "Didn't anyone teach you it's not polite to stare?"

Sylvie blinked. Chad was glaring at her. He was right; she was staring. How could she not? The closest thing she'd ever seen to someone eating like that was feeding time in the tiger pavilion at the zoo.

Vera tugged her hand. "Don't worry about him."

Sylvie forced herself to look away and let Vera lead her over to a cafeteria-style smorgasbord on the far side of the room. The kind of buffet display reminiscent of a school cafeteria, with a sneeze guard and wells for different types of food.

But as they got closer and Sylvie caught sight of Mummy G's lunch spread . . . her stomach revolted again.

This time, Sylvie did nearly vomit, the fruit-punch-and-bile mixture hot on the back of her throat. Her knees softening so much, she had to grip the side of the buffet, Sylvie clenched her teeth together, clamped her lips shut, and swallowed.

The boys didn't have a special order of pure protein. The raw meat and fish were right there on the buffet, along with the weirdest lineup of food—if you could call it that—that Sylvie had ever seen.

The raw meat led into a vat of something that looked like Grandma Marcy's famed butternut-squash soup but was labeled "PLASMA." It came with a ladle.

Actual soup came next, but it was made with *larvae*. Sylvie was fairly certain some of those larvae weren't completely pulverized in the cooking process, because *several* somethings were definitely moving around the beige clam-chowder-esque stew.

Sylvie wrenched her attention away from the soup as an amputated larva attempted to escape down the side of the stainless-steel serving well.

She suddenly wished she hadn't.

The food at the end of the line—ostensibly sides to go with your soup and raw meat—was a slew of stomach-churning treats from start to finish: a salad featuring a mix of so-fresh-they're-still-moving tentacles and earth-worms; beetles fried a deep-golden brown; fingernail fancies; something vaguely resembling pudding labeled as "toxic sludge"; candied eyeballs(!) from an unspecified source.

At the end of the display was an assortment of insu-lated carafes—squid ink, poison-ivy tea, and a big one on the end marked "Type O." In tiny letters beneath it were the words "Types A, B, and AB available by special request."

Sylvie was certain all the color had drained from her face right along with her appetite.

She couldn't eat this. She couldn't even *pretend* to eat it.

And yet everyone here was chowing down. The sounds of forks scraping across plates and snatches of conversation carved around bites of this very food rang out from the tables lined up behind her.

"Hey, Mummy G."

Sylvie's head snapped away from the carafe of blood and back to the present. The mess-hall manager was standing in a threshold between the main dining room and what had to be the kitchen. She wore a frilly, lace-trimmed apron and the same hollow-eyed look from last night. Upon hearing Vera's greeting and seeing the vampire wave, Mummy G let out a little grunt and nodded. She started to turn, as if she was going to collect something in the back, but then she turned her attention to Sylvie.

"Hungry?"

Her voice was hard to make out, all the letters crowding together into something guttural, but Sylvie couldn't deny that Mummy G *was talking to her*. The dark wells of her eyes seemed to bore into Sylvie's face, trying to figure out what she might find appetizing. Sylvie guessed the mummy knew that even full-blooded vampires ate real food sometimes.

Sylvie smiled but shook her head in answer. She couldn't do it. Not now. She had a protein bar in her backpack. She could polish it off in the outhouse. It would be fine. And she wouldn't retch everywhere.

The mummy shrugged but didn't press. When she returned from the kitchen, she had a brown paper sack in her bandage-wrapped grip, Vera's name scrawled across the front.

"Thank you, Mummy G." Vera accepted the bag with her little, closed-mouth smile. A lank of her thick red hair fell across her face, and she pushed it behind her ear in a way that made it seem to Sylvie like she was nervous.

Why would Vera be nervous?

This was the third meal she'd had since arriving here, and if it wasn't enough or didn't taste good, she could always supplement with blood or maybe the plasma . . . did vampires eat—slurp?—plasma? It was made from blood, wasn't it?

As soon as Mummy G disappeared back into the kitchen, the reason for Vera's nerves became obvious.

The pair of them had turned around and were facing the tables, figuring out where to sit. Just like the lunch-room at school, everyone had their own little pods. The witches in the back; Zephyr, Norah, Vivian, and Tatiana knotted together; Francis, Bebe, and Fade; then the were-wolf boys. As Sylvie readied the suggestion that they sit at the end of the witches' table, Chad stood and wiped his meat-juice-covered palms on his basketball shorts.

"What's on the menu today for that delicate little tummy of yours, Vera?"

"None of your business," Vera mumbled, the bag clutched tightly in her fingers.

"Come on now, inquiring minds want to know what *humans* are eating these days."

With that, Chad snatched the bag and held it up over his head, where Vera couldn't reach it.

"Hey, give that back!" Vera yelped, jumping for it. Sylvie angled for the bag on her tippy-toes, but she was shorter than Vera and jumping just thumped her backpack painfully against her spine.

"Of course," Chad sneered. Sylvie was confused for a second, but then he reached one hand into the bag and roughly began to reveal Vera's lunch one item at a time.

"Chips."

He dropped the bag of Lay's, and Vera lurched to catch it. She was able to snag the bag but not reset before Chad pulled out a green Granny Smith and dropped it too.

"Apple."

Sylvie dove for the fruit, catching it just before it hit the ground.

As both of them scrambled back to standing, cradling the food in their palms, Chad pulled out the last item—a sandwich. He let the brown paper sack float to the floor, using both hands to wrench open the wax-paper wrapping and sniff what was inside.

"Bologna. That's mosaic meat. Gross."

Nose crinkling, Chad then tossed the sandwich like a frisbee in the gap between the two girls.

Suddenly, Sylvie was right back in the park, trying to save her LARP binder from Fisher and his minions. With a cry, Sylvie shot a hand out in the gap, her fingertips snatching the hurtling sandwich out of the air. The soft bread collapsed under her fingers, compressing on the lunch meat in a way that kept the whole thing together.

She handed the sandwich to Vera, whose eyes were the size of dinner plates and shiny with welling tears.

"Not cool, Chad. She can't help it."

"Yeah, because she's not a real monster." He bared his teeth. Raw beef clung to his incisors. "Only a human would touch that food with a ten-foot pole."

"Oh, yeah?" Sylvie asked. But it wasn't really a question. Instead, she turned and marched over to the entrance to the kitchen. "Mummy G? I'll take a sack lunch if you have one. Just like Vera's."

Immediately, the mummy reappeared with a second sack lunch. Sylvie accepted it with a smile.

That smile stretched into something mean when she turned around and approached Chad, the bag clutched in both hands.

"What are you doing, vamp?"

"What I do every day as a *real monster* at human school." Sylvie fished through the bag, yanked out the apple, and, without breaking eye contact with Chad, took a huge bite. Chad snarled in disgust as Sylvie let the apple's tart juice dribble down her chin. "Get educated on what other monsters consume, meathead."

Sylvie grabbed Vera's hand. "Hey, want to eat outside?"

Vera nodded furiously, her lunch pieces safely returned to the crumpled brown sack in her other hand.

The pair swept past Chad and the rest of the tables. They were almost to the door when they heard the werewolf's comeback, shot belatedly at their backs. "You do that. Nobody wants to watch you eat that gross stuff anyway."

"You tell yourself that, Chad," Sylvie mumbled under her breath.

When they stepped into the light of the noon sun, Vera found her voice. "Thank you! That was awesome."

"It was self-defense," Sylvie said. "Sorry he's such a jerk to you."

"That's Chad. . . ."

"That's not an excuse." Sylvie dropped Vera's hand, only to snatch up her wrist and halt them. She faced her roommate and ducked her head to try to catch Vera's big downcast eyes. The moment Vera's gaze met hers, Sylvie's eyebrows flew up. "Maybe he thinks he can get away with that very unkind behavior because he can play it off as being funny or whatever, but it's still bullying. And it's not okay."

"I—I know."

"You also know it's okay to stand up for yourself, right?"

Vera nodded but seemed to look anywhere but at Sylvie. "I'm . . . I'm not very good at that."

"Good thing practice makes perfect."

Vera peered at Sylvie through a curtain of red hair. "You've . . . you've had bullies to practice on?"

"Plenty. And I'm not going to give Chad a pass to bully you just because that's how he operates."

A small smile ticked at the side of Vera's mouth. "Okay." Her eyes fell to the sack in Sylvie's hands. "I appreciate you asking for a human lunch too . . . but really, you don't have to eat it if you don't want to."

As if on cue, Sylvie's stomach grumbled, loud enough that they both laughed. "I think I worked up an appetite in there."

Vera tugged them under the very same tree they'd stood under before entering the mess. She plopped down in such a way that she could lean on her backpack.

"Is it okay that we're eating out here?" Sylvie asked, looking around. She'd said it as a mic drop to Chad, but she wasn't actually sure it was allowed. There weren't tables to sit at, and no one else was outside.

"Yeah. I did it last year. It was fine. We're not missing anything."

CHAPTER 16

You Want Me to Capture What Now?

Lunch outside with Vera felt almost normal.

Sylvie had been slightly concerned that she wasn't eating food like a real vampire would—Like, did they smell everything? Maybe take tiny bites? Or scrunch their nose up before trying something new?—but if Vera's half-vampire-eating skills were any indication, Sylvie was at least on target simply by downing her sandwich, chips, and apple like she would at Evermore Middle School.

What came after lunch, though? That was not normal in the least.

At yet another earth-shaking "CAW-CAW" from the very helpful Rupert, Scott waved down both groups to join him at the flagpole. Rupert perched atop the pole, his giant head and beak pointing straight down at them, blinking and twitching, as he watched, like a security camera gone wild.

But that wasn't when Sylvie was once again reminded that things here were not normal.

Actually, that wasn't true. They were normal—for the monsters.

And Sylvie Shaw was not a monster, only pretending to be one. And, she had to admit, the way Rupert was staring at her now—all morning, if she was being honest—Sylvie wondered if the bird knew her secret. His beady black eyes seemed to scan her like the full-body X-ray thing at the airport. It was . . . unsettling.

"Okay, let's see. . . ." Scott had a clipboard and seemed to be counting the campers rather than taking official roll call.

Sylvie noticed that Master Gert, Yeti, and Amos were nowhere to be found. Sylvie couldn't decide if that was a good thing—fewer monsters to perform for—or a bad thing because there'd be only one adult around if Chad decided that lunch was just a warm-up bullying session.

Pleased that everyone was accounted for—including Fade, whose name tag hovered near the semitranslucent ghosts—Scott ditched the clipboard in favor of two boxes, identical in every way except that one was red and the other one was blue. The manticore tucked them under his arms and did an about-face toward the trees. "All right, kiddos. This way!"

He turned, his massive lion's body stalking forward, his scorpion's tail twitching in time with each step.

"Do you know what sort of team-building activity we're doing?" Sylvie asked as she fell in line next to

Vera. "Like, have you done this before?"

Since this morning's announcement, Sylvie had wracked her brain for every team-building thing she'd done in her short life. At orchestra camp, it had been a "rosin relay." At the family climbing clinic she'd attended with her dad, it had been trust falls. Sylvie did not want to do trust falls within a five-mile radius of Chad.

"I think we'll have to work together," Vera said. "Either as a group against Fester or with both Fang and Fester working together for a common goal."

That was what Sylvie had been afraid of that morning. When everyone had a role, fading into the background was a bad idea.

The snaking ribbon of campers began to slow at yet another clearing somewhere within the Monster Camp woods, their destination ahead. Sylvie's gut did a backflip as her steps stopped completely at a rusted gate.

They'd arrived at a graveyard.

It was small and old, most of the names carved into the gravestones worn away by time. A massive marble building the size of Sylvie's detached garage anchored one side, a serpent sneering across the roofline. On the other side, a thicket of small trees heavy with immature pears leaned over obelisk-style gravestones, their points jabbing toward the clouding sky.

Though she typically liked all things spooky as a rule, Sylvie did not care for cemeteries. They reminded her too much of her mom.

"Campers, we'll have two teams today. Team Fang, stand over here to my right. Team Fester, to my left," Scott directed from a point toward the center of the grave-yard, under a massive tree. It had once been surrounded by benches. Now, all but one was upturned, beached in the patchy grass.

The groups began arranging themselves—all except Sylvie, who still stood outside the gate, and Vera, who was in the cemetery but lingered near her roommate.

"Are you . . . okay?" Vera asked, voice low so that the others couldn't hear. Sylvie noticed that she'd also angled her body to block most of Sylvie from view.

"Um . . ." Sylvie wasn't sure how much she wanted to talk about her mother with Vera or anyone at this camp. But she knew if she mentioned her mom, it shouldn't be in a rushed conversation before whatever Scott had planned.

"Hey, vamps! You're holding everyone up," Chad yelled.

Of course he'd taken notice.

Sylvie took three calming breaths. "Yeah," she told Vera. "I'm fine."

Vera raised an eyebrow, clearly not believing a word of it. But Sylvie stepped through the gate, and that seemed to dissuade Vera from prodding.

All of Group Fang was staring at them.

A reflexive "sorry" dropped out of Sylvie's mouth, even though she wasn't.

"Okay, now that we're all here, let me tell you about this afternoon's team-building activity!" Scott and Yeti had similar energies—like they'd eaten an entire gallon of mint chocolate chip before speaking to the group at large. "The name of the game is . . . capture the frog!"

A cheer went up from most of the campers. In elementary school, Sylvie had played a game called capture the *flag*. They could be similar, but a frog and a flag shared a first letter, and that was about it. Sylvie swallowed hard as the excited chattering subsided, and Scott ran through the rules.

"In the game of capture the frog, the object is to capture the other team's frog. I know, I know, that much is pretty self-explanatory." Scott laughed a little here, and Sylvie tried to pretend it didn't come out like a roar. His head was a normal human's, but the chest powering the sound was a lion's, after all. It was enough to raise goose bumps on her forearms. Sylvie tried to rub them away. "Also self-explanatory are our teams—Group Fang and Group Fester will compete against each other. Today is about teamwork; this afternoon, we're going to work within our camp teams for the very first time."

Freya very obviously rolled her eyes at Benedict and Annika, who would be on the other team.

"From there, the rules are slightly less explanatory, and they do vary, so I want to make it clear how this game will proceed." Scott held up his two boxes. "Within these boxes are our two frogs. Before we start the game, each team will congregate with their frog box on their half of the playing field."

Scott threw his arms wide.

"Your playing field is contained within this fenced area. Group Fang, your side is this way"—he pointed toward the big mausoleum—"and Group Fester, your side is over there." He pointed toward the pear trees.

Everyone nodded. Even Sylvie.

"Once the frogs are released by the teams, the game will begin. The object is to be the first team to capture the opposing team's frog and bring it back to your territory." The manticore paused. "Let me repeat, so we're all clear: it isn't enough to simply capture it; you must cross the dividing line between the territories—otherwise known as this very tree—and arrive on your side first with the frog." Scott scanned the crowd. "Everyone got that?"

They did.

"Good, now, a couple more rules. If you cross into the opposing team's territory and are tagged, you are in the dungeon until a teammate is able to make it across and tag you back in."

Scott leaned around the big tree and gestured to something Sylvie hadn't seen before: two open graves.

They were partially filled in by time and debris, but they were still at least four feet deep and shaped like a casket. Each was situated about ten feet from the center line.

Sylvie did not want to go to the dungeon. Not now. Not ever.

An open grave was not going to happen for her.

"Um . . ." Vera raised her hand tentatively. Scott nodded at her to continue. "Isn't it a little disrespectful to play a game in a graveyard? Those are human life spans on the graves, and, um, my mom and grandparents have always told me to only walk in front of the headstones so I don't step on anyone's final resting place."

Grandma Marcy had reminded Sylvie of the very same thing every time they went to visit her mom in Evermore Central Cemetery. Obviously, this was not somewhere they visited in Vera's previous camp experience.

Scott's face broke into a friendly, less feral smile. "Yes, Vera, you're right. It would be quite disrespectful to play a game in a normal graveyard. However, this one has been donated for our use by its residents."

Sylvie couldn't keep her brows from creeping together at Scott's answer, which was less an explanation than a riddle.

"Everyone buried here is a ghost," Norah said to the group, but mostly to Vera and Sylvie, who were clearly the most confused. "Our great-grandpa's bones are over there." She nodded, and Zephyr swept a hand that way. This was the first time Sylvie realized they were related.

"Nobody's at home, nobody to disrespect," Scott assured the group. "Plus, in the covenant donating the land from the Ghost Coalition, it's specified that they want us to do programming here."

"Oh, okay," Vera said, quietly.

Sylvie leaned over and said, "I'd never heard of that either."

"Now, let's continue with the rules, shall we?" Scott asked, though it wasn't really a question. "Where was I? Oh, yes. If by some fluke your entire team ends up in the dungeon at once, you forfeit because no one can save you. The other team will win, even if they have no frog. Everyone got that?"

A wave of nods went around the group.

"What do we get if we win?" Freya asked, as Chad, of course, accepted Team Fang's frog box. Scott's big mouth dropped open, but before he could say anything, Freya's little hand sprang up like a stop sign. "Please don't say bragging rights."

Scott smiled with *all* his teeth. Though they were technically humanoid, Sylvie couldn't decide if it was more or less disconcerting than when Yeti did the same.

"Normally, bragging rights would be all I'd be authorized to give you." Scott's pointer finger (claw?) sprang up. "However, today I can confirm that the winning team will earn lake time with Nessie!"

The *OOOOOOH*s and *AHHHHHH*s began almost immediately.

Vera was in Sylvie's ear. "Nessie is very particular about who's in her lake and when." This was definitely news to Sylvie. "Having her approval for an entire afternoon in her water when it's not on her usual schedule? That's nearly impossible to get."

Sylvie normally loved to swim. But the prospect of doggie-paddling in a murky lake while a legendary monster lurked in its depths was too much even for her monster-loving heart. She'd never wanted to lose a game more.

"Oh, and one more thing," Scott said. "The use of your gifts is encouraged. Fly, magick, and disappear to your hearts' content! As long as you do so safely and responsibly, that is.""

Sylvie hoped none of her fellow monsters had supersonic hearing, because then they'd be able to hear her heart beating louder than the timpani drum in orchestra class. So far, she'd managed to get by without revealing her lack of vampire powers. But what if her team expected her to use superspeed or superstrength or whatever powers vampires had in real life? The sound of Scott's voice interrupted her panic spiral.

"All right, teams, it's time to meet your frogs."

He was positively beaming as he gestured toward Benedict, holding Fester's box, and Chad, who had the red box pressed to his tank top. From where Sylvie stood, she could just barely read the word embroidered on the side of the box. "Frick."

Using two ridiculously hairy fingers, Chad slid open the slot on top of the box.

The frog stared back.

Bloodred and slick, it was the size and shape of a beating heart.

"Frick? Nice to meet you little buddy," Freya all-out cooed. "Hey, Benedict, what's yours called?"

"Frack. He's as blue as an electric eel!"

Electric eels were dark gray or brown, *not blue*, but Sylvie kept that bit of knowledge to herself.

Scott clapped for their attention. "Okay, teams, huddle on your side, talk over strategy, and decide where to release Frick and Frack. You have five minutes. GO!"

"Wait!" Tatiana's chartreuse hand shot up. Scott's finger hovered over the timer function on his watch, one eyebrow raised. "They have one more player. That's not fair."

Annika took a step forward toward Scott. "Tatiana's right. Are you planning on playing on our team?"

Bebe's wings fluttered and her water-producing fingers balled into fists as she lifted off the ground. "Hey, wait, it's not fair to have Scott on your team, he's an adult."

"Yeah, well, it's not fair that there are eight of you and seven of us," Zephyr shot back.

Scott held up both hands. "You all make good points. Group Fang, the fairest thing for us to do is for you to have a player sit out with me. Please vote among yourselves."

Sylvie's heart leapt once more, this time with joy. This was the perfect excuse for her not to have to demonstrate her distinct lack of powers. But before she could open her mouth to volunteer, Chad cut in.

"Vera won't play," he said, neglecting to even consult with his teammates. But when the other Fang members stayed silent, it was clear they didn't disagree with Chad's pronouncement.

It was obvious why.

Vera didn't even react other than to sweep a curtain of hair out from behind her shoulders so it fell in front of her face, blocking out one of her giant eyes. She wasn't surprised, but she obviously was embarrassed.

Sylvie nervously stepped forward as her escape route started to slip away. "I'm happy to sit out. Vera, you should play!"

She thought she'd whispered, but maybe werewolves did have super-duper hearing, because Lenny shut her down the second the words were out of Sylvie's mouth. "We really need a full vamp on our team if we want time with Nessie." Then he tipped his ball cap at Vera. "Sorry, Vera."

"No. It's fine." Vera shrugged her slim shoulders. Then, she mumbled to Sylvie, "At least this way, Chad can't blame me if we lose."

That was true. That had been her fear this morning. Sylvie tried not to make it her fear too.

Game on.

Group Fang vs. Group Fester

Chad came up with Group Fang's frog-hiding spot and strategy. Because of course he did.

They'd split up into two teams—seekers and guards.

Bebe, Freya, Chad, and Milo were seekers. The idea being that because Bebe and Freya could fly, they'd be able to reach the frog if it wasn't at ground level. Both Chad and Milo claimed that being werewolves made them fast and naturally athletic, so they hoped this would keep them out of jail and on the hunt. Sylvie wasn't sure why Lenny wasn't included in this scenario, but he seemed pleased to be grouped with Francis and Sylvie to guard Frick.

Sylvie was relieved, because this meant she couldn't be tagged out and put into the open-grave dungeon. Shudder. But it also meant she'd have to work with the two boys to protect Frick while also not making it obvious where the bright-red frog was located.

"But don't stand right by the frog," Chad was saying, "That'll give away his location; they'll know where he is if you're blocking him directly." He gestured widely with his arms to Group Fang's side of the playing area. "You'll need to spread out, work the border, and stay at least ten feet away from Frick, so that if one of them gets past your line, they won't know immediately where to look on the other side."

Sylvie had to admit that even though Chad was a jerk, he could create a solid plan. She didn't know if this made her like him more or less. Or if she should add those skills to the running list she had to worry about if her humanness was revealed.

It was also decided that Freya would put a temporary freezing spell on Frick so that he would stay where they put him. The witch explained that the spell in question was one she could reverse at any time, so if he was located, the frog could—in theory—hop away from his captors.

Group Fang hid Frick on top of the giant mausoleum. The body of the snake obscured him nicely as long as Freya's spell kept him still. Sylvie honestly wasn't sure if hiding him up so high would do much considering four members of Group Fester could fly—the ghosts and the witches—but she didn't dare say anything. It was her job to stop them.

"All right." Scott clapped his hands together and faded

toward where Vera was propped up against a sturdy part of the aging cemetery fence. At least she wouldn't be alone the whole game if Scott refereed from there. "Everyone good? Ready to play?"

In answer, all seven players on either side of the massive dividing-line tree stepped forward. Group Fester wore game faces with little, smirking grins. Like they knew something the rest of them didn't. Well, all of them except Fade, whose expression Sylvie couldn't read, but which she assumed would match that of his teammates'.

Sylvie took a deep breath.

"Okay!" Scott crowed from his spot next to Vera. "On your marks, get set, seek!"

Group Fang immediately split apart, the seekers darting forward—Bebe flying with her wings and Freya with a spell, while Chad and Milo sped forward with twin, growling grins.

Meanwhile, the Group Fang guards spread out, each covering a third of their territory.

Sylvie was on the end farthest from the gaping pit of their site's dungeon, and that was something she very much appreciated. Francis didn't seem to mind being close to the dungeon. As prone to smiling as he was, his green face was already split wide, his long arms ready to sweep anyone coming at him straight into the open grave. And Lenny, well, he was in the middle and . . . Sylvie caught sight of something out of the corner of her eye and yelped.

No Lenny.

No, instead, right smack between Sylvie and Francis was a *horse*.

A big, snorting, tail-swishing black horse. Exactly where Lenny had been standing. Lenny's shorts, tank top, and shoes were in a heap beside the animal, but his Kraken ball cap was on the horse's head.

"What the . . . ?" Sylvie started, momentarily stunned stiff.

"I'm a kelpie," the *horse* said in Lenny's voice.

He wasn't a werewolf? Sylvie's mouth hung open. The horse spoke again.

"Look alive, vamp."

Then, before she could verbalize all the questions piling in her head—*because what the heck's a kelpie?!*—Lenny began to run, covering the middle in a streak of black silk. Sylvie pivoted and faced Group Fester, shaking her head and staring down her competition. The shock of it would have to wait.

They'd expected it to be four-on-three, a twin strategy of attack from Group Fester.

They were wrong.

Instead, six players rushed forward. Benedict, Annika, Zephyr, and Norah flying, as expected. But Tatiana and Fade rushed forward too. At least, Sylvie thought Fade had—he'd taken off his lanyard. Completely untraceable. An advantage was an advantage, after all.

Meanwhile, the only player who most definitely

stayed back to guard Group Fester's bright-blue frog was Vivian. As soon as Group Fang crossed the border, it immediately became clear why.

The banshee tossed her head back, her long hair sweeping the dead grass like the train of a wedding dress, and started SCREAMING.

Oh. No.

The high-pitched, keening wail was long and unrelenting, and it felt like a tornado siren was parked next door.

Every thought flew out of Sylvie's head.

She plugged her ears and doubled over. Across the line, Chad and Milo were doing the same, their quick strides stumbling as they bent to the noise. Bebe was shooting water at her own ears to drown it out, but it was too late, her flight path wrenching off course as she nearly plowed into a tree. Freya had dropped to the ground entirely, mumbling words to herself that might have been a spell to make it stop.

Meanwhile, a streak of bright blue rocketed from obelisk to obelisk; Frack was on the loose.

Sylvie was about to shout at Bebe, who was the closest to the frog's current location, when Lenny started frantically whipping his head, trying to get her attention without yelling uselessly or waving with arms he didn't presently have. Sylvie looked to where he was gesturing and—

Ghosts incoming!

Norah was plunging straight for Sylvie's side, trying

to go the long way around her along the fence line.

Sylvie broke into a run, hands out and up, wondering just how exactly she was supposed to tag a ghost. Would her fingers simply slip through her like a plane through a puffy cloud?

Norah started laughing, skittering by, high enough to dust the lower limbs of the half-dead oak that shaded this section of cemetery. Looking up and ahead, Sylvie saw that there was one large limb much lower than the rest. A tight knot of branches bent down close to it, a squirrel's abandoned nest in the shade there.

Sylvie had an idea.

Racing as fast as she could over the uneven ground, Sylvie took a running leap onto a flat-topped gravestone and jumped for the limb. Her hands caught the rough bark. Norah swerved to go over the branch instead of under, but just as she dodged over where Sylvie hung, Sylvie kicked both legs up and out like she'd learned to do rock climbing with her dad. Her foot went straight through Norah's leg. A cool numbness took over, and Sylvie knew she'd tagged Norah. And the ghost couldn't hide it.

"Ouch!" Norah screeched, loud enough that all of Sylvie's side could hear it, even over Vivian's continued wail. "I have nerve endings you know. You don't have to amputate. Rude."

It was probably pretty rude to stick your shoe into another person's leg, and Sylvie's cheeks flushed as she dropped from the limb and to the grass.

"Um, sorry. Dungeon for you."

"You don't have to escort me," Norah sniffed, and pointed herself toward Group Fang's open grave.

Out of the corner of her eye, Sylvie saw Lenny flash her a horsey grin. She shrugged back, a smile creeping onto her face. As Sylvie turned back to watch Norah lower herself into the grave, she suddenly realized her pulse was racing . . . but it wasn't from fear. Tagging Norah had actually been thrilling. And, well, kinda sweet. Sylvie literally just *took down* a ghost. It was something she couldn't have imagined, even in her wildest LARPing dreams. Yes, she was still a walking snack trapped in a mass of hungry monsters. But she was *almost* getting used to it. She was even maybe starting to . . . have fun?

Returning to the front line, Sylvie glimpsed the action on the other side. Bebe was chasing a screaming Vivian around, shooting her with water in hopes of breaking her concentration, while Freya, Milo, and Chad were working together to corner Frack. It was complete chaos.

On the Fang side, Zephyr had already managed to set Norah free, while Benedict and Annika were turning Lenny in circles as they searched for the red frog. They were almost to the mausoleum. It was an obvious hiding spot, now that Sylvie thought of it.

"Sylvie, watch out!"

Vera's voice ripped through her thoughts, and Sylvie's head whipped in her roommate's direction, over by the fence. Vera was pointing at something over Sylvie's shoulder. She spun in a slow circle, but couldn't figure out what—

Hands shoved Sylvie hard.

She fell forward, palms extended to catch her body, just like that terrible day on her old, crooked brick sidewalk. Just like that time, Sylvie caught herself before her face met the earth. But she wasn't safe—she was over the line.

Sylvie popped up and flipped over, managing a backward bear crawl, only to have someone grab her by the scruff of her tank top.

"Dungeon time, Sylvie." She looked up, and staring back down at her was Tatiana, her blue tongue kissing the back of her too-sharp teeth as they gleamed in a smile.

Tatiana frog-marched Sylvie over to the dungeon.

Sylvie hesitated. She didn't know Tatiana, but still she looked back and half pleaded, "Do I have to—"

Tatiana shoved her in. Geez, goblins were strong!

Sylvie got her feet in front of her just in time not to land on all fours. Still, her hands splayed out for balance, sinking into the dank mud.

She was in a grave. A real, actual, dug-out grave.

Suddenly, Sylvie wasn't having fun anymore.

She could see over the lip of the hole, just barely. And though she realized she probably shouldn't advertise the fact that she'd been caught, Sylvie started to wail. Not as loud as Vivian, but she hoped someone on this side of the playing area could hear her.

"Hey! Hey! Hey!" she yelled, waving her hands.

Sylvie only succeeded in getting a second cellmate: Milo. She would have preferred to escape the dungeon, but having someone else with her was preferable to being alone. And that was really saying something, since that someone else was a werewolf.

"Why are you in the dungeon?" he asked. "You're a guard."

"I got pushed over the line by Fade and tagged by Tatiana." Then, because she figured she should ask, she gestured to the werewolf. "You?"

"Chad told me to tackle Vivian to make her shut up so that he and the girls could coordinate in catching Frack, who's up in the trees. But apparently because she touched me first and we were on her side, I'm out."

"That doesn't seem fair."

"I know—"

"They're coming! They have Frick! They're coming!"

Sylvie and Milo stood on their very tiptoes only to see Lenny galloping toward them, yelling his warning like Paul Revere and his horse rolled up in one.

Behind him, Francis was running as fast as he could, trying to catch the flying wall of Benedict, Annika, and Zephyr. Cradled in the ghost's belly, like a cherry inside a glob of clear Jell-O, was Frick.

Lenny ran over and skidded to a stop in front of the grave. "We need defense, now!" It was obvious he meant to tag them out of the dungeon to help him form a front, as the rest of the team was literally up in the top branches of a pear tree, trying to coax Frack free. The familiar blue lightning of Freya's freezing spell zapped through the leaves as she aimed to incapacitate the frog they were trying to capture.

Lenny leaned a hoof into the grave. Milo reached for it, just as Scott yelled out, "Only one at a time, Lenny! You have to return to your side before freeing a second prisoner."

Milo withdrew his hand. "It should be Sylvie. She can fly."

Sylvie's lips dropped open. She couldn't fly. They knew vampires couldn't fly, or they would've tried to convince her to do just that as a seeker. Why did he think—

Lenny's hoof brushed her shoulder. "You're tagged. Get up here!"

Then, Milo pushed Sylvie to solid ground, and Lenny's hoof pulled her as the rest of him reversed. It was only when she got to her feet that she realized both boys had meant for her to *climb* onto Lenny's back.

"Let's go for a ride," the kelpie announced, nudging her hard with his horse muzzle. She swung a leg up, and they were already moving. Sylvie nearly fell off, but grabbed his hair—mane?—as he got back up to speed, dodging gravestones and angling straight for the flying trio. It was a wonder his Seattle Kraken hat was still in place, given the speeds he could go. "And then, when they dodge, just 'bat' and fly straight into Zephyr! Even if you don't knock the frog loose, you'll tag him out, and they'll have to scramble to cover."

"I—"

She was drowned out by another cry, louder than Vivian's wet wail, which was starting to weaken under Bebe's current onslaught of water. Tatiana and maybe Fade were chasing Bebe now, trying to tag her out as she shot water at point-blank range, straight into Vivian's open mouth. Sylvie looked over her shoulder to see Freya shoot out of the branches of the pear tree, an immobile blue lump in her palms.

Group Fang had captured a frog too!

Flying, Freya was all the way at the very back of the Group Fester territory, but if Sylvie could keep Group Fester from crossing the line, Freya would be fast enough to cross into Group Fang territory first. On the ground, Chad was sprinting now, covering from down below.

"Ready, Sylvie?"

At Lenny's voice, Sylvie looked back toward the approaching ghost and witches. They were in a flying V formation.

She couldn't turn into a bat. But she could do something, right?

Maybe she could stand on his back and jump for it? Sylvie knew her hand would go through Zephyr, just as it had Norah. She could pluck the frog straight out. Couldn't she? And then maybe grab on to Benedict or

Annika so that she wouldn't plummet to the hard grass? Yeah, that could work. Maybe.

But at the sight of Lenny dodging around gravestones and right at them, the ghost and two witches shot up, lifting like they were riding an elevator.

Suddenly, they were twenty or thirty feet off the ground. High enough to be above the treetops.

Sylvie craned her head. She couldn't jump for it now.

But that momentary lack of forward progress gave Lenny just the time he needed to make it onto the other side of the line. The pair of them were now in Group Fang territory. All they had to do was keep Frick inside and buy Freya time to cross the line.

"Bat! Bat! Bat!" Lenny yelled, and Sylvie realized it was a chorus, Milo, Freya, and Chad, all yelling the same thing at her back.

Sylvie couldn't fly. She couldn't jump for it. She couldn't do anything a normal human couldn't do.

So, as they crossed paths with Group Fester, Sylvie picked the only option she saw as viable.

She yanked Lenny's hat off his head and flung it straight for Zephyr.

Sylvie watched helplessly as the cap Frisbee'd up on a trajectory straight for the ghost, hopeful it might knock him off course, or, if that didn't work, count as a tag with a side of dungeon time.

Instead, Annika knocked the hat straight out of the sky with some red-lightning spell.

As the cap fell to the ground, Zephyr crossed over the line, Frick in his belly.

Group Fester erupted in a cheer.

Freya dropped from the air, Chad stopped running, Milo stopped yelling.

Lenny skidded to a halt, picked up his hat. He said nothing to Sylvie as she slid to the ground.

Group Fang had lost.

It was all Sylvie's fault.

And Chad made sure everyone knew it. Loudly, so all of Fang, all of Fester, Scott, and probably all the rotted corpses beneath their feet could hear.

"What was that, vamp?" Chad sneered as Scott and Group Fester pointed themselves down the trail, chattering excitedly about their afternoon at the lake. He actually looked like he might bite her. Despite herself, Sylvie shuffled back a step. Chad's sneer curved into a sickened smile. "You might as well be human."

Sylvie froze, trying not to react further. Was this it? Was Sylvie about to be unmasked?

"Oh, give it a rest, Chad. You look like a human in need of a good brow-and-back wax." Freya sniffed. Sylvie would hug her if the girl weren't still busy eviscerating the werewolf. "Want the name of my aesthetician?"

Sylvie was half-certain Chad didn't know what an aesthetician was, but he'd gotten enough from the first part of the jab to be properly mad.

"Well, you're a human with all your wires crossed, witch!"

Freya whirled on him, her hands balled into fists, her short pink hair sticking to her lip gloss. "I dare you to say that again, pup."

"I *think* I *might* hear some unkind words from the back," Scott said from waaaaay up front. "But that can't be right, because I know all Monster Camp monsters heard Master Gert last night when they declared they would not accept monstrous actions between campers."

Freya whirled around, hooked a finger to yank the hair free from her mouth, and balled her fists even tighter before taking a pointed step forward to get back in line with Annika and Benedict. Meanwhile, Chad closed his lips over his teeth and ducked his head, eyes reading the trail before he took each step. Sylvie and Vera exchanged a glance and trudged forward in the back.

No one in Group Fang said a word the rest of the way to the main camp.

Trading for *Eternity*

You might as well be human.

Chad's words echoed around Sylvie's mind, and her heart.

She was sure Chad truly saw her in that moment. That he knew what she was. That the put-down was actually an accusation.

Sylvie had run through all the scenarios in her mind as she walked through the trees in silence behind Vera. What would've happened if Freya hadn't cut in. What would've happened if she'd reacted in a different way.

That was close. *Too* close.

Chad and Milo had peeled off as they exited the woods and pointed themselves somewhere besides the camper cabins. Sylvie's heart raced at the thought of the pair of them in Master Gert's office, laying out their suspicions about Sylvie in real time.

She wasn't fast. She wasn't strong. She couldn't turn into a bat.

Totally not a vampire.

Meanwhile, now that Sylvie could see what all the other campers could do? The fear was back and so thick in her mind she was literally nauseous by the time her cabin was in sight.

Trailing Vera, Sylvie climbed the steps of their little gothic castle, stinking of loss and fear, and all she wanted to do was collapse face-first into her coffin bed and shut the lid.

Instead, Sylvie took a shower in the cabin's bathroom—which happened to be where the little door under the rack of antlers led—and stuffed a protein bar in her mouth while the water warmed. That helped the nausea—a relief.

The shower stream ran beautifully hot, melting the exhausted whining in her muscles to something more muffled. Drying her hair as much as she could, Sylvie redrew her widow's peak—the liner was waterproof, but it did fade—and checked her fangs, which were still straight and solid.

She opened the door and walked with the pent-up steam into their cabin's main room. Sylvie felt so renewed that when Vera met her with her own half-dry hair, a shiny magazine, and a grin and asked, "Want to go to the roof and read?" Sylvie couldn't say no.

Dropping her dirty clothes into her amazing expanding

duffel, Sylvie found one of the vampire novels she'd brought with her. Like almost everything else monster-rific she owned, this one had been her mom's. Tucking the paperback under her arm, Sylvie climbed the stairs.

Something was different when Sylvie hauled herself up on the roof this time—noise.

Laughter and splashes and screaming—the good kind. When she stood up and peered over the spires topped by Ringo and George, the mist shifted enough that she could see Tatiana doing a cannonball into the lake water and Vivian standing on the edge of the dock, obviously clapping after the goblin's performance. The witches rode brooms, hovering above the surface like skiers, clinging to tendrils of magic wrapped around the ghosts, who flew over the water faster than any speedboat Sylvie had ever seen. The long neck of Nessie bobbed in the shallows.

Ugh.

"I don't know how they have so much energy. I'm zonked."

Sylvie pointedly dropped into the nearest patio chair.

Vera raised a mischievous eyebrow but didn't look up from her magazine. "See those coolers?" Sylvie did, in fact, see a pair of big orange coolers on the dock. "They're filled with straight sugar water."

Sylvie's mouth fell open. "What? Master Gert wouldn't just give them, like, hummingbird food, would they?"

"Oh, no. Of course not! Zephyr and Norah brought it from their cabin. Ghosts are sugar freaks. It's a fact. They just swallow it down, and it dissolves straight into them, like Kool-Aid powder into water. Instant sugar rush." This was not a fact Sylvie knew. "Anyway, Group Fester will be partying on long after Rupert announces free time is over."

"If that's the sugar high, I really don't want to be anywhere near them when they crash." Then, harnessing the general *eau de loser* that wafted around her, she gave a sheepish grin and decided to address the elephant—er, bat—between them. "Too bad I couldn't save them from themselves by being able to 'bat' on command. . . ."

Sylvie glanced through her lashes at Vera, hoping she hadn't made a big mistake.

"Oh, don't worry about it! Those boys shouldn't have pressured you." Vera's too-human teeth gritted together in a grimace. "You just got your fangs, didn't you? It takes time and practice to 'bat' properly. It's not like it's flipping a switch—which they would know if they actually bothered to ask a vampire about it instead of just assuming."

Oh. Phew.

"It's still embarrassing," Sylvie answered, picking at her book cover.

"Only because they made it that way." Vera's cool hand landed on Sylvie's wrist. "My cousin took two full years after getting her fangs to 'bat' properly. Getting her learner's permit to drive was way easier than becoming a bat!"

Sylvie sighed, a genuine smile spreading across her face, and decided to go double or nothing in tricking Vera into educating her. "Well, I guess I shouldn't fault them for not knowing everything about me. I totally thought Lenny was just another werewolf. I've never met one, but I should've known he was a kelpie."

The word still sat strange on her tongue. She'd gotten a chance to look it up on her phone while scarfing down her protein bar. A kelpie was a Scottish monster who haunted streams in the shape of a horse but had the ability to shift into human form . . . and be super hairy like a werewolf, apparently.

Vera rolled her eyes. "If he didn't tell you or change in front of you, what were you supposed to think? He wears that hat all the time so you can't see his horsey ears." *Horse ears?* "And it's not like he sounds like Scrooge McDuck or anything. His family relocated with Nessie forever ago. He was born in the States."

"With . . . Nessie?"

"She's his aunt. Well, not biologically. But, like, they're close. Regional-monster thing. Gert too. Sort of."

"Oh."

With those mysteries solved, Sylvie felt a little better and maybe like she was on solidish ground. Sylvie nodded toward her roommate's reading material. "Whatcha reading?"

Vera flashed the magazine's cover. There, in smart, serifed letters at the top was the word "Eternity." A man with brown skin and an intense stare looked off the page as if he were calling sunbeams to his will. He wasn't in vampiric robes or anything. Instead, he was in a shiny black suit, like he was headed to a movie premiere.

"*Eternity?*" Then, Sylvie added because it seemed prudent, "Dad doesn't get magazines."

"It's, um, like *Time* but for vampires." Then, Vera added an annoyed little exhale. "My dad gets *all* the magazines."

"There are more?"

"Wow, your dad really does have you under a rock!"

Sylvie shrugged, hoping Vera was buying it. Her roommate's cheeks bloomed with color as words rushed out of her unlike ever before. Maybe Vera really liked sharing what she knew? "There are *lots* of them. *Eternity, Fang-Fare*—that one's like *People*—there's even one that's like *Popular Science* with information on new vampiric technologies and stories about biology and stuff. It only comes out twice a year, though." She waved *Eternity* around. "The others, like this one, come weekly. And Dad is obsessed with them. We probably have fifty years of back issues of all the magazines organized neatly by year in our attic."

Wow. How cool was that? Sylvie had never wanted to hang out in an attic so bad in all her life.

"What about you?" Vera read the spine as her pale face tilted and her long red hair leaned. "What's *Snow* about?"

Sylvie held up the battered paperback so that Vera might better see the cover, which depicted an enchanted mirror with a single white rose at its center.

"It's basically a retelling of *Snow White* where Snow White's a vampire, the huntsman's a werewolf—naturally—and the evil queen wants to make a pass at eternal life through the vampiric Snow White."

It was overwrought in a way that made everything dreamy, and there was literally no kissing, which Sylvie preferred because *yuck*.

"That sounds interesting," Vera answered, staring at the rose on the cover. "Dad doesn't really invest in vampire books. Unless they're by other vampires, he figures it's all wrong, so why try? Though I know for a fact Mom has some hidden on her e-reader, because I found them one day, but I read a page and it was . . . um, lots of . . ." Vera's cheeks flushed.

"There's no kissing in this one!" Sylvie blurted out, because she suddenly very much wanted Vera to know that fact. "It's just . . . a quest."

It was. A hunt and a quest and battles and . . . maybe that was why Sylvie, LARP queen, liked it so much. It had every twist and turn she imagined for her own role-play. Plus, a really cool, awesome vampire.

Sylvie noticed Vera's attention was still snagged on the white-rose cover, even as her cheeks paled back to their usual alabaster. "Would you like to read it?"

The question broke Vera's trance, and her face immediately contorted into something . . . *shy*. She rustled her magazine. "Oh no, no, I should . . . Dad told me this profile on Ichabod Clotting is 'rousing'—direct quote."

"Um, who is Ichabod Clotting?"

"You've never heard of him? Seriously, your dad must be way too good at keeping you guys under the radar if you haven't!" Sylvie shrugged dramatically. Vera continued. "He's pioneering private space travel, but that's just a front. He's really creating a program to put vampires in space and see if they can be the first beings to land on Mars."

"Whoa, really?"

Who better than a vampire to spend years in space hurtling toward a vegetation-free rock? Easy-peasy for the undead.

"Yeah, I mean, look at him." Vera stabbed the cover, right between Ichabod's super intense eyes. "He's totally full of himself, and the technology might not work at all, but you know, it's a cool way to use the billions he's amassed over the last, like, three hundred years."

Sylvie shifted in her chair, and the little metal seat gave a squawk of disapproval. "You know, I'd love to read that article when you're done."

And she would. While Sylvie hated math, she loved science. Especially when it involved a journey to a new frontier. Plus, the more she learned about the vampire population as quickly as possible, the better chance she had at surviving this week.

"Um, you can read it now if you want. I've got more magazines downstairs—"

"How about this? I'll trade you. I've read *Snow* a million times, and I can definitely tell by the look on your face you'd much rather read about Snow White the vampire than Ichabod Clotting." Sylvie leaned in. "I'll even give you a little report so you can know what it says about Ichabod in case you get quizzed on the way home."

Vera laughed, full and strong. "Suddenly, I think you understand my dad more than I do. Yes, there will be a test. And, yes, I would much rather read your book . . . if that's okay."

"It's a million times okay."

"Are you sure?"

"Of course! I don't know anyone else who's read it." *Except for Mom.* Sylvie swallowed down the rush of feeling balling in her throat and forced a fangilicious smile. "It'd be a blast to talk about it with you!"

"Really . . . no one you know has read it?"

Sylvie shook her head. "I haven't shared it with anyone at school. And, well, Dad doesn't really like to do things that remind him of Mom."

Vera's brows threaded together. But she didn't ask why he needed to be reminded.

Sylvie drew in a breath that was shakier than she'd expected. It'd been more than half her life and still this. Every time. "My mom was in an accident. Six years ago, she died—for good," she added quickly. Then, Sylvie looped her thumb to the chain around her neck and pulled out her little crescent moon. "She gave this to me, and I wear it every day. And . . . even though Dad doesn't like to do things that remind him of her, I do. All the time. These books, her favorite movies. All of it."

"Sylvie, I'm so sorry."

Sylvie had heard those exact words for six years. Yet Vera meant every syllable of her response. Her expression was fierce, her eyes dark pools trained on Sylvie's face. Her pale hand even fluttered across the table and to Sylvie's wrist in consolation.

"CAW-CAW!"

Sylvie flinched. She was never going to get used to that.

After Rupert's warning died down, Sylvie shrugged. "I guess that means dinner and scary human stories . . . but please read this." She shoved her beloved paperback toward Vera. "I really want to know what you think."

"I'm going to start right now."

"Right now?" Sylvie was confused. Rupert's job was keeping them on task. And, well, he'd spoken. On reflex, she caught sight of the bird, perched atop his flagpole. Sylvie could swear his beady bird eyes met hers, even at this distance.

"I . . . ," Vera started while accepting the book. She gently rubbed a finger along the etching of the cover's mirror. "I don't think I'm going to go to the scary human stories."

"I thought we had to go?"

When Vera shook her head, Sylvie wondered if this was like their adventure outside at lunch—a proper bending of the rules.

Really, up until she totally lied to her dad and showed up to this camp, Sylvie had never been one to make the type of decision that went against the grain and broke or, perhaps it was better to say, *tested* the rules. Now, it seemed she was running roughshod with everything since she lied to her dad. Even if all the lying she'd done recently was for survival.

"Remember Master Gert's rules?" Vera asked once she finished shaking her head. "Be kind and be yourself? Well, I don't find the scary human stories *kind to myself.* It's . . . awkward. I don't really like them. So I'm just not going to go."

Oh. Of course. As a half human, Vera wouldn't like them any better than any monster would probably like a scary story where they were the bad guy.

Sylvie really, really, really didn't want to draw more attention to herself by missing something—Master Gert certainly noticed when Sylvie left the opening ceremonies early—but she also didn't want to abandon Vera.

Maybe she'd go another night. "You know . . . I can stay here with you."

Vera waved her pale hands in a blur in front of her face. "You don't have to do that."

"No, it's really okay. It's been a long day." That much

was true. Sylvie was so tired, she was sure her bones were snoring. Then, Sylvie added some more truth with a little smile. "I've never been around so many monsters at once. It's sort of overwhelming."

Vera nodded. "It is."

"But if you want to be alone," Sylvie added, "I can totally—"

"No, no." Vera shook her head. "How about this? We can get a sack dinner from the mess, and we can just sit up here? Like a picnic."

Sylvie truly liked that idea. And that she could get a twin dinner. That protein bar sure had helped, but a real meal would work wonders. "They'll let you take your dinner from the mess? I thought we had to eat there, and that last night was a special case?"

"Mummy G and her crew never have a problem handing over a sack and letting us eat as we please. Plus, I think it might be because there's far less cleanup if we take it with us. One less person's dishes to wash or crumbs to sweep."

Vera mimed brushing her hands.

And it meant one less meal with Chad. Or fireside with Chad. Or anything with Chad.

Sylvie squeezed her eyes shut for a second, mentally slamming the door to her mind in Chad's sneering face.

Her eyes popped open. "Let's do it."

And so they munched on turkey and Swiss, drank blood (and fruit punch), and read *Snow* and *Eternity* together until the stars came out and it was impossible to keep reading.

It was the best night Sylvie had experienced in a very long time.

The Heart of the Human Matter

Ichabod Clotting really was an amazing individual.

The profile in *Eternity* was the question-and-answer type that Sylvie read often on her favorite LARPing blogs and was compiled by the reporter after spending several days at the billionaire's walled estate near Seattle.

He'd graduated from every Ivy League school in the United States at least twice (in different decades, under different names), and he had billions in the bank, but what was most important was what Clotting did with the money he kept after paying taxes (or not), because he spent the majority of it on *science*, including the space program Vera had mentioned.

It was truly quite interesting.

Actually, *all* the articles were interesting. Every page of *Eternity* was filled with stories about famous vampires, vampire families, conferences, films, books, TV shows streaming on vampiric-specific networks. There was even a whole section on vampiric athletics leagues, with standings and predictions and everything Sylvie's dad loved about those loud sports shows where people recounted in excruciating detail the baseball game he'd just watched and all the ones he hadn't.

So when Vera held up *Snow* the next morning and shyly asked Sylvie, "Um, do you mind if I keep reading?" Sylvie's answer was "Of course!" and "Do you have any more magazines?"

Vera did. Seven of them—her dad had packed her up with one for each day of camp. Three issues of *Fang-Fare*, two more of *Eternity*, and a single copy of *Necrosis*, aka the *Popular Science*–type magazine. It had more information on Ichabod Clotting's space program.

Sylvie's vampire-loving heart had to work very hard not to drool at the amount of knowledge about real, living-dead vampires in her hot little hands. It was difficult to part with it all at the reverberating "CAW-CAW" from Rupert announcing an end to breakfast and a start to meeting time.

"Where were you *ghouls* last night?" Chad asked upon the girls' arrival to the flagpole, where Fang and Fester were already pairing off.

"The undead and ghosts are not the same," sniffed Zephyr while Norah's spectral face shot daggers toward the werewolf. The ghost boy turned to Vera and Sylvie. "But yeah, you missed some good ones. Mummy G even told her tomb-raider story!"

While a nonfiction tomb-raider story *did* sound amazing—her dad was a huge Indiana Jones fan—Sylvie was busy wondering if every new interaction with Chad was going to involve an insult.

Vera bit her lip, and Sylvie took that as a cue that she didn't want to be as frank about her reasoning last night as she'd been in the privacy of their rooftop sitting area. "The stories are fun, but not required," Master Gert said as Rupert landed on their shoulder, marking the completion of his duty. Sylvie had to admit she was relieved to hear from the camp director's mouth that they were not in violation of the rules—just as Vera had said. "We all have our own needs. Let's please be respectful of our other campers' interests."

Even Chad had nothing to say to that.

After roll call, they gathered on the long, covered porch at the back of the administration building that Sylvie had walked past upon her registration and entry to camp on Sunday.

An outdoor classroom had been set up on the porch for the day's HURT lesson, but instead of desks, there, in two rows of four, were eight magnificent, magical pumpkins.

They were beanbag height with a perfect bottom-sized indentation at the top where the stem once was. Each had a name carved in it, and when Sylvie got to hers, she noticed it was a little smaller than Vera's. And when Vera plopped down, hers was the perfect height for her feet to comfortably touch the porch planks. Sylvie's was similarly set up in height, which was a relief, because she hated the way her legs were just short enough that her feet could never *completely* touch the floor in any of her classes at Evermore Middle.

As she settled into the pumpkin seat, Sylvie couldn't believe how surprisingly comfortable it was. "Wow, we need these at human school."

"I'm sure Amos would make that happen if they let him in. He grows them himself and magicks them before each session he teaches. They're always perfect."

Sylvie had to agree.

Up front was a green chalkboard, dusty with ancient chalk. At the top, a big clip held in place a sheaf of long, laminated sheets, which were obscured by a cover that read "Human Anatomy with Counselor Amos."

The walking skeleton strode proudly to the front of the classroom while Yeti settled into the back, where Sylvie now noticed an extra, very large pumpkin sitting like an orange boulder in the corner.

"Group Fang, I hope you enjoyed our joint HURT lesson yesterday. That joint lesson is something that Master Gert thought would be important for our would-be seventh graders. And today's lesson will be similar." Amos paused. "I can assure you that if you have had a human anatomy lecture from me before, this one will be tailored appropriately to the fact that you all are now a year older and therefore can handle more complex information and understanding."

With that, Amos removed the display's cover sheet and gently set it on a small table to the side. Beneath it was a general graphic of a human body, and, honestly, Sylvie was somewhat relieved to learn that Amos wasn't going to just, like, gesture at himself and talk. Even better, he picked up a pointer, which he wielded like a magic wand.

"Now, human anatomy differs from that of monsters in a myriad of ways," Amos said, gesturing to the graphic. "Some of these differences are more obvious, depending on the type of monster you are. Humans obviously don't have the equine abilities our friend Lenny has, nor do they have the innate skill to change their exoskeletons into a wolf every full moon, nor can they shoot water out of their fingers. Not to mention that on the outside, their skin is pretty much never green like Francis's or blue like Bebe's, unless they've gotten very ill . . . or are a humanoid of an alien variety, but that's something we won't cover for a few years yet."

Lenny shot to his feet. "Wait, aliens exist?"

The skeleton grinned. "Mr. Lachlan, you'll just have to keep coming to camp to find out, won't you?"

About forty-eight hours ago, Sylvie would've thought Amos was kidding. With what she knew now? Aliens totally existed.

The counselor turned back to his board and waved his pointer in the direction of the human person, as if it were exhibit A.

"Obviously, even our human-adjacent monster friends are slightly different from humans," he said matter-of-factly. "For one, they couldn't have been able to get past our human shield, which is specifically programmed to detect monster DNA."

Holding her breath, Sylvie snaked a hand toward Vera, prepared for when Chad would make a crack at her expense. Instead, he just shot a knowing expression at Lenny, who laughed, and Milo, who was very focused on Amos and trying hard to ignore them both.

When the skeleton was able to continue without a snide remark from Chad, Sylvie exhaled and placed her hand back in her lap.

"Many of the body mechanics of human-adjacent monsters and humans are similar, which is why they can easily walk among the masses undetected." Amos held up a bony finger. "However, there are several key differences, which I'd like to list out. I know many of you have had this portion of the lecture before, so let's let some of our new campers answer first."

There was only one new camper in Group Fang: Sylvie.

Amos gave her a go-ahead skeleton smile. "Sylvie, what are some internal differences between monsters and humans?"

Sylvie's guts dribbled into a puddle within her stomach. She was pretty sure color was flushing her face, and that despite her liberal morning application of SPF 90, she was bright red.

"Uh," she started, a stumble. "The brains are definitely different."

Amos lit up. "Yes, very good, Sylvie! Human brains are very different than monster brains!"

Sylvie nearly sighed in relief.

Amos started to pace excitedly. "For example, humans only use ten percent of their brains. Did you know that?" Sylvie actually did know that. "Whereas, because of their magical adaptations, many monsters use seventy to eighty percent of their brains."

Wow.

Amos held up a finger. "Now you may ask yourself, if humans only use ten percent of their brains at most, what actually controls them?"

Sylvie's very own human brain thudded to a halt.

What the heck did he mean?

"Anyone?" Amos glanced around. "Yes, Vera?"

Sylvie hadn't realized Vera had even raised her hand. It didn't seem in her nature to draw attention to herself *willingly*, but here, Vera calmly answered, "Their hearts."

Again, Sylvie held her breath, this time because that was totally nonsensical—

"Very good, Vera! Yes, humans are powered by their hearts."

Say what? That didn't make a lick of sense based on everything Sylvie had ever learned in school. Still, Amos clapped his hands together in a cheer, nearly dropping his pointer.

Amos swept back to his display and ripped off the full-human sheet. Below it was an illustration that detailed the top half of a human with its heart, lungs, brain, and everything inside and in between. "A human's heart guides their emotions and actions, all from a central location."

With the tip of his pointer stick, Amos thwacked the heart on the diagram for emphasis.

"Have you ever heard the human phrase 'home is where the heart is'? Or 'the heart of the matter'? Or perhaps 'I had my heart set on it'? All those phrases directly hint toward the nucleus of the human experience being located in their chests."

Um, that wasn't even remotely true.

Not in the slightest.

Sylvie sat on her hands and hoped that Amos was finished picking on the newest camper.

"Then, there are all the ways humans discuss being in pain or dying based on one's heart. 'Died of a broken heart,' 'cross my heart and hope to die,' or even the very common and medically sound 'heart attack.'" Sylvie's mind raced as understanding dawned on the faces of her classmates. All of them, even Vera, were buying this baloney. "Those are just some of the bits of proof we monsters have that confirm the human body revolves around the heart like the earth to the sun."

Sylvie was so discombobulated that she barely even noticed Chad and Milo appreciatively nodding with Amos's last addition.

"Basically," Amos concluded, "we can learn a lot about human anatomy from their own metaphors, which I dare say is mighty pleasing."

Chad raised his hand.

"Is this a question or a comment?" Amos asked, and Sylvie got the feeling that comments would have to wait until after the lesson was over.

"A question," Chad answered definitively, and Amos gestured with a click-clack of his bony hand for the were-wolf to continue. "What happens to the anatomy of someone who is half monster and half human?"

And there it was.

Chad's tone wasn't mean, not like it had been previously, but everyone knew, including Amos, that this was a complete dig at Vera. Something in Sylvie switched. The anxiety she'd felt moments before at being called out in class was instantly replaced by a rush of anger at Chad and all the cronies like him who made themselves feel big by making others feel small. She'd had enough. Not even monsters should be able to get away with this kind of behavior.

Sylvie reached across the aisle and placed a hand on Vera's arm. Then, she looked Chad in the eye and said loudly, "It makes them a superhero. Spider-Man was a human with monster spider DNA. Heck, if you think monsters are gods, may I remind you that Hercules was half god, half human, and he was very strong."

"Oh, like Percy Jackson," Milo blurted out, and Sylvie

marked him as both a reader and an independent thinker.

Chad did not appreciate that betrayal.

After giving his cousin the stink eye, Chad turned to Sylvie and bared his teeth in a snarl. "Except none of those examples are real and breathing."

"If I may," Amos said, clearly trying to gain control of the discussion. "While I love the idea that creatures borne of monster and human DNA are superheroes or demigods, and it *is* quite special for a monster to reveal themselves to a human, let alone have a long and successful relationship with one"—here, he clearly dipped his chin at Vera—"the truth is that human physiology and monster physiology mixing is quite *normal*."

Now, that was a surprise.

"In fact," Amos continued, "it's likely far more common these days than pure monster bloodlines. Which means, Chad, that monsters of mixed blood like our good friend Vera are more common than anyone else in camp."

This time, Sylvie wasn't the only one shell-shocked.

"But if that's true . . . ," Lenny began, "humans would know about us in ways that should mean we don't have to hide."

Chad literally sneered. "It's because our human-adjacent friends hide in plain sight and make it impossible for the rest of us, because they don't own up to what they are. The witches taught us exactly what happens when a monster becomes careless around humans. Trials and witch barbecue."

Freya shot to her feet. Her pumpkin nearly pitched over, but she didn't steady it. She was busy staring daggers at Chad.

"You're invoking *Salem*? Like that was *our* fault?! How dare you! Would you like to become a beagle this time?" the little witch asked, flexing her fingers. Her dark eyes flashed. "Or perhaps a teacup chihuahua? If I'm going to be punished for spelling you, I want to make the outcome as annoying for you as possible."

Amos spread his hands in the air, a blur of white. "No, no, no magicking! And no prejudicial assumptions."

At the back of the class, Yeti half rose from his pumpkin, ready to intervene. Somehow, the combination of the two adults' reactions was enough, because both Freya and Chad clammed up and turned away to scowl.

Sylvie had to admit she was relieved. Though she did appreciate that Freya was still one to act if Chad got out of line when going after the human-adjacent.

The skeleton regrouped and explained, "What is often common is that, unless the monster DNA reveals itself outwardly right away, as in the case of someone like me or Yeti, the presence of monster blood just might not . . . be a topic of conversation in a love story. Which makes someone like our friend Vera a very special case indeed, in that her vampire father proudly told her mother what he was, and they are raising their child to know her monster side and have experiences like this camp."

Sylvie again patted her roommate's arm. Vera, for her

part, was staring very, very hard at her interlaced fingers.

"Moreover, our experiences vary greatly, even within the same community," Amos said. "Chad, I think you're likely aware that it's often much easier for full-blooded female werewolves to present as humans and can often slip in among nonmonsters undetected."

In response, Chad sighed. Meanwhile, Milo grinned and said, "My older sister and my mom go into town a lot." He scratched the back of his neck. "Sometimes that makes me a little jealous of Lena, but I know they're just trying to keep me safe."

Huh. Maybe girl werewolves were naturally less hairy and more human-esque?

"Yes, that exactly, Milo. They are keeping your family safe while still trying to maintain connection to the human world, which benefits you also, doesn't it?"

Milo nodded, and Amos matched it, a little more enthusiastically.

"I understand that it is easy to create divisions among ourselves here, based on our traits and experiences," Amos said, sagely, "but it is important that we stick together, because we face enough hostility in the outside world, no matter how we present. Which means petty jabs like sneaky questions and magical threats targeting your fellow campers are unwelcome."

Both Chad and Freya stared at their feet.

The rest of the HURT session had a lot less participation and a lot more completely incorrect facts about humans that one might pick up from observing them.

Like "Humans can literally digest anything, including Play-Doh. This makes them akin to the animal known as a goat" and "The funny bone is located in the human's elbow, and it is a fact that a human can be born without one and never laugh. If a human breaks that bone, they will have a hard time laughing until it is fully healed."

Honestly, Sylvie was suddenly quite nervous about the idea of vampiric scientists putting fellow vampires in space, because if they were this bad at biology, perhaps astrophysics might not be the best monster-regulated activity.

Though maybe the only incorrect knowledge monsters possessed pertained to humans and nothing else in the scientific world. Amos had pegged goats right after all. They really would eat anything. They even "mowed" the grass near the highway outside Evermore twice a year.

Finally, Amos doffed his pointer and clapped his hands together. "All right now, let's pack up and head to the mess for lunch."

The skeleton nodded to the building just feet away with gleaming eyes. Suddenly, Sylvie wondered if Amos ate food or if he got his energy from something else. What would a person without a digestive system subsist on? It was probably impolite to ask.

"You'll need to fill up those little monster fuel tanks," he continued with another grin, "because I know Master Gert has big plans for you this afternoon!"

What's Going to
Work? TEAMWORK!

Everyone got a sack lunch on Tuesday and instructions to follow Master Gert into the woods for a Group Fang "teamwork opportunity." Which, of course, Chad insinuated while gnawing on a fresh side of raw cow in the middle of the trail, was because they were "losers" from the day before.

In the back, Sylvie just pointedly ate her apple, surreptitiously checked her fangs in her compact—straight and neat—and kept walking with Vera through the evercreeping brush and shadows clawing at her ankles. Luckily, Master Gert's apparently stellar monster hearing caught what Chad was getting at and corrected him.

"Group Fang," Master Gert announced, deftly walking backward over the rocks and roots with a swish of their cape. Sylvie could swear the forest jumped away from them as they moved . . . completely opposite of how the surely sentient woods treated her and Vera. "I assure you that Group Fester did this very same teamwork opportunity this morning under the watchful eye of Scott and myself."

"Where *is* Scott?" Milo asked, like he'd had that question bottled up for quite some time now.

"He's preparing the course for us."

The *course*? That didn't sound good.

Vera looked just as stricken as Sylvie felt, which Sylvie took as a nonverbal cue that, no, they hadn't done this the year before either.

"We'll meet him there. Come along now." Master Gert swished back around, magically avoiding a slim tree trunk that had planted itself toward the middle of the trail as if on accident. It was like the director had eyes in the back of their head, and Sylvie realized with a start that *could* be true.

A few minutes later, they arrived at another clearing. Master Gert waited patiently for all of them to emerge from the trail and into the clearing before beginning their explanation. But as Sylvie arrived as the group's caboose, it wasn't Master Gert who spoke first, it was Scott—yelling from far away.

"Hey there, Group Fang!" The manticore waved, his scorpion's tale wiggling at his back from his spot all the way on the other side of the clearing, up on some sort of structure that put him a good twenty feet in the air. He tossed both lion's arms (legs?) wide and yelled some more. "Welcome to the Boneyard!"

Scott's voice echoed a little, and a lot in Sylvie's head.

She recalled a sign on the flagpole labeled "Boneyard" but, honestly, after their trip to the cemetery the other day, she'd just figured that was what it referred to.

Looking around now, she realized her assumption was very, very wrong.

The clearing was a final resting place.

A skull as massive as Cabin No. 7 was to Sylvie's left, its jawbone sucked into the soil like a bare foot in wet sand on the beach. Beyond the skull, jutting from the earth at varying levels of exposure, was the rest of what appeared to be a massive, intact skeleton. It was lying stomach-side down, from the curve of a spine to a splintered cage of ribs poking in all directions to an extended tangle of femurs and tibias.

The legs had come to a rest crossed, throwing the whole thing askew, starting at one hip bone higher than another and ending with the skeletal remains of feet as big as school buses crossing in a mound in the far distance. Scott stood atop the citadel of heels, hooked into a harness and wearing a helmet.

"This, my friends," Master Gert was saying, "is Old Jake. He was a famed giant until he was felled by a porcupine some millennia ago. Picture it as the Dark Ages equivalent of stepping barefoot on a Lego."

Everyone winced and sucked in a collective breath.

Ouch.

"Old Jake's caretakers, which includes Yeti, requested

that his bones be enjoyed by children and used in an educational manner." That sounded familiar to Sylvie—the ghost cemetery had been similarly donated. "So, this year, as rising seventh graders, I present to you the greatest teamwork opportunity of Monster Camp: Old Jake's Relay!"

A relay? Sylvie was suddenly wishing she'd joined the Evermore Middle track team in the spring as her dad had *heavily* suggested.

"The eight of you will work *together* to traverse the obstacles of Old Jake's bones. That means each of you will have a role and touch the baton." Sylvie saw Chad's whole face fall at this, his hands coming to rest on his waist. "To be successful, you must get the baton all the way across the length of Old Jake's body. From there, the final team member will attach themselves to the zip line with Scott's expert help and safety inspection—and deliver it down the zip line to the finish line."

There was a lot of standing on tippy-toes, and even some hovering in the air, but nobody could see the finish line from where they were standing, Old Jake and the trees in the way.

Chad's eyes narrowed. "So, we just have to complete it? Do we get a number of tries? Is there a ticking clock?"

Sylvie was annoyed yet again that he didn't raise his hand before interrogating one of the adults. He'd made it clear he didn't attend human school, but even if you weren't accustomed to raising your hand, there was such a thing as common courtesy.

"Well, yes—"

An earthshaking "CAW-CAW" swallowed Master Gert's answer as Rupert arrived overhead and circled around Old Jake's entire length, before gliding neatly to Master Gert's shoulder. Clasped in its beak were two things: a folded piece of paper and a lanyard.

Master Gert plucked both from the giant bird and took the time to read the note, though everyone had an idea of what they were going to say before they finally did.

"Group Fang, this may come as a surprise, but it appears we've lost Fade once again. Has anyone a clue to where he might be?"

They held up the lanyard.

Slowly, everyone—including Sylvie and Vera—shook their heads and glanced around as if looking for the invisible boy. Only Francis—Fade's roommate—spoke up. "He came with me to breakfast and roll call." He held up his empty and crumpled sack lunch. "Didn't see him when we were at the mess hall, though."

"Yes. I suppose that's where we lost him; he did this very challenge this morning." Master Gert ducked their head. "Give me a moment; I need to write Amos."

The director whipped a pen out of the recesses of the day's cape—this one shimmered like stars in the light instead of rainbows—and jotted down something quick on the paper. As he waited, Sylvie could swear the bird watched her like, well, a hawk. Like she might do something suspiciously human in the moment Master Gert's eyes were averted. But a second later, the director refolded the paper with a flourish and sent Rupert on his way.

As the bird shot back over the canopy of trees, Master Gert gathered themself. "Okay, where was I? Oh yes, the parameters. You will get as many tries as it takes, Mr. Wolff." They inclined their chin to Chad. "That said, let's make a deal. This morning's group finished in a flat five minutes. If you can beat their time, we'll head straight to the mess and get a frozen treat."

Sylvie's mouth started watering at the very hint of something cold and hopefully creamy. And, well, not bug-filled.

"What's the catch?" Chad asked, his hairy arms now wound in front of yet another sporty tank top.

Master Gert grinned. "The catch? You mean the rest of the parameters, no?" Chad didn't answer. "Whatever you want to call it, the rest of the information you need is this: As I said, all of you will need a role, and all of you will touch the baton. If any of you drop the baton, all of you will have to start over from square one, even if you're right at the end. So, don't drop it."

"But what is the baton?" Sylvie raised her hand to ask, because this seemed vitally important, especially considering yesterday's game pieces were quite slippery and, er, jumpy. Chad glared at her, probably because she beat him to the question.

The director's grin widened further, which made Sylvie even more nervous.

Again, Master Gert reached into the recesses of their cape. This time, instead of a pen, in their hand was an egg. It was oblong but didn't look like the kind Sylvie had in her fridge at home. No surprise there, really.

"Snake egg?" Milo asked.

"Very good, Milo, yes!" Sylvie's stomach turned. "Don't worry, if you drop one, a snake won't pop out! But you will have to start over."

Sylvie was somewhat relieved that a whole reptile wouldn't emerge if they dropped the baton.

"How many eggs do you have in your pockets, Master Gert?" Lenny asked. Another good question.

"I have three eggs, which means you have three tries to finish the course with the baton intact." Three tries, eight people, and a zip line. Okay. "I'll give you five minutes to discuss strategy and place your relay members along Old Jake. You can station your team members wherever you like, but you do have to have one who starts at the edge of the clearing, feet on the last of the trail, and someone who Scott will harness in for the zip-line portion. How you want to divvy up the rest of Old Jake is up to you, so long as *everyone* touches the baton."

Sylvie was pretty sure Master Gert was looking directly at Chad when they repeated that last stipulation yet again. If he noticed, it didn't affect the werewolf at all. Just as the day before, he intended to call the shots. This time, he made that clear by motioning for everyone to shift from their line into a close circle, so they could discuss a strategy.

Or, more accurately, so Chad could tell everyone the strategy.

"Okay, we need to play to everyone's strengths here." In a surprise, Chad did not pointedly look at Vera and make it clear he thought she was weak. Sylvie attempted to give him the benefit of the doubt that maybe the goal of teamwork had made him slightly less terrible. Or maybe it was just that Master Gert could hear every word from where they stood. "That means we figure out the parts that are difficult to travel by foot and assign those to Bebe and Freya, so they can fly over them."

"The ribs and hips," Milo answered without hesitation. "Both are treacherous enough that flying is the best bet."

Chad nodded and Freya popped in. "I'll take the hips. Bebe, you good with the ribs?"

"Yep. Got 'em."

Chad had the rest figured out and assigned everyone else a piece of the relay. Which worked out more or less, except when it came to Vera, of course.

"You're zip lining," Chad told her, not even bothering to use her name. "No monster balance required, and being half vamp, you should have the strength to hold on the whole way. And if not, the harness should at least make sure you make it to the end of the line without dying."

Vera immediately blanched. "I—I can't."

"Why not?"

Vera practically receded into her curtain of red hair. "I'm afraid of heights."

The thin line of Chad's lips began curling into a sneer, his eyes flashing with "Can you believe this?"

"I'll do it. We can switch." Sylvie had been assigned the lower spine. "I'm fine with heights, and the lower spine isn't more than four feet off the ground."

Chad's lips curled up, baring his teeth as he gutted out, "Fine. Use that freakish vamp strength to hang on tight. You drop the egg, and we have to start all over on the last step."

Oh, how Sylvie wanted to snap back. But that wasn't constructive. She answered as evenly as possible, "It won't be a problem."

The final relay lineup was set.

Lenny, shifted into his superfast kelpie horse form, would start them off. He'd give the baton to Francis, who would climb the skull and hand it off to Milo. Milo would traverse the upper spine and deliver the baton to Bebe, who would then fly over the ribs. She'd land at the lower spine and give it to Vera, who would then run it to Freya, who would fly over the twisted hips and femur. She'd hand it off to Chad in the depression of Old Jake's right kneecap, and then he'd run up the incline of the tibia, meet Sylvie at the heel, and then she'd zip line down.

Master Gert looked on as everyone got into position. They said nothing about the strategy. Just simply handed off the first snake egg to Lenny with a "Mr. Lachlan" as he got into position and waited for Scott's signal that he had Sylvie harnessed up to the zip line.

"You're ready to go, Sylvie." Scott gave her a high-five while giving the signal to Master Gert.

Sylvie had been in a harness many times and wasn't afraid of heights, but her heart started pounding as Master Gert began to count down to the start. This was it—a chance at redemption after the way they lost the day before.

All they had to do was work together.

"Monsters . . . in three, two, one . . . GO!"

Lenny broke onto the course with amazing speed, making it to the skull in a blink or two. Sylvie couldn't see Francis or his exact route, but from her climbing experience, she had to guess he swung up and shimmied through the nose indentation, using the sides of the eye sockets as grips. In any case, he appeared at the top of the skull, faced Milo, and SPIT the egg out of his mouth and into Milo's waiting hands.

Milo didn't even flinch at the saliva—instead, he carried the snake egg in a single palm, crossing the ridges of the upper spine like he was running over the top of the monkey bars at the playground. His balance really was impressive. For as much as Sylvie was not a fan of werewolves, there was no denying that these two were athletic.

Bebe accepted the egg with two blue hands. Her sharp teeth zippered into a grimace as she flew fast and furious over the cavernous rib cage, before fluttering down to the lower spine to hand it off to Vera.

Vera . . . who even at this distance looked so very nervous.

She bobbled the exchange, the snake egg squirting from her grip and hanging in the air for one dangerous second before her reflexes kicked in and she caught it.

"Come on, Vera," Sylvie whispered, afraid that if she cheered, it'd spook her and send her straight off the spine and into the dirt.

Vera moved slowly, her steps unsure. The hand that didn't hold the egg was thrust out in front of her body, ready to snatch a vertebra if her steps faltered.

"Faster, Vera! Get the lead out of your pants! Let's go!" Chad yelled.

The werewolf's eyes weren't on Vera; they were glued to his watch and the seconds ticking by, so he didn't see the way she stumbled at the sound of his voice.

Vera fell forward, that protective hand catching the top of the nearest vertebrae. But with her feet already staggered on different pieces of bone and her upper body fixed on the single point of her hand, Vera began to twist the second she caught herself.

The hand with the egg swung out wide, sweeping within an inch of the ground. Vera used every ounce of strength she had to keep from falling into the void with the egg. Forget spooking her—the girl needed a jolt of confidence.

"You've got this, Vera!" Sylvie yelled. "Steady, steady! Up to Freya. You can do it!"

Vera's shoulders twitched; she shook her hair out of her face and paused, all four limbs back on the vertebrae now.

"Yeah, Vera! I'm right here. Just a few more steps," Freya yelled.

The witch was on all fours, balancing in the twisted dip between the hip bones, as low as she could get to the spine, one arm out. It really was just a few feet.

"Crawl if you have to, just keep moving," Chad yelled, and Sylvie couldn't tell if that was truly him being helpful or if he was making fun of her. "We're past two minutes! Come on! Go!"

Either way, Vera wrenched her mouth open, her jaw gaping much wider than any human's Sylvie had ever seen, and took a page from Francis's playbook, tucking the egg safely inside.

Oh, yuck. A good idea, but yuck. Both hands free, Vera pushed into a low bear crawl and made her way much faster over the remaining vertebrae than she'd done on the first half while standing and balancing.

She delivered it safely to Freya, who got both hands on it and made up time, as Vera shakily settled into the dip in Old Jake's hips. Sylvie held both hands overhead in a double thumbs-up. "Good job, Vera! Goooo, Freya!"

And now that the egg was safe, the others began to join in.

"Nice save, Vera!" Bebe called, clapping her hands so hard they shot spurts of water into the air.

"Go, Group Fang!" Milo yelled, both arms thrust in the air on top of the skull.

"Almost there! Fly, Freya, fly!" Lenny cried, taking

the opportunity to run the length of Old Jake until he was right in line with the soaring witch as she approached the kneecap.

"Yeah, Freya!" Vera yelled, finding her voice.

Even Chad joined in, glancing up from his watch to prepare for Freya's approach. "Easy does it! Good hand off in . . . three, two . . . one!"

The witch placed the egg in Chad's hands, and the werewolf flung himself around and ran straight up the right tibia.

As much as Sylvie didn't like Chad, he moved even better than Milo, his balance uncanny, his steps sure. He was coming at Sylvie like a freight train.

Behind him, the cheering continued.

"Go, Chad!" Milo and Francis.

"Almost there!" Freya.

Clapping: Vera.

"Whoooo! Fangilicious!" Lenny, running alongside. "Get ready, Sylvie! He's coming at ya!"

He was indeed. And Sylvie was ready.

Ready to prove she was a team player, that yesterday was a fluke, that she could do this with all the expected strength of a vampire.

Chad crested Old Jake's lower leg and landed on top of the little platform made up of the giant skeleton's crossed heels.

He deposited the snake egg into Sylvie's waiting palms. It was leathery, wet (Sylvie didn't want to think about that), and far more pliable than she expected. The shell wasn't hard like a chicken egg, but definitely still delicate.

As he offered Sylvie the egg, Chad's eyes narrowed. Just low enough that Scott couldn't hear, he whispered, "Don't screw up, vamp."

"I won't."

Sylvie secured the egg in a single hand, wrapped the other hand over the bar of the zip line, and stepped off the platform.

"Gooooo, Sylvie!" Vera shouted the second Sylvie became airborne.

More voices joined in as the bony platform fell away. In front of Sylvie, a straight shot, maybe twice the length of Old Jake's remains over rocky and rooted soil.

Sylvie was flying. Fast and free, through the trees. The wind whipped the hair out of her face, the air whistling through her stick-on fangs as her mouth hung open in a smile.

"Almost there! Yes! Less than four minutes!" Chad's voice.

Sylvie glanced over her shoulder to see her Group Fang team members scrambling down the embankment from the platform to the trail below. Lenny was in the lead, running hard enough his Kraken hat flew off, and Freya caught it as she and Bebe zoomed through the air in his wake. Vera popped up over the side, jogging behind next to Francis. Milo, Chad, and Scott came down the other side.

Sylvie's mind registered that Master Gert wasn't with them. But just as she did, her name came again. Not from behind—from ahead.

"Sylvie!"

There, somehow ready and waiting, was Master Gert. They were standing on a platform attached to a tree at the line's end.

How did they get there so fast?

Sylvie hadn't seen them move at all. And she was sure they were standing there when she accepted the baton from Chad.

Yet there they were, at the end.

As Sylvie dropped into a flat section, slowing down, Master Gert lifted a hand in her direction, long fingers outstretched.

Suddenly, it was if Sylvie were a feather, floating in the breeze. The speeding zip line slowed, and Sylvie landed as gently as Mary Poppins and her umbrella on the platform.

"3:39," Master Gert said as a greeting. "I do believe that's a new course record."

Sylvie grinned from ear to ear.

"What? Really?"

"Yes, indeed. And you know what I think? I think you modeled excellent teammate behavior, and that helped Group Fang be successful." Sylvie's heart swelled as Master Gert placed a warm hand on her shoulder. "You stepped up for a teammate when they expressed vulnerability, you started *positively* cheering when the team needed it most, and you stayed calm when pressured by a teammate very focused on the final outcome." They squeezed Sylvie's shoulder. "Great job, Sylvie."

"Did we do it? Did we do it?" Chad was yelling, thundering in at the very same time as Lenny at this point. "I had 3:42, but I was judging from far away and—"

"Even better," Master Gert said, holding up Sylvie's hand with the snake egg safely inside. "Sylvie crossed the line in 3:39—a new record!"

All of Group Fang erupted into cheers.

A Human Connection

Filled to the brim with victory and vanilla soft serve (everyone else had slugs, plasma crunchies, and other stomach-churning mix-ins), newly showered Sylvie and Vera climbed to their castle roof and collapsed into the chairs of their patio table, reading materials and drinks at the ready.

The sky was a brilliant, cloudless blue, and a light breeze would dry their wet hair in no time. The day had been an exhausting one, and, honestly, Sylvie had been craving this quiet time. When it was just the two of them, the call of birds, and errant shouts and squeals from campers on the common, the fields, or in the lake.

Sylvie had decided she'd read *Necrosis* that afternoon, because she really, really wanted to believe that vampires weren't as incorrect about humans and, well, science, as Amos's lessons had led her to believe. But before she'd even turned to the table of contents to pick her first article, Vera's light hand tapped at her forearm.

Sylvie looked up and found her roommate's large eyes completely overfull.

"I should've said this earlier, but . . . I knew I couldn't do it without this." Vera gestured toward the obvious wetness gathering in her gaze. "Um, but . . ." She took a shaky breath. "Thank you for describing me as a super-hero at HURT today."

Sylvie's heart lurched, but she tried to maintain levity for Vera's sake.

"Well, you are. Duh. Or a demigod. Whichever you prefer."

"I don't feel like either." Vera offered a tight little smile, her fingers toying with one battered corner of *Snow*'s spine. "I know this experience is supposed to help me get in touch with my monster side, but it doesn't."

"Can I help in some way?" Sylvie asked, though it felt like a feeble offering. What could she do, really? Other than listen?

To that end, Vera shook her head. It seemed like her slim shoulders were up to her ears, though her long ropes of half-dried hair obscured everything.

"I mean, being here is supposed to be good for me. That's what my parents say. Both of them, even though Dad's really the one who pushes it. But . . ." She took a big, shaky breath. "I wish they understood what it's like for me here. Mostly, the whole week just reminds me how different I am."

Vera slumped in the chair, her chin tucked to her chest, her curtain of damp red hair draped heavily over either side of her face, like horse blinders.

"It really isn't fair how much it's been pointed out that you're part human," Sylvie said. "If not by Chad, then, um, by well-meaning people like Amos. It really shouldn't be mentioned at all.

"Honestly," Sylvie continued, a knot of anger on Vera's behalf welling in her gut, "if anything, they should use your half-human side as an opportunity. We're literally learning about humans in HURT for half our week. How awesome is it that we have you, who spends every day with her real live human mom, right here with us? I mean, it's sort of an embarrassment that they haven't made you a voluntary human expert. You're a gold mine, and they just continue to insult you!"

Vera's little snort was the saddest semi-laugh sound Sylvie had ever heard.

"Nope, they've never asked me. But . . . ," Vera said, her brows threaded together and her chin lifting, "if what Amos said is true, if there are more people like me than full-blooded monsters, I wish there could be more like me *here*. Just one more person who was half human—or any-percent human, really—would go a long way toward making me feel less like such an outsider."

Sylvie's guts balled up tightly.

"Please, please don't get me wrong," Vera amended quickly, her eyes suddenly wide and fearful. "It is so much easier with another vampire here, and I'm super thankful that you came this year. But being a vampire is only half the reason this week is such a struggle for me."

Just as on the first night, the truth scurried onto Sylvie's tongue. It would be so very easy to let it spill into the air between them. Sylvie's heart began to pound as her secret tried to claw into the air. She began to sweat. It would help Vera to know she wasn't alone, yes, but . . . but beyond that, Sylvie had no idea how she'd react.

The odds of Vera feeling betrayed by all of Sylvie's lies might be just as high as the odds of her feeling relief. And a coin flip didn't feel like a safe bet when monsters were literally in the cabins next door.

And, well, right in front of her.

Sylvie scrabbled for her mother's necklace, and after running her thumb along the crescent moon's arc, that boiling feeling under her skin receded just enough that she was able to say, "You've talked to Master Gert about this, I know . . . did they say how other half humans feel when they come to camp? Surely if they run different weeks for different age groups, they hear nearly every week from half humans with similar issues. They could—should—connect you."

Vera shrugged her slim shoulders into her long ribbons of damp hair. She was as pale as the classic vanilla cones they'd both just enjoyed.

"They don't. They just tell me it's normal to feel this way and suggest I spend more time with the witches in camp. Seeing as they're human-adjacent and all. But that's different." Something like a flash of bitterness soured Vera's pale face. "I mean, they don't even have to lower the human shield for them. Just for me."

This was news to Sylvie. "They can lower it?"

Vera's bitterness was suddenly replaced by sheer panic. "Wait! That's a secret! Shoot."

Sylvie held up her hands, trying to staunch her roommate's concern. "Don't worry, I won't tell anyone." Sylvie pantomimed zipping her lips for extra emphasis. "I promise. I wasn't trying to pry. I was just . . . surprised. Master Gert made the human shield sound like a big deal and really secure right after Chad was turned into a show dog."

Sylvie was also wondering if it was lowered for Vera, then maybe she happened to wander through the trees to the camp at just the right time.

"Yeah, well." Vera seemed to fold further into herself, her arms straight but crossed at the elbows and twined again at the wrists and fingers. She glanced up balefully. "They *do* have to bring the shield all the way down so I can enter camp. Last year, I bounced off it."

"What? Really?"

Vera released a sigh deep enough to clear the mist off the lake. "It's very powerful, and I guess you have to reach a certain magical DNA threshold to get in. I don't reach it.

The witches and other human-adjacent monsters do . . . but I'm too human for the dumb shield, I guess." Vera glanced down and swallowed while Sylvie scavenged her brain for literally anything she could say that wouldn't seem like a platitude. Vera sniffed. "Anyway, it takes several minutes to get back to full strength when they lower it. When it's down and when it's revving back up, the camp is basically unprotected."

Unprotected.

Considering what normal humans might stumble into with the shield down, that would be bad. Sylvie suddenly had visions of Dustin breaking out his Monster SLAY 3000 moves, plus whatever he was learning at his special camp, and going all Knight of the Night on real live unsuspecting kid monsters.

Not. Good.

Vera was watching Sylvie's thoughts page across her face, waiting for some sort of response. Sylvie decided to be honest. "I didn't notice it was down when I came in."

Vera smiled weakly, her mouth a bloodless line. "You can't see it. So, it's not like humans know it's down or how long it takes to get back up or anything, but . . ." She let out a big sigh and unpeeled from her chairback. "I just feel guilty making them take it down at all."

Sylvie could understand that. It was like locking the door when leaving the house—which her dad always reminded her to do.

"Don't feel guilty about it." She leaned forward and put a palm atop Vera's hand. It was unnaturally cold. Sylvie swallowed. "They wouldn't have lowered it if it was going to be an issue. But I won't tell anyone. Promise."

A Small Dose of (Pretend) Reality

The next morning, Sylvie saw HURT with new eyes.

No matter what they had planned for their Wednesday session, Sylvie was going to do all she could to make the experience as good for Vera as possible. And if the day's lesson again veered toward Vera's differences, Sylvie was going to do everything in her power to right the ship.

Yet as game as she was for whatever Yeti and Amos had planned, Sylvie was still completely surprised when the pair of instructors revealed the day's lesson in the shadow of the flagpole.

"Today, Group Fang, our Human Understanding and Resources Training gets *real!*" Yeti tossed his massive head back and shouted the words like he was a talk-show host giving away brand-new cars to everyone in the audience. Like it was a good thing.

But Sylvie's heart skidded to a crashing halt in her chest.

Real as in . . . *how real?*

Yeti exchanged an exaggerated grin with Amos, then both of them looked out enthusiastically at the campers before them. It might have been Sylvie's imagination, but she thought Vera stiffened next to her.

"Today," Yeti announced in that same big voice, "we're going to run through role-play scenarios so that we can practice our skills interacting with humans!"

There was an audible, collective sigh among the campers. Yeti and Amos chose to ignore this.

The skeleton raised a pointer finger. "Working on role-play strengthens our human-relations skills and is one of the most useful exercises you'll learn at Monster Camp that you can use when you return home."

Sylvie nodded her head because this made sense. But several campers, most notably every single one who wasn't human-adjacent—Lenny, the werewolves, Francis, and Bebe—all looked like they'd rather feast on glass shards while standing on hot coals.

Yeti recognized this reaction and was prepared.

He tossed out his big hands in a welcoming gesture. "We know that this exercise might seem . . . *superfluous* to some of our monster friends who don't easily blend in with humankind. This is something Amos and I know very well."

Yeti caught eyes with his fellow counselor. They both nodded sagely.

"We know firsthand that many of you who present

more obviously monster-y than others may not have much interaction with humans." Yeti nodded. "But the truth of the matter is that as you grow older and become employed by other monsters or even by the very select members of humankind who know of your existence, you will have to interact with humans."

Yeti paused, letting it sink in. Above him, Rupert peered down from the top of the flagpole, as if listening in. Sylvie told herself his beady bird eyes didn't linger on her.

"We can teach you all we know about humankind, but none of it matters if you can't have a simple interaction with humans, regardless of whether you're being open about your monster self or hiding it."

Amos nodded along, and Sylvie was suddenly aware that Master Gert was standing on the porch of the administration building, watching silently, the rustle of their cape and their long shadow the only clues to their presence. Sylvie stole a glance, and the director caught eyes with her and nodded, face unreadable at this distance.

Sylvie turned her attention back to Yeti, who had folded his hands in front of his body. Like he did that first night at opening ceremonies, he rocked his weight and put it all in his heels, lifting his giant toes off the ground for a moment. When he was firmly planted again on the ground, he took in all members of Group Fang in his gaze.

"If I'm being honest, this is the most important skill we will teach you this week by a mile." Gone was the showman quality to his voice. It was low, serious, and direct. "And I say that knowing full well that 99.9 percent of humans believe I'm a mythical creature. I have had the chance to interact with that .1 percent, and I'm still standing here because I did it correctly."

It suddenly occurred to Sylvie that Yeti or Scott would be tremendous prizes to the wrong human with a big gun and an even bigger ego. Were there monster hunters eager to kill and display monsters to prove they're real? To prove that they were the first to know and then best them?

Horror sliced through Sylvie at the thought.

As fearful as Sylvie had been after her realization that she was a human locked inside an invisible bubble with real live monsters, she now feared what would happen if humans who weren't as friendly to the idea of monsters as, say, Vera's human mom, found out about this place and these people.

Because monsters were people. The workers were adults. The campers were kids.

They were all people.

Yeti plastered a new grin on his face, segue clear. "Okay! For role-play, we're going to pair you up!"

Sylvie immediately got so close to Vera, they knocked shoulders as everyone else shuffled about. Yeti clapped his hands. "But—wait—let me rephrase. *I'm* going to pair you up."

There was a collective moan of "Awwww . . ."

This made Yeti smile bigger. "It's important that we practice talking with people we don't know very well. If we just pair up with our roommates and good friends, what's the point?"

"But you'll purposefully pair us with someone we don't like," Freya whined, shooting daggers at Chad.

"If you don't like someone, that's a *you* problem," Chad slung back.

"Perhaps," Amos ventured, "you may think you don't like someone because you don't know them very well."

"Or because they're a jerk," Vera mumbled.

"Okay," Yeti said, "with that in mind, I'll pair you up for a few exercises—"

Another long, collective groan.

But Yeti doubled down. "Unless we have a volunteer who would like to pick a partner they don't know very well?"

The monster raised a fuzzy eyebrow and waited. As he did, from the corner of Sylvie's eye, she caught Chad whisper something to Lenny and Milo. His brown eyes skittered to Vera.

Oh no, you don't.

Sylvie's hand shot up just as Chad's own hand began to raise (for once).

"I will!" she half shouted for extra emphasis.

"Sylvie?" Yeti smiled, surprised. "What an excellent example from our newest camper. Who—excluding your roommate—would you like to pick?"

"Chad."

The werewolf's eyes narrowed in surprise. "Me?"

Vera clutched Sylvie's arm. "Him?"

Her roommate's question came out as a fearful whisper. Sylvie nodded once to Vera but answered Chad. "Yep."

Yeti and Amos grinned their winsome and weird smiles.

"Oh, I think that would be a great match," Yeti said. "You two stand over here."

He directed them to the side. Sylvie patted Vera's hand as she moved away, hoping to convey that she'd be just fine. As the others paired up, Chad stomped over, stood next to her, and then asked in a low, annoyed voice, "Why did you pick me?"

It was clear by his tone that she'd ruined his plans of tormenting Vera. Over Chad's shoulder, Sylvie could see that Vera had teamed up with Bebe, which was a relief.

"Maybe we got off on the wrong foot," Sylvie answered. It really was the truth. "We literally *collided* when we met."

"You were in the way."

"That's your point of view."

After a moment, the werewolf's eyes narrowed again. "You know that they'll switch us up and I'll be paired with your half-human bestie at some point, right, bloodsucker?"

Sylvie thought that might happen, and with Chad's

previous camp experience, the threat was likely some version of the truth of how this morning would play out. But if she could save Vera the initial pain, she would. Sylvie could handle Chad.

Before Sylvie could come up with a pithy answer, Yeti presented an ancient-looking witch hat to the group, flourishing it in a swooping loop.

"Now, each one of the pairs will pick a scenario from our scenario hat!"

Yeti wiggled the hat and lowered it, allowing Amos to dump a handful of folded slips of paper inside.

When the skeleton finished, Yeti held the hat aloft again and crowed, "Each of these scenarios would be a common interaction situation for a human and a monster."

Somehow, Sylvie doubted this.

Yeti strode forward and presented the hat to Sylvie and Chad, the first team in the line. Vera and Bebe were at the end, and between herself and her roommate were pairs consisting of Francis and Lenny, and Freya and Milo. Sylvie wondered how many times Milo would become a bespectacled Pomeranian between now and lunch . . . though he did seem to live up to Vera's estimation of being "not so bad" for a werewolf. Especially away from his cousin.

"Would you like to draw?" Sylvie asked Chad, attempting to be polite.

The werewolf kept his arms folded over his chest. "Nope."

Okay, fine.

Sylvie thrust her hand into the hat and didn't bother to search around. Her fingers clasped on the first slip of paper they touched. She pulled it free, and the pair of them inspected their scenario: the first day of school.

Well, that was one Sylvie could do.

Chad, though, muttered like she'd set him up. "I've never been to human school, and I'm never going to go to human school."

Sylvie didn't know what to say to that.

From down the line, Yeti waved the hat. "Everyone have their partners? Everyone have their scenarios?"

There was a lot of aggrieved nodding.

"Great. Now, you can go anywhere within the circle of the track to practice your scenario. Be far enough away from each other to allow for yourselves to fully feel immersed in the scene, but please don't stray too far." Yeti spun his big body in a circle, arm flung out to the common area. "Amos and I will be walking around, observing your work, and providing feedback and suggestions as necessary. Good luck!"

CHAPTER 23

A LARP Queen's Gambit

Immediately, everyone began to scatter to various corners of the Monster Camp infield.

"Let's take the chessboard," Chad said, and Sylvie had to admit it was a good suggestion. It was a defined space, and maybe if they got creative, they could use the life-sized pieces as stand-ins for other students or teachers.

As the werewolf marched them over to the chessboard, Sylvie's mind combed for all the things she would've said to other kids had anyone seriously joined her LARPing club. At the beginning of any LARPing relationship, boundaries and relationships were set up, and characters established.

In this case, the boundary was anything educationally oriented, and the relationship was between classmates, and the characters were students. Really, if Chad wanted to think about it that way, this was not that different from the first day at camp. Sylvie kept that thought in her back pocket just in case Chad was a complete stick-in-the-mud about their scenario.

Wordlessly, they arrived at the board. All the pieces were in their starting positions—and this close, Sylvie realized they weren't your usual characters. They were monsters, because of course they were. Vampires, were-wolves, skeletons, witches—nearly every monster type at camp was represented right there in black and white.

They dumped their bags and water bottles along the side.

"Do you want to be the human or the monster?" Sylvie asked, because that seemed like the polite thing to do with no set roles in this role-play.

One side of his lips curled up. "I've never been to school. I don't know the first thing about it."

Sylvie drew in a deep breath and tried very hard not to seem too eager. "Okay, then I'll be the human. You be the monster."

Chad just kind of nodded. And Sylvie suddenly understood she was going to have to set this up fully herself.

She thought about every LARP technique she'd ever read in any of her books or magazines or online. She needed to create a quest. One with a goal.

On the first day of school at Evermore Middle, there had been one immediate goal as all the sixth graders stood in the entrance, staring at identical printouts of their individual class schedules: finding their first class.

Sylvie laid out the role-playing concept as directly and politely as possible.

"Okay, Chad, the scene is the first day of school, and you and I are brand-new middle-school students. We've never been inside the building before because we missed orientation, and we need to find our first class."

His eyes narrowed under bushy eyebrows.

"Are you showing off right now, vamp? I know you think I'm an idiot because I'm homeschooled, but I do watch movies, you know. And my girl cousins go to human school—they aren't as hairy. I know how middle school works."

It took everything within Sylvie not to put up her hands in retreat. Being competent shouldn't equal being a show-off, especially when the other party refused to participate. Plus, he'd just said he didn't know how school worked. Mixed signals, much?

"I'm not showing off, I'm setting the scene for the role-play and basing it on my experience." Okay, maybe to his ears that did seem show-off-y. She really wasn't trying to offend him. Sylvie extended an olive branch. "Unless you'd like to base it on a movie? A scene you know?"

Chad's nostrils flared. "Maybe later."

Sylvie drew in a calming breath. "Okay. So, we'll do the new-students-looking-for-class scene? Do you have the setting in mind? Are you ready to start?"

He nodded.

Well, at least that was something, even if she wasn't sure which of her questions he was answering. She hoped all of them.

Sylvie retrieved her discarded backpack, slung it on, and mimed herself holding a piece of paper. She purposefully glanced down at it and back up before squinting around, brows drawn together in obvious confusion.

Her eyes landed on Chad, who hadn't adjusted to enter the scene at all. His arms were still crossed defensively over his chest, and his furry brows hung low over his narrowed eyes. He didn't put on his backpack. Whatever. Props were nice but unnecessary.

Sylvie worked up a friendly smile. "Um, hey, I'm Sylvie. . . . You don't happen to have Miss Tottenham for homeroom, do you?"

Chad said, "Yes."

"Oh, great! Do you know where the room is? I must have left my map at home. I'm sorry, but what's your name? I don't mean to be rude."

Sylvie waited for Chad to say something, feeling like she'd fed him enough leading questions that he could latch on to something. Anything. Even Dustin could've taken that opening and run with it (right before yelling, "You're lost and alone? Perfect for SLAYING!").

But Chad didn't latch on.

Instead, he just stood there, all of him still except his chin, which he tilted to a ridiculous angle.

"This isn't how humans act."

Sylvie was determined not to break the scene. She was human. And she'd react as a human to every single thing he said. "Um, what?"

Chad's eyes narrowed even more. "You just came up to me and asked me my name?"

"Ha. What elementary school did you go to?" She squinted at him in a closer inspection. "I'm going to guess Walton Heights. Am I right?" Sylvie smiled and waved a hand. "Anyway, at Ever Day, that's what people do when they don't know each other. They ask each other's name."

Chad seemed utterly determined not to react to any of it.

Sylvie took a step toward him, reached forward, and pantomimed tilting an invisible school schedule up from his clenched fists. She leaned in as if to read it.

"Ah, Chad. Oh! We have math together too." Then, returning to the stated goal of the scene, Sylvie continued, "Um, so, Chad, do you know the way to Miss Tottenham's homeroom?"

She watched him with interest painted all over her features, trying to will Chad to say anything that made sense to all her questions. He didn't.

Sylvie decided to employ another tactic. She gave Chad a little shove, as if she'd been knocked by another student during passing period, and to her surprise, he took a step. "Oh, we better go now, or we'll be late. I don't know about you, but I don't want to find out what happens if we're in the hall when the bell rings!"

Instead of musing with her, Chad raised an eyebrow as he continued to walk forward. "Aren't you going to ask me why my hair is so thick?"

Sylvie mimed putting her schedule in her pocket and looped both thumbs under her backpack straps. "Um, no?"

Chad ran a hand down one of the big ham-hock sideburns that covered his cheeks. "You don't find it unusual that I have facial hair in middle school? Have you seen my arms?" He thrust out one of his arms, bare in yet another tank top and nearly as furry as Magnus, if she were being honest.

Sylvie shrugged. "It's *hair*? Did kids at Walton Heights make fun of you or something?"

"Yeah."

Finally! A productive answer.

"Well, um, that's stupid. And I don't care."

"You don't?"

"Why should I? So, you're hairy? I'm super pale. Whatever. It's dumb to be all hung up on looks anyway."

Sylvie steered them toward a sorceress-looking black chess piece that she assumed was supposed to be the queen.

"Hi, Miss Tottenham, I'm Sylvie Shaw."

Sylvie swiveled to Chad, waiting for him to play along.

The werewolf drew in a deep breath. "I'm Chad Wolff."

Sylvie put on a terrible British accent, speaking out of the side of her mouth so that it might seem to be coming from the sorceress standing in for Miss Tottenham. "Great to have you in class, Sylvie and Chad. Come in, come in!"

They moved past the chess piece.

"Hey, so you want to sit together?" Sylvie asked.

Chad shrugged.

"I'll take that as a yes, Chad."

Sylvie plopped down and slung off her backpack, miniquest complete.

"Bravo!" Sylvie and Chad spun around . . . and there was Master Gert. Silent and as dark as a shadow, their face completely alight as they stepped out from beyond the forest of white chess pieces on the other end of the board. "That was the most realistic human-monster scenario I've seen in my thirty-plus years of Monster Camp."

Wow. Really?

Sylvie was so stunned, in fact, that Chad beat her to the punch in addressing what they'd said. "You're serious?"

Master Gert smiled so hard, *Sylvie's face* ached for them. "Of course, Chad. I'm always serious. That was heartfelt and real and so very delightful."

"I concur." Sylvie and Chad again whirled, and there was Yeti.

Had they both been watching this whole time?

"You know what?" Master Gert asked, but it didn't

seem like a question. Their dark eyes settled on Yeti's. "Perhaps we should have them give a demonstration at the bonfire tonight? Ahead of the scary human stories? I really do think it might be beneficial for the other campers."

"You . . . want us to perform?" Chad asked, like he was actually shy. He was not. But he sure did seem stunned.

The camp director's dark eyes twinkled, and their long face gave an encouraging grin. They moved forward and clapped Chad on one bare and hairy shoulder.

"Why, yes! I want you to do exactly what you just did. Or if you can't remember it exactly, that's okay; the point is the energy and the interaction. It didn't feel like a performance; it felt real."

Sylvie's mind raced. It didn't *feel* like a performance because it *was* real.

She was a real human asking real questions of a real monster that she didn't know. And he was reacting like a monster who was almost never around real live humans.

A chill spread up Sylvie's spine. Did they know? Couldn't they see? They'd been wrong about so much about humans during HURT, but what if they really knew a human-monster interaction when they saw it?

Maybe she could say she wasn't up to it. But if she didn't want to demonstrate, would that make things worse? Would that be fishy?

Sylvie drew in a deep breath. The nature of her vampire farce had changed, and she had to stay on her toes or risk wrecking it all.

"We'd love to. I mean—I would," Sylvie answered finally, her words coming in a furious rush.

Maybe Chad would back out. Maybe she could do this with someone else. Anyone else. She could take all comers.

But before Sylvie could get any further in that thought, she heard Chad's voice. "Yeah. I'll do it."

Chad took her acceptance as a challenge. Because of course he did.

Master Gert was instantly delighted, lighting up their black robes with joy. "Excellent. Perhaps tonight? So you all are fresh?"

Tonight? That seemed so soon.

Sylvie suddenly wished they could have time to practice. Maybe a whole day to get their performance together . . . and for her to figure out some way to mask how painfully obvious it was that she knew so much about humans because she was a human.

But Master Gert was smiling, and Yeti was smiling . . . so, when Chad nodded his shaggy head, Sylvie nodded too.

CHAPTER 24

Potions, Pig Eyes, and an Impending Performance

I can't believe they asked you to *perform*," Vera mused to Sylvie, not for the first time, as they huddled over a miniature cauldron in the Potions Shack that afternoon.

Sylvie's stomach was already being greatly tested by this new camp experience, and it wobbled wetly in her gut as she struggled to figure out what to say this time.

Because tonight wasn't really a performance, just role-playing, but it sure did feel like being on display.

With Chad.

Chad, who was currently whispering wildly with Milo over their own cauldron across the shack from where Sylvie and Vera had tucked themselves into a literal corner. Like by a bunch of extra bins and overturned buckets.

Sylvie told herself that if the adult monsters hadn't sniffed out her humanness by watching their earlier scene, they wouldn't as they performed.

As long as Chad didn't actually bite her, she'd be fine tonight.

Sylvie tried to play it cool. "If it helps give someone fresh ideas on dealing with the outside world, I'll take it."

"If that's what they needed, they should've just hired my parents," Vera said, dipping a thermometer into their bubbling cauldron. According to Mummy G, they weren't supposed to touch anything on their tray until the "liquid gold" inside hit its boiling point of 570 degrees. Sylvie had no idea what this liquid gold actually was, except that it totally looked like the shimmering insides of those bracelets you could win at the Evermore Middle School carnival.

"Why haven't they?"

"No clue."

Sylvie bit her lip.

"Oh! We're at 570!" Lenny cheered, both hands shooting up so quickly, his hat fell off and nearly landed in the cauldron he was sharing with Freya. He swiped it and squashed it back down over his equine-like ears.

"Good. Good," Mummy G said from the front of the class and her own bubbling cauldron. The shack was actually set up a lot like Sylvie's sixth-grade science class, complete with a demonstration table up front. "Let's wait for everyone else to get there. In the meantime, familiarize yourself with your ingredients and tools."

Also like her science class, the Potions Shack was plastered with informational material. In this case, they were curling posters of various potion ingredients and their properties. Some Sylvie recognized—chamomile, lavender, lemon balm—and some that she had to read twice because, well, that couldn't be right.

Skullcap (herb). Meadowlark foot (actual bird foot). Dried axolotl gill (weren't those endangered?).

There was even an entire periodic-table-like presentation of every kind of animal eye in existence—including human!—and their individual properties.

Now, Sylvie had many of those ingredients out in front of her on a little silver tray with a handy rim. Her stomach wobbled even worse every time she accidentally glanced down. Sylvie's science class had dissected earthworms last year, and that was pretty gross, but this was about eighty million times grosser.

Sylvie snuck a peek at their own thermometer. They were at 550 and climbing fast—much more efficient than the Bunsen burner she'd used at Evermore Middle. She couldn't procrastinate any longer. With a steadying breath, Sylvie adjusted her safety goggles, and started studying the ingredients—which, honestly, was something she'd been avoiding for the last twenty minutes.

A laminated place mat lined the bottom of the tray, and each ingredient and implement arranged to match the label below it.

Scalpel. X-Acto knife. Tongs. Whisk.

Eyeball (pig). Heart (crow). Saliva (rhino x 1 cup). Dirt (x 5 lumps) from a fresh (1 month or newer) zombie grave. Peppermint sprigs (x 10).

"Are we all at 570 degrees?" Mummy G asked.

Sylvie had gotten the impression in the mess hall that Mummy G was mostly nonverbal, which sort of made sense given what she knew about mummies. But she'd been completely wrong. Mummy G could speak; she just didn't *prefer to*. Unless she was telling a tomb-raider scary human story or giving potions instructions, apparently.

Her voice was low and about as well-worn as the shabby ends of her bandages. She sounded like she'd gargled rocks and spit them out like bubblegum that'd lost its flavor. "Okay. First things first. You'll need to slice your eyeballs thinly and as evenly as possible. You will have the most success with a combination of your X-Acto knife and tongs, *like so*."

Mummy G began demonstrating with a chef's grace, but Sylvie could not watch.

That fruit punch she'd sipped all morning and at lunch sloshed wetly in her stomach as a wave of nausea crossed over Sylvie. Her head suddenly felt like a helium balloon, and she wondered vaguely if her passing out would be a dead giveaway of her humanness.

Maybe it wouldn't totally ruin the potion recipe if she dumped the eyeball straight in without slicing it. Any liquid that hot would just melt it, right? Maybe it would be a little less smooth, but . . . that'd be okay?

Sylvie honestly had no idea. And she was afraid to ask. Across the table, Vera's tongue was poking out of the side of her mouth as she very carefully, very slowly sawed through some poor pig's eye—

"NO, FRANCIS."

Sylvie's head snapped up in time to see Mummy G, with speed Sylvie did NOT expect, whip out one of her mummy bandages and lasso an eyeball clean out of Francis's green grip. The monster stared at his empty hands, then blinked at the mummy. She wagged a bandaged finger in front of his face, and then mimed eating the eyeball before repeating, "NO EATING INGREDIENTS."

Sylvie was not going to have that problem.

Mummy G dropped the eyeball back onto the tray and pointedly circled the whole thing with her finger. "This is not for you. This is for the Greenland Refugees. You will have your pick of candied eyeballs at dinner. Do not be selfish!"

Francis's green ears turned a startling purple red as he slumped in his seat.

"If I see any of you eating or wasting these ingredients, I will have you stay after during free time to write a letter to the Greenland Monster Initiative explaining why we're missing a jar of their promised Pollution Salve."

Sylvie swallowed.

Mummy G, with Master Gert standing at her side, had explained at the beginning of today's lesson that they'd be creating some Pollution Salve to help monster refugees who'd been forced out of their home in Greenland to a new area with much higher levels of pollutants. Mummy G's salve was supposed to help them adjust.

Mummy G was right. Messing up the salve was self-ish. Sylvie took a deep breath—she needed to slice up the eyeball.

"Sorry, buddy," Sylvie whispered to the eyeball as she picked it up with her tongs and placed it on the work area in front of her. She really wished she didn't know it had belonged to a pig. A faceless animal would've been much better than those cute little dudes.

Tongs clenched tight, and her teeth gritted so hard she was sure she could feel her fake fangs stiffen, Sylvie focused on making a straight, clean, precise cut—not what she was slicing.

As further distraction, Sylvie returned to the con-versation they'd been having before Francis's attempt at a snack. "Um, Vera, I know you don't really like the campfire stuff and you already have your human-coping mechanisms because of your mom and your genes, but . . . would you come tonight?" Sylvie kept her eyes on her work, almost afraid to look up. "Please?"

Vera let out a soft laugh and whispered, "And miss out on your performance with Chad? Are you kidding? I need to be there just in case you actually impale him."

Sylvie was relieved and started to wonder if maybe she should ask for a critique from Vera, based on her half humanness—was that something a real vampire would do?—when a knock came on the doorframe.

Master Gert stood there, Rupert on their shoulder. Staring straight at Sylvie, of course. Again.

"Group Fang," the director began with a sigh, "this will surprise no one, but it appears Fade has gone missing yet again. Has anyone seen signs of him?"

Everyone in the room shook their heads.

Master Gert nodded, unsurprised. "Well, I suppose it's time to pull out the glitter his mom sent us. Thank you, all." But before making to leave, they paused and clapped their hands together. "Hope to see each of you at tonight's campfire for something so special that Fade might actually make an appearance."

Then, Master Gert winked at Sylvie and was gone.

Live-Action Role-Play...
With an Audience

That night, Sylvie held fast to her "You Suck" tumbler, the red fruit punch sloshing merrily as she walked forward, furiously hoping she wouldn't pass out.

"Don't be nervous," Vera was saying as they approached the campfire circle carved out of the vast trees. Smoke was already billowing high enough to drift past Rupert's nest and higher. "You have nothing to be nervous about. Remember? Master Gert literally said this was the most realistic thing they'd seen in thirty-plus years!"

Though she'd convinced herself otherwise earlier, the worry that perhaps the adults recognized Sylvie's human-ness resurfaced the closer the clock crept to showtime, and it all made her nerves jump and her pores ooze per-spiration. She'd rubbed the pad of her thumb raw on her mom's necklace, and even that wasn't enough to keep the sweat at bay. A fine sheen of it coated her palms, her hairline, under her arms, and up her back, made worse by her backpack, which she'd filled with her textbook-sized LARP manuals and brought as a prop.

Upon entering the campsite, Sylvie and Vera selected the same log they'd sat on that first night. Master Gert, Amos, Yeti, Scott, Mummy G, and the campers filled nearly every space on the logs. Master Gert had been right, even Fade had appeared—and there was no way to miss him, because the director had indeed covered him from head to toe in a crust of Mom-approved rainbow glitter.

Everyone was there—except for Chad.

The campers and adults talked among themselves, waiting. Finally, after a hushed conversation with Milo and Lenny, Master Gert nodded to the other counselors, released Rupert from their shoulder and to his nest above, and, with a flash, they disappeared in a plume of smoke.

"What the . . . ?" Sylvie asked aloud, almost reflexively.

If Vera heard her, she didn't even try to answer—she didn't have time. A few seconds later, Master Gert reappeared in a flash-bang and a whip of their cape. When the cape unfurled, Chad was standing there, looking sullen.

He didn't say anything; instead, he just sat down next to his cousin as Master Gert addressed the crowd.

"Okay, everyone," they said cheerfully and without a second look at Chad, "as you may have heard through the grapevine, as an opener to our nightly scary human stories, I've asked two campers to demonstrate the role-playing techniques they used earlier today. I've done this because I think the group as a whole might find them exceptionally helpful." There was a pause, and the director tilted their head. "That said, one of our participants isn't up to demonstrating and would prefer to watch."

"Um, what?"

Sylvie hadn't realized she'd said it out loud until Chad answered her.

"I don't want to do it."

Master Gert ignored Chad's excuse and waved at Sylvie. "Would you come up here, Sylvie?"

Mind racing, Sylvie left the safety of her log and approached Master Gert.

"Now, Chad doesn't believe me, but during their HURT human-monster role-playing scenario this morning, he was the perfect picture of an incredulous monster interacting with a human, played by Sylvie."

Just that little bit of recognition was enough to send a warm glow through the chill of Sylvie's nerves. Meanwhile, though Master Gert lavished praise upon Chad, the werewolf didn't glance up.

"I have seen many a role-play scene in my day, and almost a hundred percent of the time, it's impossible to tell the monster from the human," the director elaborated.

Sylvie's blood turned to ice, the inner glow of recognition immediately snuffed out. Sweat renewed its prickle at her skin, heat flaming immediately in her cheeks, just in time for Master Gert to wave a hand at her in hopes that everyone would look.

They did.

Sylvie gulped.

The director nodded enthusiastically. "What I saw this morning that was so interesting to me was, while Chad was the perfectly closed-off, suspicious monster, Sylvie did an excellent job acting like a normal human might."

Chad clearly realized that what made him good in that scene was that Sylvie was good in that scene. And he didn't like it. His snarl came out as he finally glanced up.

"No, she didn't," he groused. "She didn't question me at all or raise her voice or comment on my hair. That's what humans do. They freak out."

Master Gert smiled gently at Chad and then addressed the whole group. "What I think is important for you to remember about humans is that they see what they want to see. They lack imagination, which means they can't even imagine they are talking to a real live werewolf."

Bristling, Sylvie wished she could argue this point. Maybe adults seemed a little lacking in the imagination department sometimes, but kids their age? Their imagination machines worked just fine.

Master Gert kept building to their point. "We spend a lot of time at Monster Camp discussing human differences and the ways that humans can treat us when they're scared of us. But . . . honestly, if I'm being truthful, that might be doing you all a disservice." Sylvie found Vera in the back, her thin lips dropped open at the director's words. "Because humanity isn't one-size-fits-all, just like all us monsters aren't the same."

Sylvie wanted to whoop and holler and point out that it wasn't, that they should most definitely stop focusing on differences and also certainly ensure a better environment and experience for half humans like Vera, but instead, the smile froze partially built on her face as Master Gert again waved a long-fingered hand at Sylvie.

"Sylvie acted exactly as a human might who has been conditioned by society to gloss over another's unique traits. Humans often believe they're being polite in ignoring someone's differences instead of seeing and recognizing them. They believe, mistakenly sometimes, that by not acknowledging differences, they are doing the different person a favor, when really, they are purposefully ignoring what makes that person special and oftentimes defines their important life experiences."

For the first time at Monster Camp, a monster's description of humankind actually seemed accurate? Sylvie recognized the exact phenomenon Master Gert was describing.

"And so, humans, except for the very young or very old, might not question your monsterness at all. Which means it's the monster's job to not only protect your identity, but to keep up the illusion."

Sylvie had been so intent on acting like a normal

human, she hadn't realized she'd done any of this. But she most certainly had.

Master Gert placed both hands on the girl's shoulders. "Now, who would like to give role-playing a go with Sylvie? I believe the prompt was a scene at school, isn't that correct?"

"It was a first-day-of-school interaction."

"Ah, yes! A very important time for any monster walking among humans," Master Gert confirmed. "Everyone is equally confused and nervous and interested in making a good first impression. Now, who would like to give it a go?"

Vera raised her hand. "I will."

Sylvie's heart leapt. This would be good. Vera could work on her monster side, and Sylvie wouldn't have to role-play with Chad, and—

"Thank you for volunteering, Vera, but because you're roommates, I was hoping someone who didn't know Sylvie as well might try first?"

The other campers just stared back.

When no one jumped at the chance, Master Gert bent down and tapped Sylvie on the cheek. "Come now, I promise she won't bite!"

"I'll do it."

Freya stood, and Sylvie was suddenly extremely relieved. The witch seemed cool, and she went to human school, so she'd know the scene without a lot of hand-holding—

"Wait, if they're going to do this, they can't be at school."

For someone who didn't want to role-play, Chad sure did have a lot of opinions.

"Why . . . do you think so, Chad?" Master Gert asked, genuinely flummoxed.

"At school, humans are supposed to be nice to one another. They aren't always, but there are enough adults around to keep kids in line." Clearly the movies about school that Chad watched didn't include scenes where kids were getting food tossed at them in the lunchroom or mean-girl stuff in the bathroom. "I think maybe we should change the scene to be somewhere there aren't any adults to police them."

Master Gert inclined their head. "What did you have in mind?"

To Sylvie's utmost surprise, Chad turned to her. "You walk among the humans, Sylvie. Where are they mean? What's more accurate?"

Sylvie was stunned—Chad was genuinely asking. He didn't even layer a twist of sarcasm to the delivery of those questions, though it would've been easy to add a sneer or growl or any of his other little bits of flare. Maybe he really did want to know?

So, in the spirit of his seemingly genuine curiosity, Sylvie dug deep and reached for the last time a human was truly mean to her, on purpose, with no adult intervention.

"How about the park?"

Master Gert was already nodding. "Human kids who are your age go to the park all the time without grown-ups. Usually, it's a big open space, minimal supervision. Excellent." They looked to Freya. "Does that sound okay to you, Freya?"

The witch shrugged and glanced at Sylvie. "What are we at the park to do?"

Sylvie was about to bring up LARPing, because that was the reason she preferred the park, but Amos cleared his nonexistent throat. "Perhaps we keep it truly improvisational and ask the audience?"

"Oh yes, marvelous idea." Master Gert addressed the group. "What are they there for?"

Lenny shouted out an answer first. "They're there to play soccer!"

"Okay, yes. You are both there, playing soccer separately, and you have a conversation. Yes? Yes." Master Gert clapped their hands. "Let's give that a go. Sylvie, you're the human. Freya, you're the monster. Ready?"

It seemed as if the director was trying to set things up as fast as possible so there'd be no more adjustments, changes, or additions.

They backed away and perched on a log crowded with camp staff. "And go!"

Sylvie had never played soccer outside of gym class. She didn't know if Freya played at all. But that was the point of this live-action role-play. It wasn't a quest.

Instead, it was a simple scene that fit into a bigger story.

Sylvie could do this.

And she could guide Freya if need be.

Sylvie's eyes snagged upon a nearby fist-sized rock, and she immediately knocked it between her two feet, gently and controlled, as if it were a soccer ball. Freya's brown eyes lit up on what Sylvie was up to. There were no errant rocks near her, something that she and her witchy friends seemed to realize at once. With a swirl and a whoosh, Benedict the warlock fashioned a ball from a fallen acorn and rolled it over to Freya.

Titters of laughter snaked through the crowd. Sylvie gestured to Freya's blown-up acorn, which was much closer in size to a soccer ball than her prop. "Hey, cool ball. Where'd you get it?"

"Uh, thanks. My friend gave it to me."

"Neat." Sylvie stopped dribbling and paused, putting her foot atop the rock as she'd seen soccer players do in movies. "I'm Sylvie. Would you want to practice drills with me?"

"I'm Freya. And yeah, sure. Want to use my ball?"

"Yeah. Sweet."

Freya kicked the acorn ball over to Sylvie, who managed to stop it without too much nonathletic flailing.

"Wait, wait, wait!" Chad shot to his feet and waved his arms. "This is too fake. No one is that nice. The point of this scene was to show how human kids might act around monsters when no one is looking."

Sylvie's teeth ground together. If he was so determined

to be a nonplaying character, she was going to yank him out of NPC land and into the scene. Before she could overthink it, Sylvie kicked the acorn ball straight at Chad's head.

Chad covered his face, and the ball bounced off the flat of his palms and straight into Lenny's hands. Sylvie waved at the boys. "Hey, guys! That's our ball. Can you send it back over?"

Lenny immediately grinned and hugged it to his chest as he rose to his full height. "Nah, I think we'll keep it." He glanced over at Chad, who was getting the picture and stood.

Visions of Fisher and his minions playing keep-away with her precious LARP binder in the park hit Sylvie like a ton of bricks. Yeah, she knew this scene. She wasn't a witch like Freya, but she'd practically summoned it.

"Hey," the witch spat, her bracelets clacking together as she angrily crossed her arms over her Monster Camp T-shirt. "I don't think so! My friend gave that ball to me as a gift. Give it back."

Chad's eyes narrowed, and his teeth flashed. "Yeah, what are you going to do about it, pip-squeak?"

"Oh, you don't want to know, hair ball," Freya replied with a near snarl of her own.

Sylvie half expected Master Gert to pipe up with something about how they weren't supposed to be awful to one another, but they stayed silent. In fact, all the adults simply watched, just like the kids.

Okay, Sylvie thought about the role-playing construction here. Was she the only human? Or were Lenny and Chad playing humans too? Until she got some context clues, she was going to have to play as the only monster-pretending-to-be-a-human here.

"No need to name-call, Freya," Sylvie said, first glancing over her shoulder at the witch, then to the boys. "Let's play them for it. Two-on-two, sudden death, first goal wins."

Sylvie had no idea if that was a thing in soccer, but it would move the action forward.

Whether it was or wasn't, Lenny gamely dropped the acorn ball and kicked it hard. Sylvie and Freya immediately ducked to avoid a being drilled in the head . . . and Yeti caught it with a single hand.

Clapping erupted from the direction of Master Gert. "And scene! Bravo, bravo, everyone! Great job! Role-players, take a bow and return to your seats."

That . . . sounded like success.

After everyone returned to their respective logs, the director continued. "Okay, now. Did anyone catch a moment where Sylvie, pretending to be human, glossed over something?"

Milo's hand shot up. Master Gert inclined their head to the werewolf, and he adjusted his glasses before answering. "She had to have noticed how hairy Chad was when Freya pointed it out."

"Exactly! But she ignored it and instead moved to set

up a game of two-on-two. Sylvie did an excellent job of showing us how blind humans can purposefully be in the name of social norms and how they avoid situations that make them uncomfortable."

Sylvie's cheeks were burning. She squirmed involuntarily in her seat, hoping no one noticed, though Vera was close enough she could probably see both the squirming and the new line of sweat misting Sylvie's brow.

This was nice, but it was too much, it was too suspect.

And then it got worse.

"What I want to know," Annika began, "is did you really learn all this at human school, Sylvie? Because I go to human school, and I never could've done that without watching someone else do it first."

Oh. No.

Everyone turned to Sylvie.

"Yeah, how do you know so much?" Francis asked.

Then, Bebe: "Like, do you take human lessons or something?"

Sylvie looked to Vera, hoping she might have a clue of what to say . . . because if other human-adjacent monsters were asking, that couldn't be part of the answer. Vera's ashen eyes held nothing but more questions within them. That wasn't good. Sylvie's mind emptied out; her lips dropped open . . . but she just blinked back at all the monstrous faces focused upon her. She took a deep breath, opened her mouth, and—

"I'm a LARPer." The words were out of her mouth before she realized what she'd said.

"Uh, what?" someone mumbled.

Then, from Master Gert: "What did you say? I'm afraid I don't know what that is."

"A LARPer," Sylvie answered, louder now. "It stands for 'live-action role-play.' LARP. LARPer."

Then, Sylvie told the most complete truth she had in days. "It's my favorite thing to do back home. It's sort of like acting, but basically, you build a character and go on a quest. It means you have to think critically, interact with others, and achieve a common goal. And I play with humans. The best part is we're all pretending to be someone else, so if something unbelievable comes up, you can pass it off as part of the game."

"Whoa, really?" That from one of the ghosts, Zephyr.

"Yep. We have a club at school." Sylvie nearly pulled out her books to show everyone, but maybe that would seem a little too convenient.

"Excellent," Master Gert said. "Commit that to memory, campers. Perhaps if you join a LARP group at home, it'll give you a great chance to work on your interpersonal skills with humans!"

Sylvie couldn't keep a smile from spreading across her face. Yes, LARPing would be an excellent place for monsters to interact. Why hadn't she thought of it before? She'd been so worried that her LARPing would be proof that she was faking it as a vampire that she'd completely underestimated the benefits of LARPing to monsters who would have to interact with humans.

Vera leaned over to Sylvie. "Do you really do it all the time?"

"Yeah."

"Why didn't you say so earlier?"

"I . . . um . . . people at my school think it's nerdy."

That was true, even if it wasn't an answer.

Up front, Master Gert clapped their hands together. "Okay! I believe it's Yeti's turn for a scary human story tonight. Yeti? Where are you?"

Everyone craned their necks, looking around—usually the monster was pretty difficult to miss, with his massive size and stark-white fur. But he'd vanished from his log, completely disappearing.

"I said, 'Yeti! Where are you?'" Master Gert repeated, cupping their hands around their mouth to further project the sound.

Immediately, there was a rustling, and the massive monster stepped out of the shadows, suddenly taller than ever before, because atop his great head was a giant, powdered beehive wig, which perfectly matched the old-timey gown wrapped around his huge body. He looked just as perfect as the drag queens who ran the special lunch-hour reading session at the Evermore Library.

"Here I am!" He spread elegant arms, pinched out both sides of his voluminous skirt, and dipped in a very regal curtsey. Everyone, Sylvie included, broke out into applause. He twirled and batted his eyelashes—which were his usual ones, no special makeup added to achieve this new, glamorous look. "Buckle up, kids, this story has everything: a beheaded queen, delicious cake, and *leeches!*"

In the next several minutes, Sylvie laughed so hard that she couldn't look away. Yeti was a masterful story-teller. He did voices, mimed big events, and wasn't afraid to go into the crowd, bringing various campers in to tell the story with him. Tatiana and Vivian became cake-eating ladies in waiting, Francis a king, Norah the specter of death. On and on until the big, bubbling finale and a huge group shout of "OFF WITH HER HEAD!"

When Sylvie stood to clap, cheering and laughing, and glanced over to Vera to see her reaction . . . she realized she was sitting on the log all by herself.

An Apology at Dawn

Vera's coffin bed was closed when Sylvie got to the cabin.

Her shoes were off, and her copy of *Snow* was sitting on the floor, where it hadn't been before. She'd made it back. Alone.

Sylvie knew Vera didn't like the scary human stories. She'd explicitly said so.

Tonight was special and different, and maybe Sylvie had just expected Vera would want to stay and listen. Just this once, because she was already there, and Yeti really was such a fantastic storyteller. And the humans really were awful in the story in Sylvie's one-hundred-percent-human opinion.

But Sylvie felt a little guilty for staying.

She wasn't sure why, but she couldn't let it go, and spent the next several hours tossing and turning, wishing for dawn, and finding nothing but the flat black of her coffin at night.

Finally, in the first hints of rising light, Sylvie hauled herself, groggy-eyed and puffy, from the coffin and into the shower, a protein bar clutched tight in her fist.

She snuck into the bathroom, wolfed down the bar, which by that point was starting to taste like a whole lot of nothing, and splashed water on her face.

It didn't do much.

As she retraced her widow's peak, brushed her teeth, and put on fresh stick-on fangs, Sylvie was vaguely aware that if anyone had an inkling in their head about her not being undead last night because of her human knowledge, well . . . she looked rough enough to halt any suspicion in its tracks.

When she opened the bathroom door, she blinked. The cabin lights were on, and Vera's coffin was open and empty.

Confused, Sylvie sank to her coffin lid, took a sip of her fruit punch, and continued to rehearse what she'd say to Vera—who most definitely was avoiding her.

Thirty minutes later, the door yawned open, and Vera entered, sopping wet. Sylvie confusedly asked, "Did you shower somewhere else?"

Was Vera really so mad that she didn't want to share their space?

As good as Sylvie was at reading people and feeling out a scene, she felt very much in the dark.

"I asked Nessie for permission to do a morning swim." Vera shrugged and disappeared into the bathroom.

Sylvie was starting to feel like Vera was upset. It seemed like she might need to offer an apology, even if she ended up apologizing for something she didn't understand.

Ten more minutes, and the moment the bathroom door opened again, Sylvie was on her feet.

"Um, are you mad about last night?" Sylvie blurted out.

Vera's giant, dark eyes widened, and her pale face seemed to wane like the moon. But when she didn't reply, Sylvie's brain lurched into motion, and she stumbled through an apology. It came out in one big, messy, jumbled exclamation.

"I asked you if you wanted to come for my part but didn't ask you if you wanted to leave. I didn't realize you'd left until the end, and I felt bad, and then I came back to the cabin, and you were asleep, and I'm sorry."

Vera blinked. The silence stretched. Neither of them moved.

A lump was forming in Sylvie's throat. She swallowed it down. "Please say something."

Sylvie nearly grabbed Vera's wrist to implore her further but didn't. That seemed rude or manipulative somehow. They'd known each other for three days and some change. And she had a feeling like she'd wrecked their relationship just by . . . what? Laughing at a story?

Friendship was confusing.

Finally, Vera blinked. Her eyes shrunk back to their usual-but-still-huge state, and her frowning lips settled into a line.

"It's . . . fine."

Sylvie's ears filled with cotton, some sort of protection as she waited for more. A real answer. A real show of why Vera left and how she felt about Sylvie staying.

When Vera didn't elaborate, Sylvie said, "But you left."

Vera's answer was immediate and almost as rehearsed as everything Sylvie had planned to say before confession came out as word vomit.

"I was there for your performance. That's why I went. And when the story started, you were so into it, I didn't want to bother you, so I slipped away. Sylvie, we're good. It's fine. We don't have to do everything together. You wanted to stay; I wanted to go." That little, tight-lipped smile tilted on Vera's face, and it was almost more of a reassurance than her carefully constructed words. "This morning I swam; you were here. It's fine."

Finally, Sylvie said, "Okay." She bustled out of the way to let Vera pass. And as she sat back down on the edge of her coffin, she told herself it really was fine.

Still, Sylvie realized that she'd opened a door to herself last night, and she wanted to share it with Vera . . . if she wanted that too.

When Vera finished getting ready, Sylvie met her with her LARP manuals. They were large enough to give someone a concussion if they happened to fly across the room and toward another being.

"If you want to learn about LARPing, I can show you." She presented the books, stacked high like a layer cake of LARP.

Vera's face lit in surprise. "Your duffel is like Mary Poppins's bag. You had those in there this whole time?"

"Um, yeah," Sylvie replied.

Vera considered this and touched the topmost book. "I didn't know they made books about LARPing."

"Oh yeah, there are books and board games and conventions, like everything a normal, uh, activity would have." Suddenly, Sylvie was feeling very self-conscious. She stood there, waiting for judgment to wash over Vera's face. Or maybe suspicion. "I told you I was a nerd for this stuff."

Relief flooded through Sylvie as that last bit drew out the slightest tiny Vera smile. "We're all nerds for something. You can't get embarrassed about something if you aren't passionate about it."

"That's very wise, Vera."

"Well, my dad is two hundred years old—his wiseness rubs off. A lot." She shrugged. "Hey, so, can I borrow one of these? So I can learn more?"

Sylvie fanned the stack and picked the middle one— *LARPing 101*. "This one does a really good job at laying out the components of a beginner's LARP."

Vera grabbed the book and set it atop her coffin bed.

"Great. Want to head with me to the mess?"

Sylvie couldn't help it; her heart swelled, and she automatically grinned wide and unabashed. Things were okay. Her therapist had been right—confronting the problem head-on before it could fester was the way to go.

"Yeah, I'd like that." Sylvie grabbed her "You Suck" tumbler and her backpack. "Ready when you are."

Basic Training

When they arrived to roll call Thursday morning, they came to the news that Amos wouldn't be with them for their HURT lesson that morning—he'd been tasked with giving a still-glittery Fade an all-day private HURT lesson because he'd missed every single one since their joint session Monday.

Despite Amos's absence, Yeti was leading them on a "little hike" as part of the morning's HURT session. Unfortunately, their path was zigzagging straight up to the highest point in camp—called the Monsterhorn, which was apparently named as a nod to some famous mountain in a book, which no one but the camp staff and Milo had read.

Both Sylvie and Vera were breathing hard, taking labored, uphill steps side by side. A layer of sweat had already formed over Sylvie's slather of SPF 90, and everything about her skin felt both clammy and hot. She didn't envy Group Fester, who'd be doing this exact same jaunt in the heat of the afternoon.

"Maybe I should ask for private HURT lessons next year," Vera whispered as the pair of them snaked through a part of the Monster Camp forest they hadn't been to yet.

"I didn't even know that was an option," Sylvie mused when she'd caught her breath enough to form a full sentence. It certainly hadn't been in her brochure.

"Me either. But it sounds like an excellent way to avoid the stuff that sucks."

Sylvie elbowed Vera. "*Sucks.* Spoken like a true vampire."

She expected Vera's small little grin to flash in her periphery at the joke. Instead, the other girl's ginger brows pulled together over downcast eyes.

And suddenly Sylvie realized what she'd said. "Not that you're not a true vampire! . . . It was just a joke."

"I know you didn't mean it that way. Sorry . . . I just . . . I'm—"

"You don't have to explain. I need to be more thoughtful."

Though they were hiking on a dirt path rife with rocks and roots, Sylvie had the distinct feeling that she was again walking on eggshells.

"Group Fang!" Yeti shouted from a rocky turn in the path above. "We have arrived!"

The line of hikers crawled to the finish and dumped themselves out onto a flat summit ringed with rocks. Chad was muttering something to Milo about how he was only tired because of the coming full moon. Milo just groaned in response.

Meanwhile, both as pale as could be and red from exertion, Sylvie and Vera sat with heaving lungs on the nearest rock. Over the pounding of her heart, Sylvie was pretty sure she could hear other kids' happy screams, though whether that was Group Fester or the camp next door, she didn't know. Or, well, maybe she was hallucinating.

Yeti, however, wasn't panting or short of breath. He looked vibrant, standing in the middle of the ring of rocks. Somehow, he'd gained energy in the upward hike instead of expending it. One look at the other kids told Sylvie this was an exclusively yeti-monster trait.

"Everyone, take a few moments to catch your breath." At least he didn't dole out that suggestion with an ounce of smugness, only adult-y concern. "Drink plenty of water and eat snacks if you have any! Then, let's settle in for today's lesson."

"Wait, there's a lesson on top of this hike?" Freya asked, crunching on a hunk of ice from her water bottle.

Yeti didn't even blink at the crankiness in her voice. "Yes! And the lesson is this: with hard work comes a great reward . . . s'roars for everyone!"

From his pack, Yeti produced all the ingredients for

s'mores—graham crackers, marshmallows, slightly melty bars of milk chocolate—plus skewers.

Chad and Lenny automatically offered to help Yeti make a fire in the center of the ring while the other kids scurried around, searching for bugs to roast. Apparently, the difference between a s'more and a s'roar was the added layer of bug exoskeleton.

Within minutes, dozens of protein-rich beetles—popular on the lunch buffet, Sylvie knew—had been procured, plus extra goodies like juicy worms, fuzzy caterpillars, daddy-longlegs spiders, and leather-skinned toads had been gathered based on individual tastes.

As Sylvie focused nearly all her concentration on eating her regular old s'more alongside Vera while blocking out the crunching and slurping noises of the monsters enjoying their s'roars, she felt a tap on her shoulder. And there, chocolate edging their lips, were Milo and Freya.

"Hey, um, Sylvie," Milo said, pushing up his glasses nervously. He glanced at Freya, who at first seemed like an odd sidekick, but then Sylvie remembered they'd been paired together during the role-playing the day before. "Would you have a second during free time to show us how to LARP?"

Sylvie's jaw dropped.

What?

This had to be a joke. But no.

Freya put up a little, pink-tipped hand, her bracelets

clacking. "We know you probably want to spend your free time doing something else, but . . . but we'd like to learn. You clearly know more about humans than we do, and this seems like a great way to interact with them without suspicion."

Sylvie gaped at Freya. Then, in a snap, everything spun into motion, and suddenly, her hands shot forward and grabbed Freya's as she bounced on the toes of her sneakers, almost jumping out of her skin.

"Yes, yes, it's all those things! I can totally teach you!" She reached blindly behind her and put a hand on Vera's arm. "I was just showing my LARP manuals to Vera this morning; want to meet at our cabin at free time? We have an awesome rooftop, and we can sit up there and go through it."

"That would be really cool," Freya said, and she meant it. She truly did. She didn't even try to pry her hand from Sylvie's grip.

Milo nodded. "Uh, which cabin's yours?"

"Seven. It's the castle."

"Ah, of course it is." The werewolf grinned, and . . . it didn't seem mean or pointy or like it might actually be a misread snarl. He did have some beetle stuck between his teeth though. "See you there."

Both Milo and Freya nodded to Sylvie and then to Vera . . . and that was when Sylvie realized she hadn't asked her roommate's permission to invite them over. That felt like another eggshell to walk over, but Vera had asked for the very same thing Sylvie had just offered Milo and Freya.

She couldn't be mad. Could she?

Sylvie glanced at Vera and found her roommate's face blank, a smear of wayward chocolate on her chin.

CHAPTER 28

"Okay, vamp, how does one LARP?"

Vera did not seem interested in talking much at lunch. Or during the afternoon's lesson. Which was archery with Scott.

Honestly, on the archery range, they were spaced so far apart for safety reasons even with suction-cup arrows, it was impossible to have a conversation with anyone.

By the time they were finished and Scott was doling out generous high-fives, Sylvie's fingers had made their way to her necklace. She rubbed the crescent-moon a dozen times before she decided she *had* to say something.

Sylvie had learned in the past day that Vera seemed to clam up when something bothered her, and that seemed to bother Sylvie more, because it made her anxiety leap as she second-guessed herself.

By the time they reached the steps leading to their little castle, Sylvie had finally gathered enough courage to make a guess as to why Vera had become so quiet. With a deep breath, she touched her roommate's arm and said, "Hey, I should've checked with you before inviting Milo and Freya to the cabin. I'm sorry, I just got so excited and figured because we were talking about it, they could join, and . . . I didn't think about how I offered your space and time too."

"It's fine."

That seemed to be her default response to deploy. "It most clearly isn't."

Vera shrugged her slim shoulders into her heavy hair. "We do have the coolest cabin and best space for LARP-ing."

Then Vera entered the castle without another word. Somehow, that didn't seem reassuring to Sylvie's anxiety. Not at all. Especially considering they were roommates. They had to be around each other and share space. Sylvie had gone to camp before, but never a sleepaway one before this, and was completely at a loss as to if she'd truly done something as wrong as she felt she had. That was part of her anxiety—overthinking—and she knew it . . . but still.

Sylvie's spiraling thoughts went nowhere but down before a knock came on the castle door.

Vera didn't jump up from where she'd sat herself on her coffin lid, organizing the leaning tower of chip packets she'd collected in the past few days . . . so Sylvie grabbed her two remaining LARPing books plus her binder, hoping to be the very picture of a competent instructor. "Hey, won't you come in . . . ?"

The greeting died on Sylvie's lips as she looked out the castle's door and met the eyes of not only Milo and Freya, but the other two witches, Lenny, Chad, Bebe, Francis, plus Fade's glittery form.

"Uh. Hey, guys."

"I hope you don't mind, but they want to learn LARPing too," Freya said, cocking a thumb to the additional campers and brushing a lock of pink hair behind her ear.

With a jolt of shock, Sylvie realized she was on the precipice of a dream come true.

Maybe, just maybe, if she could show them how . . . she might finally form a LARP group. Not a joke of a club like she had with Dustin at Evermore Middle, but an actual, excited, interested, animated band of live-action role-players.

"Oh, excellent!" Sylvie replied. Behind her, she felt Vera's presence as she moved away from her coffin bed and peered out the stained-glass window to the site before them. "But I'm afraid you all won't fit on our roof."

Milo shrugged. "We figured. Which is why I asked Master Gert if we could use the main firepit. Unlit, of course. Would that work? I did some Googling and found an enclosed space might be best to start, just so we'd have set parameters."

Sylvie blinked at Milo. "Yes, that would be great."

The werewolf looked relieved. "See, told you it would

be fine, cuz," Chad offered from the back. "It can't be that complicated if humans do it. Duh."

They marched to the fire ring in the woods. Rupert met them, watching quietly from his nest with a cock of his great head. In the daytime, the fire circle was bright with afternoon sun but shaded enough they wouldn't all sweat their pants off as they began.

It actually was a perfect place to start.

"Okay, vamp, how does one LARP?" Chad asked, seating himself as always in what amounted to the front row—in this case, the log directly before where Sylvie had planted herself in front of the dormant fire ring. Milo and Lenny sat next to him. Instead of sitting themselves around the circle, everyone piled onto that log and the one right next to it.

It had been months, *so many months* since Sylvie had plotted that first Evermore Middle Monster LARP-ing Club meeting. It'd been back in August, on the very first day of sixth grade, when she'd found out the middle school was accepting proposals for new clubs. She'd run right home, just bursting with every which way she was going to blow away the faculty sponsorship group with her application and obvious enthusiasm for both LARPing and monsters.

She'd been so full of hope at finding others passionate about LARPing, creating memorable characters, going on quests, and achieving things together . . . only to realize the audience for her dream was . . . two.

Maybe one and a half.

Dustin barely counted.

But before Sylvie had known what a tough sell monster LARPing would be, she'd created character sheets and a set of rules and a basic outline for club meetings.

Rule number one of LARPing: if you're going to live-action role-play, you need a character.

Sylvie blinked back to the present. Everyone was staring at her. Vera, with her dark eyes and stark red hair; Fade next to her, his glittery body bent and propped like The Thinker; the furry pair of Chad and Milo; Lenny, adjusting his ever-present ball cap; the blue and green faces of Bebe and Francis; the witchy trio of Freya, Benedict, and Annika.

It hit her then that she was looking at exactly what she'd wanted all those months ago. Something deep within Sylvie wobbled with a feeling that might have been joy.

With a heavy exhale, Sylvie released her long-ago hopes into the muggy air of a June afternoon.

"Live-action role-playing or LARPing is exactly as described. We play characters in real time, telling a story of our choosing."

A hand raised—Benedict. "Wait, how is that different from acting? Isn't that just improv?"

"Good question. LARPing is a lot like improv, but there are set guardrails: character, story, rules."

Milo's big brain was instantly confused. "Don't guardrails usually come in sets of two?"

"It's a metaphor, man, don't be so literal," Lenny drawled.

Milo frowned but didn't say more.

Sylvie clapped her hands together in hopes of keeping things moving. "First things first, we need to start with a character. You're role-playing, but who are you going to be? That's the first question that each of us need to answer before we LARP—"

Bebe's blue hand shot up before Sylvie could continue. "What's your character, Sylvie? I need a good example."

It was a compliment in a way, and yet Sylvie's heart bottomed out.

She was her character. Right now. In this very moment.

There was literally only one safe way to answer this. And she was a good example—her survival since Sunday proved it.

Sylvie pasted a huge smile on her face, fangs out in force. "Well, I've found that the easiest thing for me to do when LARPing with humans is to play as my real self."

"Wait, so you role-play as 'Sylvie the Vampire'?" Chad asked, disbelieving.

By the expressions on everyone's faces, he wasn't the only one.

Sylvie swallowed and revamped her smile. "Yep."

"And you don't think that makes them more suspicious?" Chad pointedly gestured from the top of his bushy head down to his extremely hairy legs. "Believe me, if I joked to an actual human about being a werewolf, they'd stake out my house on a full moon."

Sylvie remembered how she'd immediately tagged Chad as a werewolf before he'd smashed into her that first day. From across an expanse of the open yard, she'd known. And up close, she'd cataloged his teeth, his snarl, his sideburns. Yeah, he was different, and by pointing it out, maybe, just maybe, he could beat humans to the chase.

"Remember what we talked about last night with Master Gert?" Sylvie asked Chad but tried to address everyone. She wasn't used to speaking to a crowd as an authority figure. "Humans see what they want to see. I've been complimented for how much I *look* like a vampire."

Again, she grinned, full fang, trying to sell it. Even if Fisher's bullying wasn't truly complimentary, it was full of tons of cracks about her being "Draculette," which was most definitely a nickname he'd come up with because of her vampireness.

"What I'm saying is that we can use our differences to create characters that allow us to be closer to our real selves around humans."

"Okay, but isn't live-action role-play pretend?" Milo asked, eyes scrunched behind his glasses. He really was extremely concrete.

Before Sylvie could figure out exactly how to answer Milo, Lenny leaned over to his friend and said, "Well, yeah, we're better versions of ourselves. Like, video-game versions."

Sylvie was starting to wonder if Lenny was her Milo translator.

"Yes! That exactly! You're playing yourself but as a character. You're an exaggeration."

Bebe's wings flickered, and suddenly, she was hovering in a twinkle of blue light. "I'm Bebe, a water sprite, and not only can I shoot water from my fingers, but I can freeze you in your tracks, frozen solid! Oh, and I can fly!"

"Yes, yes, you but better!" Sylvie cheered.

Francis hopped to his feet beside Bebe, his black eyebrows leaping up with him. "I'm Francis the Green Monster! I can rip dictionaries in half and play disc golf with them!"

"Yes!"

Milo frowned. "Wait, but how does it help us on a LARP quest if he can rip dictionaries? I mean, it's cool, but is it useful?"

"If I play disc golf with half dictionaries, I can accurately cut down attackers in a quest-fight with said dictionaries and a flick of the wrist." Francis tapped his temple with a finger. "Big-brain idea, no?"

"Yes," Sylvie answered before yet another Milo question. "So, basically, you want to build a character around yourself. What's your name and monster type? What are your goals? What are your strengths and weaknesses?"

Milo squinted. "Like literally or . . . ?"

"Physical strength, mental strength." Sylvie gestured first to her biceps and then to her temple. "For example, as Sylvie the Vampire, I have superhuman strength and fighting ability, but garlic makes me sweat, sunlight makes me itch, and a stake through the heart will always do me in."

As Dustin had managed to do many, many times.

Sylvie continued, pacing now, like she'd seen so many teachers do in lecture. "Eventually, you'll want to make a sheet cataloging all the details. But for now, let's do the basics, and everyone can flesh out their character from there."

Sylvie did have the extra character information sheets in her binder, but absolutely no pencils, and the ratio of people to pockets in this group was not a good one. And rustling paper kind of ruined the feel of a story. And, truthfully, it was so much more fun to build organically rather than filling out the paper like it was a medical form or something. So, Sylvie made the executive decision to hold off on the character sheets for now, and just write everyone's names on the LARP outline of their choosing.

Chad raised his hand, which was definitely a surprise. He was treating her like he did the camp counselors—polite and in accordance with social structure. Actually, maybe better because he didn't just shout out what he wanted to say. It was weird. She nodded at him. "Um, yeah, Chad?"

"Do we have to use our real name?"

Sylvie shrugged. "I mean, no. That's how I do it, but my friend Dustin always plays as 'Knight of the Night.'"

The werewolf grinned his pointy grin and waggled his

bushy eyebrows. "Well then, you're no longer looking at Chad but 'Prince Hairy.'"

He was so proud, chest puffed out and grin expectant, waiting for everyone to get the joke, that Sylvie couldn't help but bark out a laugh. A mostly collective giggle rose up in its echo. Even Vera's face lightened, just a touch.

The two cousins and Lenny bent together in whispers on one end of the log, Vera and Fade talking closely on the opposite end of the neighboring one.

In fact, now that Sylvie looked around, everyone was talking among themselves. Spitballing characters and "powers" and laugh-inducing weaknesses, all with varying tones of amusement, wide-eyed and . . . happy.

They were happily LARPing.

Sylvie's heart gave a little tug. This. Exactly this was what she'd always wanted from her LARPing experience. It was almost too much to ask that it was happening here and now. She touched the necklace at her throat, almost as if holding on to it would anchor her to this moment so that it wouldn't slip away. She'd wanted this so much and for so long that it felt impossible, even as it unfolded in front of her in real time.

After an amount of time Sylvie couldn't discern, the group was back to asking questions. Freya whirled around from the little triangle she'd formed with Benedict and Annika.

"Wait, so if Bebe can fly as part of her character . . . if we have magic, can we use it in a LARP?" Freya asked, brow cutting. The other two witches had similar expressions.

"If it's part of your character, I don't see why not."

"Sweet," they replied in a three-way echo.

"But no turning Chad, er, Prince Hairy into a Pomeranian, or Master Gert is going to end this before it's even begun," Lenny shouted in the general direction of the witches.

Freya rolled her eyes. "Ugh, fine."

"Promise?" Chad pushed. "No Pomeranians, Chihuahuas, Yorkies, or anything that barks. I *howl*, Freya. I do not bark."

Freya's eyes hooded, annoyed. "Yes."

Chad, Milo, and Lenny all turned to the remaining two witches, who sighed in tandem. "Yeah. Fine. We won't."

Perhaps it was time to divert this ship before it kept going. Again, maybe a little too much like Miss Tottenham, Sylvie clapped her hands for everyone's attention. "Okay, now that that's solved and everyone has a general grasp of who they're role-playing, it's time for the second guardrail: the story."

"Do we make that up as we go along?" Milo asked before thrusting a hand at Sylvie's LARP materials. "Or is there something in one of these books? My Google search returned a myriad of results on the best way to go about a story."

"Even better than any of that, we can vote!"

Then, Sylvie hopped atop the nearest log bench and

raised her LARP binder high over her head with a flourish, squeezed her eyes shut, and announced the words she'd planned so long ago that she'd never gotten to say.

"Inside this binder is our first quest. All we have to do is pick it. There are no wrong answers, only the story we want to experience together!"

To her surprise, the monsters began clapping.

Sylvie's eyes sprang open, a little nervous that maybe she'd overdone it and been too geeky, but no . . . they were well and truly applauding, her own excitement reflected back in their bright, monstrous faces.

Sylvie hadn't been this thrilled in, well, forever.

She hopped down, and the group converged around the binder, which she opened to the first page, using the log and stacked LARP books as a makeshift table. "Who's ready?"

"Me!" shouted Milo and Lenny together.

"Here! Me!" Freya yelled, two arms thrust in the air so forcefully that her pink-tipped fingers sparkled with magic.

"Us!" sang Annika and Benedict, with Francis and Bebe chiming in. To the side, Vera grinned; to her right, Fade bobbed his head.

And when Chad closed the show of agreement with a shout of "All of you are going to bow to me, Prince Hairy!" Sylvie's heart leapt with the certainty that LARPing really was the best thing in the world.

Secrets Don't Make Friends

To Sylvie's genuine surprise, the group picked the very first LARP in the binder.

It was a quest for a magical *Goonies*-style pirate ship full of treasure.

The basic layout: Crack the magic safe for the treasure map. Begin the quest at where X marked the spot, fight other monsters, best a challenge by a centaur (happily played by Lenny in horse form), and then storm the castle and become rich.

"Hey, um, can we come?"

The LARPers turned from where they were still crowded around the binder to find the rest of Group Fester—Norah, Zephyr, Tatiana, and Vivian—standing there behind them at the edge of the campsite clearing. Above, Rupert watched from his nest, as focused as a security camera.

"We saw you from over there," Vivian said in her soft voice, her long hair sweeping across the dirt as she gestured toward the basketball courts, and Sylvie realized she'd been the one to speak before they'd noticed their presence. "Are you doing that thing you talked about last night? The . . . SLURPing?"

"LARPing," Sylvie supplied. "And, yes, the more the merrier. Please join us."

It took barely any time at all to explain the formation of characters to the newcomers, as well as the goals of the quest. Accordingly, like Bebe, they all wanted to fly, if they were able.

The scenario was another matter.

"Wait, so, like, all of us go together?" Annika asked, and Sylvie realized that the witch's ability to arch her eyebrows nearly to her hairline might have been magical rather than just dramatic. "There are fifteen of us."

Sylvie actually didn't have an immediate answer. Doing this with a party of ten others had been a dream come true only minutes ago. A group of fifteen? Unthinkable.

But Annika was right—they were almost at an unreasonable size.

"What if we broke into two competing parties?" Chad inquired in a way that wasn't asking as much as it was announcing his newest greatest idea.

"Oooh, yeah," Lenny exclaimed. "That would be cool."

"Sylvie," Milo began, uncertainty in his voice, "is that something we can do? Or would it denigrate the validity of the LARP?"

"Wait, what?" Tatiana asked, her chartreuse face squished into confusion.

"He's asking if two groups will screw things up," Lenny informed the goblin.

"It will *not* screw things up. Have you monsters never watched a sport before?" Chad had his hands on his hips and exasperation in the cut of his shoulders. "Competition always makes things way more dramatic. And considering this is role-playing, we *want* more dramatic. Prince Hairy has spoken."

"Yeah, but your word means nothing here, your highness," Freya replied to Chad. "We need to hear from our expert on this. Sylvie?"

The witch turned to Sylvie—as did everyone else, even Chad. The werewolf *did* look annoyed, but even then he didn't argue. Which was . . . weird.

"Well, um," Sylvie started, buying time, waiting for her wealth of knowledge about LARPing to kick in and fill in the hole left by a vast lack of actual LARPing experience. "Yes, that's a classic of large-scene LARPing. Having rival groups means more opportunities for tension on the quest and gives each individual more, um, 'screen time,' if that makes sense."

"Of course it makes sense, which is why I suggested it, vamp." Chad's smile was ridiculously wide, and if he puffed his chest out any farther, he might tip over.

"Okay, but, like, how would that work with the goal of our quest?" Vera asked. "Are we both after the treasure? And if so, why can't we just work together to find it? Or share it? I mean, it's a whole boatload. Literally."

It was a good question, Sylvie thought.

"Easy," Chad answered, clearly thinking it was *not* a good question. "We don't work together. We're rivals."

Nope. No way. Sylvie shook her head. "Okay, but wait, the whole theme of Monster Camp this week has been to work together. Wouldn't it fly in the face of our entire camp experience up to this point to be rivals?"

Lenny broke into a fit of giggles. "Good one, Sylvie. Literally the first full day at camp, they had us compete against one another."

"That's true, but it was under the guise of working together," Freya answered.

"Which is exactly the same as us being in rival groups, trying to achieve the same goal?" Francis asked, his voice going high.

There was far too much nodding for Sylvie's comfort level.

"You know," Fade said, toying with his lanyard, "the other theme of Monster Camp this week: interacting with humans. I mean, that's the whole reason we wanted to LARP. No offense, Sylvie, not that this isn't fun, but you totally learned a lot about dealing with humans from it, and we want that too. So, let's add humans to the mix."

Ugh, she thought Fade would be on her side about this with how he seemed to feel about HURT, considering he'd purposefully missed two sessions.

Sylvie tried to catch Vera's expression, but she'd looked away. That was probably information enough about how she was feeling about this line of conversation.

"Oh, yeah." Chad rubbed his hands together like he was about to tuck into a giant feast. "This is good. Let's fight a band of humans."

"We don't have to *fight* them; we have to *interact* with them. It's different." Freya waved a hand. "What if they're after the treasure too? We could work together with them."

Sylvie fought a sigh. This LARP was quickly getting away from her. "Yes, so perhaps a group of humans wander onto the Monster Camp grounds while our group of awesome LARP campers is searching for buried treasure. They become an obstacle, and we have to put them off our scent, both to the treasure and to us as monsters. So it's doubly difficult."

Sylvie wished anyone besides Vera and Freya would nod as they chewed on her suggestion. She was getting to her wit's end with everyone's second-guessing.

Milo shoved his glasses up his nose and squinted once they were back in place. "But that wouldn't happen, because the human shield would keep them away."

"Oh, come on, we don't even know that it works,"

Chad answered. "It's not like they use real humans to test it."

Sylvie rolled her eyes. "Look, what if the interaction happens when the shield is down?"

"The shield doesn't come down, Sylvie."

Sylvie's irritation was about to spill over. "It does so. Can we just move on?" She implored the group but really just to Chad, totally annoyed. "Our LARP won't set itself up. Who wants to adjust their character profiles so we can plant this interaction? I can lead the human group, Prince Hairy can lead the monsters, and—"

"Wait, hold up, go back." Chad held up a stop-sign hand. "Sylvie, how do you know for a fact it can come down?"

Oh. No. "I—I don't. I just want to move the LARP forward," she sputtered, panic edging her voice. And even though she tried her very best not to, Sylvie couldn't stop her gaze from flicking quickly to Vera.

Vera, whose eyes were welling up with tears.

Chad gasped with recognition. "No way."

Sylvie froze.

With a couple of words, Sylvie had betrayed Vera. And with one look, she'd confirmed her source.

Sylvie whirled around. "No, it's not what you're thinking—"

"You're a good LARPer but a terrible liar, Sylvie." Chad was sneering now, his courtly Prince Hairy act stripped away. "It's absolutely true. They bring down the human shield for Vera. I was wrong the first day, it doesn't have a leak; it literally has a bypass code for anyone too human to be recognized, doesn't it?"

Sylvie spun back to Vera, an apology on the tip of her tongue.

Vera was already backing away from the group, every eye on her. She bared her too-human teeth. Tears spilled onto her cheeks, sadness and fury warring on her heart-shaped face. "How could you?! I never want to talk to you again, Sylvie! NEVER."

Her words hit Sylvie like a slap.

Then, Vera raced away.

Even as stunned as she was, Sylvie felt the urge to chase after Vera surge through her muscles. Righting herself, she toed forward in the dirt, one hand out, that apology still at the ready—

"CAW-CAW!"

Rupert's dinner bell rang through the woods in a deafening echo, as if he'd been right over the top of them that whole time and, from that vantage, was everywhere all at once.

When the call died down, Chad was the one who spoke first, of course. But what he had to say was a complete surprise.

"Come on, Sylvie, let's go get dinner."

That . . . sounded like an invitation.

"But—"

"If it's true, and it sure sounds like it's true, you don't

need to apologize." Sylvie blinked at Chad. "It's not like you made up a rumor about her."

She hadn't done that. Somehow what she'd done was worse.

But the remaining faces before her weren't looking at Sylvie in disgust. They were sympathetic?

"It's her problem," Chad was saying as Milo and Lenny, and even Freya, nodded along. "It's not yours. Just come to dinner, and let's plan tomorrow's LARP."

Still, Sylvie hesitated. She was the one who'd done something wrong. Not Vera.

She took a step toward the trail—where Vera was retreating, sprinting down the path faster than any human could.

"Hey," Freya said, putting a hand on Sylvie's shoulder, her bracelets clacking. Sylvie looked away from Vera and to the little witch. "I know you want to go after her, but I think she wants to be alone."

Sylvie swallowed. Freya was right—Vera didn't want Sylvie around. She'd said as much.

With a big, shaky breath, Sylvie nodded. "Yeah. You're right."

And then Sylvie accepted the invitation.

The Quest

Vera had meant what she'd said.

She had no plans to ever talk to Sylvie again.

That night after both a mess-hall dinner and scary human stories, Sylvie had returned to a silent and dark Cabin No. 7. Vera's coffin was not only shut but covered with a blanket. It practically screamed "Do Not Disturb."

In the morning, Sylvie got ready without a single Vera sighting.

She wasn't at the mess to grab breakfast, either.

Instead, the first time Sylvie saw Vera after spilling her secret to everyone was on the covered back porch of the administration building. Right where they'd had HURT class on Tuesday, Vera was in close conversation with Master Gert. The girl's head was tipped down, the words aimed at the toes of her shoes, a curtain of red hair swallowing her pale face nearly whole.

A pang of guilt tugged at Sylvie's gut.

She wanted to apologize. She began to move toward the administration building, but she'd barely taken two steps when Vera turned and caught her eye. The look she gave Sylvie made her blood run cold and stopped her dead.

If Vera really wanted nothing to do with her, Sylvie would make sure she'd get exactly what she wanted.

"Hey, Sylvie!"

Sylvie turned at the sound of her name being called from up by the flagpole. Freya's voice. But Milo and Lenny were waving. Even Chad gave an up-nod greeting.

Sylvie waved back and jogged toward them, her backpack thumping against her fresh black tank top and black jean shorts.

"Hey, guys." She smiled with fangs.

Vera and Master Gert joined the group, and nothing was different other than Vera's silence and slight separation. She insisted on standing off to the side during roll call, all of Group Fang squeezed together feet away.

She didn't say a thing that morning at HURT during a rundown of monsters famous for working in and around unsuspecting humans. The gist was that these were monsters that people their age could learn from, model behaviors and maybe future careers after.

Most of them were like Ichabod Clotting—tech scions with money to spare. Very few, very old references were made to famous monsters who were not human-passing.

A fact that Group Fang was still discussing that afternoon on the waters of the Monster Camp lake. Nessie had allowed for Friday to be a swim day for everyone. And though Sylvie had always been told that one shouldn't swim within an hour of eating, monsters didn't seem to play by those rules, because Group Fang was on the water immediately after lunch.

"I don't even know what we were supposed to learn from that HURT session," Lenny groaned. He was in full kelpie horse form, sleek black coat incredibly shiny, even in the mist-filtered light. He seemed so at home in the water Sylvie wondered if he preferred being a horse and was only human-shaped for ease at camp. "I mean, what's the takeaway for someone like me? My options are always to stay hidden or join the circus and hope no one looks too closely."

"I don't know. It was cool to learn about Fade's great uncle." Milo shrugged from the dock, where he sat with his goggles and nose plugs, water streaming off his body after several minutes of swimming. "We can't all be spies during the Cold War, but, like, cool use of his invisible talents."

Like Sylvie—and Chad, surprisingly—Milo doggie-paddled. Sylvie had half expected the super athletic werewolves to move through the murky water like Vera, who, true to her background on a swimming team, was motoring through furious laps as far away from the dock area as she could get.

Ignoring them.

Even Nessie seemed to have an inkling of the social strife happening above, because the big monster had planted herself between Vera and the rest of Group Fang, her long body stretched out in a half-submerged line of demarcation.

Us. Vera. Nessie.

Sylvie hauled herself up out of the water and onto the dock near Milo. Her arms and legs were exhausted from basically treading water in her inefficient doggie paddle.

"Ah, but there's where you're wrong," Sylvie said, elbowing the blond werewolf. "We can all be invisible Cold War spies during the magical adventure that is LARPing."

"Touché, vamp," Chad answered in a joking way that was a hundred-percent less snarky than what he'd said to her any other day that week. He was still in the water and somehow acquired an unused life vest, which he wedged under himself for extra flotation as he talked.

"You know, there's no shame in sitting on the dock if you need a rest," Bebe assured him as she did a dead man's float past him, her wings splayed out like a wide, flat pool noodle. The water sprite was more at home in the water than out of it, even if she was able to fly. Sylvie wondered if she was made up of more water than a human, which seemed almost impossible given that humans were seventy-percent water and she didn't look any more liquid than a human. Just, well, blue.

"I'm not tired," Chad insisted. "Just saving my energy for LARPing tonight!"

"But not too late. It's the full moon. Remember?" Milo added.

"Yeah, yeah, don't worry. I'll be ready."

Sylvie was sort of curious about what exactly Chad and Milo had to be ready for other than, you know, changing into wolves.

"It'll be great, right, Sylvie?" Chad asked.

Sylvie blinked and really looked at Chad, bobbing in the water, his whole mess of thick hair smashed against the sides of his head. He was grinning at her. Friendly. Like he actually liked her. Beyond the Nessie divide, Vera hit the end of a lap, her head appearing for the slightest moment above water.

She didn't even look their way.

"Um, yeah, right. It'll be fun. A true LARPing adventure."

Sylvie was as uncomfortable as she was thrilled.

She was finally LARPing with a big group! But she was also participating in a quest that made her skin itch.

Vera hadn't come. In a way, that made things a little easier, because now they had an even number and could break into two even groups.

They'd decided not to divide into Fang versus Fester.

Instead, it was two groups of monsters. Each one with half a treasure map. They were to work together to get through all the hurdles of the original quest.

The basic, revised layout: Crack the magic safe for the treasure map. Find one half, the X ripped totally apart. Encounter the other monsters, who have the other piece; decide to work together; best challenges together; storm the castle; become rich.

Chad insisted on leading one group, which was no surprise. Freya, the other.

Then, they picked LARPing teammates like they were in gym class. Flashbacks of Fisher choosing sixth-grade kickball teams burst into her brain, but she shoved the memory away before Fisher ensured "Draculette" would be picked last. This wasn't gym class, it was LARPing, and she was the de facto expert.

Chad's group: Milo, Lenny, Francis, Bebe, Norah, Sylvie.

Freya's group: Benedict, Annika, Tatiana, Vivian, Fade, Zephyr.

Though Sylvie did not like the natural friction supplied by the two groups or the fact that Vera wasn't there with them, she tried to focus on the positive.

They were LARPing. Truly LARPing.

Winding up a trail through the dense trees, teasing vines, and snaking shadow fog, no whining at all, everyone babbling *in character* about what they would do with their riches should they finish a successful quest.

To Sylvie, this was magical in more ways than one.

They came to a clearing and suddenly stopped. Sylvie

wasn't sure why, but it was clear Chad had something planned. She decided to let it play out.

"We've made it . . . to the edge of camp," he intoned dramatically in his "Prince Hairy" voice. "The human barrier lies just beyond these trees . . . which means this is where our rival humans will appear! I say we get ahead of their plan by forging through the barrier and reaching the treasure ourselves!"

Sylvie's stomach dropped. This wasn't part of the plan! She couldn't let them cross the barrier—which was buzzing faintly like an electric fence, she could hear it now, even if she couldn't see it. There was no way she'd be able to get through, and her lies would be exposed. She had to think of something, and fast.

Sylvie threw up her hands. "Wait!"

Everyone turned to her in a half spring, spooking a massive bird out of the trees behind them.

"What if, um, we let the humans come to us? And we propose a truce?" Sylvie gestured toward the human shield, buzzing invisibly. "We could wait for them to appear here and then, uh, make a new game plan with them?"

Beside her, Freya piped up. "I guess that makes sense? We're supposed to be learning how to make friends with humans after all, not enemies."

The other witches and Vivian, human-adjacent as they were, agreed.

Sylvie breathed a small sigh of relief.

Then, Chad opened his mouth.

"Stay here if you want, then," the werewolf crowed with a gleeful snarl and plucked both sides of the map from Milo's hands. "You're with me, boys, or you're not, but we're going to get to that treasure with or without you!"

Clutching the stolen map to his chest, Chad sprinted for the barrier. Milo and Lenny darted after him, giggling wildly at this turn of events, Francis, Bebe, and Norah too. Until Sylvie was the last member of Chad's group that stayed behind.

Then, Sylvie watched as, without so much as a hitch in their strides, the monsters sliced across the human barrier like it was butter.

Like it was nothing.

They emerged on the other side, fierce quest faces locked in as they beckoned over their shoulders and up the incline at the rest of the quest group.

A cold sweat trickled down Sylvie's neck.

She was stuck. If she tried to follow, they would know. The second she couldn't cross, they would know that she was human. They'd all know. And then it would be over.

"They stole our map! Let's get them!" Freya shouted, and then the other team was racing toward the barrier.

Sylvie was still frozen.

Something that Freya realized as she waved her entire group through.

She crossed the shield a second time, rushing up to Sylvie and cuffing her upper arm. "Come on, Sylvie, you can join our team. Let's go protect those humans and get the treasure."

With that final sentence, the little witch crossed the barrier. Sylvie's feet still weren't moving, and Freya dragged her. "Come on, our group doesn't bite. You'll be totally fine with us, vamp."

Freya's entire body was on the other side of the shield now, except the hand wrapped around Sylvie's bicep. The little witch yanked hard . . . and Sylvie's arm hit the human barrier like she'd punched a brick wall.

The force field shuddered and wobbled like Jell-O.

"What . . . ?" Freya examined her own hand as if she were the problem.

A few monsters in Sylvie's periphery moved back toward the shield and got a much closer look as Freya extended her hand again, the clear force field letting her arm pass through. She again clamped on to Sylvie's wrist, and before Sylvie could pull herself away, Freya yanked harder.

Sylvie slammed into the human shield, the entire right side of her body bouncing off it with a teeth-rattling *THWACK*. She stumbled to the ground.

The monsters rushed the barrier. And when Sylvie rolled over, onto the butt of her now-dusty black jean shorts, they were all staring at her with round eyes and gaping mouths.

"Sylvie, what's happening? Are you . . . are you a human?" It was Freya's voice, but it might as well have been any one of them.

Sylvie popped to her feet, searching furiously for anything she could say.

"What? No. No, I'm not—"

"Your fang is hanging off your lip," Milo said with a tilt of his shaggy blond head.

Oh, God. It was. Her left fang was stuck to her lip like an errant piece of corn from a demolished cob.

Sylvie brushed it away. "Oh no, I just lost a tooth—"

"You're lying. We can see you haven't lost any teeth. That was clearly a fake fang. You're human. Totally, a hundred-percent human." Chad stepped through the barrier now, and Sylvie immediately backed up, her shoes scraping on rocks and brush as she backed away.

They were all advancing now.

"I knew I didn't sense magic in you," Freya spat, arms crossed.

"I knew your 'blood' smelled like fruit punch," Lenny added. "I'd know Capri Sun anywhere. Even across the mess."

Sylvie swallowed.

But, of course, it was Chad with the nail in the coffin, so to speak.

"When we were role-playing partners at HURT, I had a funny feeling you knew too much about humans," the werewolf said with an Elvis snarl to his lips. "It wasn't human school or LARPing, it was because you're *an actual human*."

Sylvie was backed into a tree now. There was no way

out but straight down the trail, and she highly doubted she could outsprint any of these monsters. Not to mention several of them could fly, and at least three of them could zap her with a spell to tie her up or encase her in ice or something else to stop her in her tracks.

She opened her mouth to say something—to plead? To apologize? She wasn't sure what. But before she could get out a single word, a voice cut through the clearing.

"Sylvie, I'll need you to come with me."

There at the top of the path was Master Gert, Rupert on their shoulder. The message was clear—Rupert had seen it all, following them like he had the day before, and had reported back exactly what had happened.

Maybe he'd gone for Master Gert the second one of them crossed the human shield—that was probably a no-no written deep within their seventy-seven-page camp packets—but it didn't matter the reason, only what everyone now knew.

And, just because this could only get more embarrassing, Vera was with them, hanging back, her thin arms wrapped in an X-shape over her middle.

The director extended a kind hand toward Sylvie. "I'll escort you away now."

"Master Gert, she's human! We can't just let her *leave*," Chad argued, fury in his eyes. "She *knows*. About us. And she's not an adult with security clearance."

Unbothered, Master Gert directed a long lock of hair from their eyes with a tilt of their head and looked to the other campers with the solemn weight of a promise. "Sylvie will be no trouble; you have my guarantee."

"She better not," Chad muttered.

"Come on, Sylvie."

With that, Master Gert placed hands on Sylvie's shoulders as if to steer her away.

CHAPTER 31

Monsters Are Real ... And They Don't Want You

Fang-free and wilted, Sylvie slumped in the guest chair in Master Gert's office.

It was the most magical workspace Sylvie had ever seen. Shelves were crammed with knickknacks that at once seemed both ancient and worn with daily use. Compasses and rough amethysts and a little stone Celtic cross that looked heavy enough to bust several toe bones if dropped from shelf height onto a foot.

The walls were blanketed in maps and pictures and paintings—gifts from campers, mementoes from trips; there was even some sort of massive black dog in several of the pictures, perhaps an old, beloved pet. Everything about that tiny room spoke to a life well lived on these grounds and everywhere else.

And nowhere did Sylvie fit in.

Master Gert skirted around their desk, sat, and planted

the points of their elbows on the well-used blotter, leaning in. This close and in the lamplight, their dark eyes glinted with flecks of gold. Even when they'd been up close before, Sylvie hadn't seen that. It was like a little treasure she'd unlocked in this light.

One she'd never see again.

All at once, Sylvie realized she didn't even know what kind of a monster Master Gert was. They were immortal and had clearly lived all over the world, that accent British yet well-traveled. But Sylvie didn't seem to have the vocabulary to guess what they were beyond that. And she wondered if maybe she didn't know on purpose. Maybe that was something Master Gert didn't share with nonmonsters.

Sylvie couldn't blame them.

She searched her hands as the director seemed to choose their words very carefully. Finally, they spoke.

"I don't think we need to prolong this conversation. I think it's been made clear to both of us that you do not belong in Monster Camp."

Sylvie's head felt like it weighed a thousand tons.

She let it sink into her shoulders, her gaze pointed at her lap. Master Gert was right, and the shame was unbearably heavy.

"I regret to say that you must leave immediately," Master Gert continued. They truly sounded sorry. Sylvie was too. "Amos is already in the process of lowering the human shield. Let's get you home."

Master Gert reached down below their desk, and there

in their grip was Sylvie's duffel, all packed up. "I'll give you a few minutes to use my office phone to call your dad. Cell service is very spotty here. Hard to have a conversation."

Oh. No. Her dad! In all of the chaos of the last few days, Sylvie had completely forgotten she'd lied to her dad. What was she supposed to say?

"Hi, Dad, it's Sylvie. So, I lied to you, and I'm at a camp with real, actual monsters, but they realized I was human, and now I have to leave. Can you come get me?"

The thought made her sick to her stomach. She'd already disappointed enough people without her dad coming into the mix. But maybe there was a way to avoid that . . .

"Master Gert? I already texted him." She hated lying here, but it felt like the lesser of a dozen evils. "This is embarrassing, but I didn't tell him I was attending Monster Camp . . . I told him I was at the survivalist camp next door. It's where he dropped me off and where he expects to pick me up. Can . . . I go over there to meet him?"

Sylvie held her breath while Master Gert looked at her shrewdly.

"Is that so?" Master Gert inspected Sylvie's face. Too close. Sylvie looked away. "Well, I must admit I'm not wild about the idea of sending you away without physically seeing your guardian. Are you enrolled in the camp next door? Would they have a record of you and your father's information on file?"

"Yes." This was true. She was enrolled there as a backup. Though she'd put down her own number for her dad's so he wouldn't get a call when she didn't show.

"I suppose that would be all right." Phew. "Come, let's send you on your way—but first, I require your cabin key and lanyard."

Of course. The key they needed for next week, and the lanyard literally had "Monster Camp" written all over it. She couldn't take that home.

Master Gert continued, "No other checkout is needed."

Again, Sylvie was nodding. This time, even if she wanted to say something, she couldn't. All her airways seemed blocked. Nothing about her body was working right.

With noodle-y arms, Sylvie removed both items from her neck. She handed the lanyard and key off to the director.

Master Gert's hand fell to the knob, the metal jangling as their heavily-ringed fingers connected. They pulled the door open and stood to the side. "It's time for you to be on your way."

Sylvie picked up her things and walked outside with her eyes fixed on the floor. She was too ashamed to look Master Gert in the eye. Once she stepped across the threshold, the door whispered shut behind her.

Sylvie was alone.

Monster Camp had been a dream, then a nightmare before the fear burned off and it became a dream yet again. Now, it was cold, hard, unrelenting reality. One where her mom was still gone, she'd become a grade A liar, and every friend she'd made this summer hated her guts.

Tears pricked Sylvie's eyes yet again. How did she have any left? She was so bone-dry now, she felt woozy. Her stomach twisted. But she didn't want to eat. She didn't want to sleep.

She didn't want to be here another moment.

And so, Sylvie Shaw, one-hundred-percent human, hauled her bag over her shoulder and slipped into the falling night.

The Darkest Night Under the Full Moon

Sylvie cut toward the same border of trees she'd navigated when she first arrived at camp. She just hoped the human barrier was deactivated. She didn't want to risk waiting around and having to see any of the other campers again.

Her stomach lurched sideways as she stumbled over brush. Her skin felt raging hot, but her heart was a block of ice in her chest as the last of the day died into a starry night—a full moon, Chad and Milo had said—above the canopy of trees.

Was this a panic attack? It felt different than the ones she'd had before.

Sylvie's fingers clawed at her neck, searching out the soothing curve of the pendant's crescent moon. Her skin sat clammy and waxen under it, the rush of her skittering pulse beneath.

But she kept moving forward, and again, Sylvie tripped over something her Converse couldn't navigate with her mind numb at the steering wheel and the forest vines as eager to trip her as ever. This time, her body keeled, pulled by the heaviness of the bag. She put both hands out to catch herself, her palms finding the promise of a sawed-off stump. She landed upon it with an audible *WHOOMP*.

Stunned, Sylvie inspected her hands. They were scuffed but not cut. Her wrists ached but weren't injured. Her heart pounded wildly in her ears as she blinked toward the hazy forest ahead.

The sun was totally gone now, the night a cloudy gray. It was going to be tough finding Camp SLAY in the dark. She had a flashlight somewhere in her bag. That would help her navigate through the trees.

She really didn't want to have to stay at Camp SLAY, just buy herself time to call her dad. Maybe he could pick her up early? He might go for it if she sounded upset enough, which wouldn't be hard to fake. She pulled out her phone and tried to dial, but she got a message that her call couldn't be completed. Oh, well. He was probably out with Lara anyway. Was tonight the night they were in Frankensport at the play? Or maybe it was just one in a string of in-town, non-Sylvie nights out. Adults had dinner late on dates, didn't they? Their food probably hadn't even arrived yet. They were just sitting across some tiny table, mooning at each other over a tea candle and breadbasket—

"Sylvie?"

At the sound of her name, Sylvie stood from the stump and spun as best she could with the heavy bag still slung about her shoulder.

And there, not far, was Vera. She was as still and silent as she had been the first time they'd met. It was strange how Sylvie could sense the otherworldliness of her here and now when she had been blind to it before.

Vera stood like a shadow, even as moonlight made a halo of her red hair. Her face was pale and wan, her dark eyes spearing Sylvie from across the distance. Her limbs were lean and stiff, as quiet as the dead. In her hands, a sack full of food and a to-go cup from the mess hall. Her nightly blood.

Actual blood.

Because Vera was an actual vampire.

The others could divide Vera up into percentages of her father and mother, but from where Sylvie stood, any-one who drank actual, 98.6-degree blood every day was a vampire. Full stop.

The meeting must have just finished. Or Vera skipped out early for her blood and time alone. Alone, because she really was the only vampire at camp.

The last time she'd spoken to her, Vera had said she never wanted to talk to Sylvie again. But yet she stood there, calling her out by name.

That was an opening, wasn't it? An olive branch? An opportunity? Maybe?

Sylvie took a step forward. Vera inched back.

That hurt. A lot.

Vera the vampire was afraid of Sylvie the human.

They'd slept in the same room, right next to each other. They'd spent nearly every minute at each other's sides for five-ish days. And now . . . Vera was afraid Sylvie would hurt her.

And yet she had already.

As Sylvie watched Vera through the trees, her skin went all pins and needles in the moonlight, her heartbeat so wild it seemed to ping-pong through her rib cage.

"I thought you were leaving?" Vera asked. Another question. Another opening.

One Sylvie was going to take.

Sylvie drew in a big, messy, shuddering breath. "I was. Or am. I just needed a second. I know I need to go . . . that I don't belong here."

Vera didn't react, but she also didn't leave. After a moment of silence, she spoke again. "Why'd you do it, Sylvie?"

Somehow, this question was worse than Master Gert throwing her out of camp. "I'm sorry for sharing your secret. I was frustrated, and . . . I don't expect you to forgive me, I just . . . I wanted you to know."

Vera blinked those huge, dark eyes of hers.

"That's not what I'm mad about."

"It's not?"

Vera shook her head and pushed a hank of hair behind

her ear. "No. What hurt the worst was that you knew my secret, but you couldn't share yours. I thought we were real friends."

Something cold wrapped itself around Sylvie's heart.

No words welled in her throat. No other sound. Nothing.

Vera licked her lips, and Sylvie saw that her mouth was quivering as she held it open to draw in a shaky breath. "If anything, you've confirmed for me that despite Amos's assertion that a bunch of half monsters are running around, I . . . I don't belong anywhere." That little, tight smile she always used came then, just a bare movement in the rising full moon. "I should've been able to tell that you were human. I should've known. And yet I couldn't even do that."

Sylvie's lies had shown her humanness in the worst way possible. She was willing to lie and cheat and share Vera's secrets—accident or not—to get what she wanted.

Friends. An air of authority. Acceptance.

If she'd been honest with Vera that first night and told her the truth, she might have been able to keep Vera as the one true friend she'd made at this camp.

Instead, here they were, and no amount of apology was enough.

Something tore open in Sylvie, and suddenly all her limbs vied to move at once. She couldn't stand here in this shame a moment longer. Sylvie's words came out low and hoarse.

"Bye, Vera."

As soon as she'd laid the goodbye between them, Sylvie was sprinting in the opposite direction. Her bag thudded heavily against the backs of her legs, her toes scraped and shuffled on rocks and roots and dropped pine cones. But she didn't care.

She had to get out.

"Sylvie! Wait! Where are you going? You're going to get hurt!"

Vera's words almost didn't register. Sylvie was hurt already. And she'd hurt Vera beyond words. What was a little more pain on Sylvie's end?

She deserved it.

"Shoot"

Sylvie ran and ran until the only sounds were the rush of her breath, the beating of her heart, and the stumble and scratch of her wayward footsteps through a fog as dense as a flight through the clouds.

Even though she could barely see her hands in front of her, she could feel her bare legs getting covered in burrs and scratches. She also felt slightly sick, like a flu was coming on. Guilt and embarrassment were a potent, terrible combination. Her therapist was going to have something to say about that.

Another thing to dread.

When she couldn't catch her breath anymore, Sylvie slowed to a walk and hauled herself across some sort of ravine.

It felt significant. Like a border. Which meant the human shield was down. She was off Monster Camp property. And now truly on her own. She knew it like she knew her next breath.

Then, as if in answer, the fog around her ankles dissipated, and the forest greenery that snatched at her skin receded.

Sylvie inhaled deeply.

She took two steps away from the ravine, and everything was clearer, brighter, somehow. Sylvie used the opportunity to search her bag, finding her flashlight and her phone. Juggling both, she zipped up the bag and hauled it onto her shoulder.

Sylvie wandered forward, flashlight beam lighting the way. The moon was growing stronger as the blue of early night drained to black. She didn't like how the silver light slithered on her skin. It made her want to vomit.

A low sound reached her ears.

It was a buzz. The kind created by movement, low voices, the crackle of flame.

Slowly, her breath held tightly in her chest, Sylvie peered around the tree.

It was a clearing. Full of tents. A fire blazed in the center, bodies bent around it, faces dark with paint and serious expressions.

She'd made it to Camp SLAY. Eager to get all this over with, she pulled out her phone to see if she could call her dad, but when it blinked to life, there wasn't any service. Not even a single bar.

Sylvie sighed, hoisted her bag, and stepped around the

tree and toward the camp. She watched the people scurrying every which way. Mostly kids, but some adults. All of them looked busy, but she figured the more she watched as she walked forward, the easier it would be to find just the right person to help her.

But then, a boy crossed her field of vision just a few feet from her—and she realized she recognized him.

"Dustin?"

Her voice was quiet, and he didn't hear her. Sylvie latched one hand onto her duffel straps and started to jog after him. He was headed toward the tents, a girl walking with him, dressed in the same camo uniform, dark smudges under her eyes. Sylvie didn't recognize her.

As Sylvie closed in, she called his name again, whisper-shouting it at his back, his body too far away for her to tap a finger on his shoulder as she did it, though she reached a hand out toward him anyway.

"Dustin?"

He whirled around, his eyebrows scrunching as he tried to make her out in the weak light. And honestly, she was doing the same—there wasn't a cell phone glued to his palm or over-ear headphones, but it was definitely Dustin. His brown hair a little longer, his face paint-smeared in some places.

Dustin's confusion broke into a goofy grin. "Sylvie! What are you doing here?"

She gestured toward her bag. "Um, I was in camp. Left early and got lost . . . You wouldn't happen to have your phone on you, would you? I've been trying to call my dad, but I don't have a signal. Maybe you do?"

Sylvie's story invited more questions than it answered, but Dustin had never been one for details. "Um, no. Our phones are in lockup. I texted you about that, right? But we can radio an ATV to take you to our admin building. It has service. Maybe that'll work?"

He glanced over at the girl with him, and she shrugged, unsure. Dustin motioned at her and mouthed, "Friend from school."

Again, the girl shrugged. And Sylvie wasn't sure why he felt the need to whisper in front of her. It didn't matter. She was so grateful for the opportunity, she could forgive him nearly anything.

"Can we give that a try?" Sylvie's voice edged close to cracking. "I . . . I just want to go home."

"Yeah, yeah, come on," Dustin said in a rush, almost as if his words could stem the flow of tears she had pushing against her eyes. He started gesturing toward a cluster of tents. "Here, come hang out in my tent a second. You want a snack? It might take me a bit to line up an ATV."

Sylvie followed Dustin through an open flap into a little tent, with a bedroll, backpack, and a lantern hanging from a hook off in the center. His partner stayed outside, and Sylvie was pretty sure she heard a dramatic little "huff" as Dustin rooted around, locating a half-eaten bag of pretzels in his backpack and tossing them at Sylvie.

They bounced off her chest with a rustle and thump as she made to catch them.

Dustin checked his watch, cursed under his breath, and immediately began undoing the catches that held the tent flaps open. He unrolled the flaps, closing the tent. "We've got things going on, and it's best if you stay here while I get the ATV."

Sylvie clutched the pretzel bag, confused.

"I could walk. Just point me in the direction of the admin building and—"

"No!" Dustin snapped. Then, rubbing a hand through his hair, he lowered his voice and started whispering again. "No . . . uh, just stay here. We've got an activity going on, and I . . . you'll be safe here. Just eat some pretzels and chill. There's probably a Snickers bar in my backpack somewhere. I don't mind if you go through my bag. Take what you like."

From outside, his partner's voice nagged, high and annoyed. "We're supposed to be at the border at twenty-one hundred hours. You know the intel. We can't delay—"

"I'm not going to be late," Dustin answered, voice low and confident as he stuck his head out the flaps, his back to where Sylvie was standing with the pretzels and her duffel. "It'll just take a few minutes for me to get the ATV. I'll make it back. Besides, Sarge won't want a civilian in the woods once the hunt begins."

Something cold slithered down Sylvie's spine.

A hunt? Sylvie knew the camp was about survivalism,

but it seemed kind of intense for kids to actually go out and kill an animal. At night, no less.

"Sylvie, I'll be back. It'll probably be a few minutes, but it might be longer. Just, don't move. Okay?"

Dustin didn't wait for her to answer, just stepped out of the tent and into the night. Sylvie sunk down on his bedroll, gloomily picking at the pretzels he'd given her.

She could hear lots of movement outside. Clearly this hunt was a major operation. Then, twin silhouettes came into focus to Sylvie's right as two campers walked up to the side of Dustin's tent. A voice spoke out.

"Did you complete the weapons inventory, Private?"

"Yes, Sarge. All silver nets are present and accounted for, and we've located the quantity of wooden stakes that were missing. We've distributed them as ordered. All units are armed and ready to proceed."

Sylvie's heart stuttered.

Silver nets? Wooden stakes?

Those weren't normal weapons used on a normal hunt for normal animals.

Sylvie dropped the pretzels onto Dustin's bedroll, forced the tent flap open a slit, and peeked out. She could just make out the campfire ahead, bodies moving all around. In packs, organized. Mobilized.

Everyone was dressed like Dustin. Not just in camo and face paint.

They were dressed for battle.

Each had stakes lined along their belts. At their backs,

sheaves of arrows made to fit the crossbows clipped to their sides. In the hands that didn't hold lanterns were batons. A few even had nets, shining with pure silver—large enough to catch a person.

Or a monster.

All the blood drained from Sylvie's face, and her entire body wasn't just frozen now; it was pure ice.

Camp SLAY wasn't just a camp for kids who wanted to put their survivalist skills to the test; it was a camp for *monster hunters.*

And thanks to Sylvie, the door to Monster Camp was currently wide open.

Sylvie grabbed her heavy bag, slipped out of Dustin's tent, and ran.

The Good Human

She needed to warn the monsters right now.

Get the shield back up. Move them to safety.

Oh, and Vera! How far had she followed Sylvie into the trees?

If Vera was anywhere near the border, she wasn't safe.

Sylvie moved in double time through the woods. The moon must have ducked behind some clouds, because the slim slice of her flashlight beam barely cut a path through the darkness of the tight tree canopy and the muted moonlight.

Her stomach no longer ached. Her skin didn't tingle. The thump of her giant bag didn't impede her stride. All that shame and embarrassment that welled inside of her seemed dormant, receding in favor of the biggest danger Sylvie had ever encountered in her life.

Not a danger to her, but to her friends.

Sylvie reached the ravine and slowed, trying to better navigate it—a twisted ankle now could literally be deadly.

That dense fog rolled over the Monster Camp side.

Sylvie half hoped the shield was up and that she wouldn't be able to set foot in that fog. That would be the best thing. If she couldn't get in, Dustin and his new monster-killer friends couldn't either.

But the barrier wasn't there.

As she picked her way over the steeply sloped rocks and back up the bank to the Monster Camp side, she heard footsteps on her heels. Shouts rang around the thick forest behind her, like bird calls. *Birds*—if only Rupert had followed her. Surely she could direct him to help alert the others. He probably had some sort of emergency "CAW-CAW," like a tornado siren or fire alarm.

But there wasn't a Rupert. There wasn't any way to warn them at all, except to show up and hope they'd listen.

Sylvie tore through the woods as fast as she could, each step a tiny leap of faith because she couldn't see anything in this fog—and hoped whoever was chasing her couldn't see her either.

She ran with her arms out in front, ready to swipe at tree trunks, push away the clawing fingers of branches, catch herself if she tripped and went down. She probably looked like a victim in a horror movie in the moments before the monster caught up. Only here, the monsters were humans, and the victims were the kids who went bump in the night.

Sylvie's heart was pounding so fast that she couldn't hear anything now over the blood thrumming in her ears and the *thump thump thump* of the duffel against her hip. Both palms stretched wide as she ran between two trees, she took the chance to turn and look back for a clue her hearing wasn't giving her.

She looked left, she looked right, she scanned slowly back between the two.

Nothing but black trunks, rising fog, and leaves blotting out the moon.

They could be two feet from her or two miles.

Either way, Sylvie knew they were on the way.

She spun around, heavy bag swinging with her, and started angling herself toward the mess hall, thinking that perhaps she'd find Vera before Dustin or any of his hunter buddies did. But as she lurched forward, something caught her by the throat, thin and tight. Like a garrote.

Panic surged through Sylvie as she fought to pull free. She had to get to her friends. She couldn't be trapped here now.

Sylvie gritted her teeth, hooked both thumbs against the thing at her throat, and lunged forward.

Snap!

The hold broke and she spun around, twisting and coughing and stumbling forward, trying to keep moving. Her duffel slammed into her back, and she barely stayed on her feet. As she righted herself, she put a hand to her neck, the other one still out in a protective position. But as her fingertips dabbed at the irritated skin, it struck Sylvie what wasn't there.

Her crescent-moon necklace.

She clawed at her neck, searching and failing to find the necklace's weight.

No silver chain. No pendant. Nothing.

Sylvie whirled, realizing now that she hadn't been caught from behind by a pursuer. She'd been caught by a branch.

"No, no, no, no . . ." Sylvie dove to her knees, her hands patting at the ground, searching for the thin, silver pendant and chain in the blanket of fog.

Nothing.

Her necklace. Her ever-present gift from her mom. Her most treasured item in the whole world.

Gone.

Tears immediately pricked Sylvie's eyes, loss and grief pulsing through her veins, growing with each rapid puff of breath as her lungs struggled to keep up with the physical and mental pain. She'd lost her mom's necklace. How could she—

"We're getting close, troops."

The voice echoed through the trees. The sounds of boots stomping through the forest were faint, but they were everywhere.

Sylvie couldn't leave her necklace. Her mom's final

gift. Her favorite reminder of her mom. But she'd already lost too much time.

Time her friends didn't have.

"Just up ahead," the voice called again. Closer.

She'd lost the necklace. That was something with which she could come to terms. But if she lost her friends tonight? That would be something she could never get over.

Swallowing, Sylvie silently slipped the duffel off her shoulder. It had been weighing her down more than she wanted to admit. Maybe it could be a distraction and buy her time. She wasn't sure but she would try anything.

Then, Sylvie got to her feet and started to run.

She was weightless now, out of the woods and really sprinting. In the space of a quick minute, the mess hall came into view, dark and looming. Empty.

Sylvie didn't pause; she just kept running.

She thundered past the dark silhouette of the administration building and into the common area. No one was about.

Was this because of her?

Did the kids have to hide with the shield down?

And where were the adults? Were they hiding too?

Wait. Twenty-one hundred hours. That was nine o'clock. Curfew.

Which meant the monster kids were sitting ducks if this hunt found them.

Sylvie sprinted across the open common to the row of camper cabins. The full moon followed, coating Sylvie in a deathly, glittering light. It made her dizzy, nauseous, knowing what was coming. She swallowed and stared at her shadow, dark and urgent. Silent.

A few of the cabin windows still glowed—it wasn't lights out yet.

Sylvie didn't dare make a sound until she arrived. And then, when she did, it wasn't too loud, only enough to get their attention. She knocked on every door and whisper-shouted, "Guys! Hey! Monster hunters are coming! Monster hunters are coming!"

As she flew down the row, more lights blinked on. By the time Sylvie reached the end, all lights were on. Doors were hanging open, faces leaning out, lit by the hide-and-seek moon, the glow within, and the fireflies lazing about with not a care in the world.

Lenny. Freya. Chad. Milo. Bebe. Francis. Tatiana. Vivian. Fade. Benedict. Annika. Norah. Zephyr.

Vera.

"Sylvie?" her former roommate's quiet voice drifted into the night, a note of fear in it.

"Oh, thank goodness!" Sylvie skidded to a stop. She waved one hand over her head while the other was braced against her knee as she doubled over, chest heaving. "You. Guys. Are. Okay."

"What are you doing?" Freya's voice.

Sylvie swallowed, drew a heaving breath, and blurted, "Monster hunters. From the camp next door. They're coming. To hunt you. You have to hide. You have to—"

"Why would we listen to *you*?" Chad finished, loud enough to cut her off. He stepped onto the walkway that linked the camper housing. The light from his cabin spilled out and illuminated one side of his furry face. "You, Sylvie, who just spent the last week lying to us?"

"No! I'm serious!" She flung her arms around uselessly. If only Master Gert or Amos or someone in charge were here, maybe they'd understand—they knew who their neighbors were. Didn't they? "They're coming! With batons and crossbows and stakes—"

"And what? You're the good human, coming to save us?"

Chad's eyebrows pinched together, his arms crossed over the chest of a Monster Camp T-shirt and his silver bracelet glinting in the dim. Despite the full moon, he hadn't changed into a wolf, which was a relief, but that didn't soften the way he glared at her now.

"Well, yeah." Sylvie gulped. "I know how it looks. But it won't matter if they see you. They have 'intel' that monsters stalk the woods on the full moon. Please—"

"There's no way they know we're here." Now it was Milo stepping forward, his blond hair sparkling as the moon slid out from behind yet another cloud. "Monster Camp's entrance is shrouded by a spell, as is the sign, and the human shield makes it appear as a void on all maps. The camp website is only available on the Monster Incognito Web. It's literally impossible for a bunch of humans to stumble upon us."

She was a human who'd literally stumbled upon them!

Sylvie stamped in frustration, and her voice bubbled with hysteria. "Well, they found out somehow! Please, Master Gert took the shield down so I could leave. The camp is unprotected, and they'll be here any second!"

No sooner had the words left her mouth than glowing beams of flashlights winked through the trees.

The monsters stood as still as statues, frozen in disbelief. Sylvie whipped around to face the SLAYers. She spread her feet and balled her hands into fists. She wasn't about to let Dustin and his cronies hurt the monsters. Not when she was the one who put them in danger.

Dustin's voice rose, loud and fevered. "Sylvie? Is that you?"

On instinct, the ghosts sank back through the walls of the nearest cabin. But Lenny, Francis, Bebe, Tatiana, glittery Fade, and the werewolves didn't have an easy option to vanish or to appear human like the witches, Vivian, and Vera.

"Stay still, Sylvie! We're coming to save you! Don't move!" Dustin yelled at her, then to his team, "Approach with caution, Alpha Group. We don't want to hurt the human."

That confirmed it. They'd *all* been spotted.

With a deep breath, Sylvie watched the trees as Dustin and a half dozen monster hunters emerged from the foggy forest.

Truth, Consequences, and (Wooden) Stakes

I t's okay, Sylvie. We're here to rescue you."

Dustin's voice was cool and confident as he and his team approached the group, not by snaking through the aisles of lawn between cabins, but all the way around the haunted house at the end of the row.

The whole statement was meant to calm her, but instead, Sylvie's heart felt like it was going to leap out of her mouth and skitter across the grass.

Swallowing a shaky breath, Sylvie knew it was up to her to stop the worst of what could come next.

When the monster hunters appeared in the open grass with fog snatching at their ankles, dark shapes and dark faces lit only by the porch lights on the closest cabins and the faded glow of the clouded moon, it was clear to the monsters that they were exactly as Sylvie had said they'd be: all decked out and ready to hunt. Their ankles were raw and glinting in the weak light, the forest doing what it could to deter their progress.

One of them went for his crossbow, loaded it, and brought it up to aim at the monsters, sharp silver tip winking. Then, others moved to do the same.

Dustin stood in front of his team, Sylvie's duffel over his shoulder. He paused, one arm reaching as if trying to will Sylvie to step forward. Like she was a toddler who fell into the tiger pit at the zoo.

Sylvie didn't move.

Dustin read her inaction not as hesitation but fear. "I know you're scared, Sylvie. But just put one foot in front of the other. The closer you get to us, the better we can protect you."

Sylvie realized exactly what Dustin meant by "protect."

The second she was out of the way, those crossbows would go off.

Sylvie was literally the only thing standing in the way of these monster hunters claiming their first victims.

The thought was horrific.

Yet instead of terror, Sylvie's mind cleared to reveal a fresh plan. They were trained, but so was she. And suddenly, Sylvie knew exactly what to do.

"What are you talking about, Dustin? What are you supposed to be protecting me from?"

She crossed her arms and tried to look incredulous.

"Sylvie . . . was this the camp you left early? Were

these the people you were with? You should've trusted your instincts and stayed in my tent, because I don't know if you know this, but"—he cupped one side of his mouth with his hand and stage-whispered—"*those are monsters.*"

Sylvie called upon all the times Dustin had ruined her LARPs and executed what she thought was a convincing eye roll.

"Dustin. You can't be serious. We're just LARPing." She gestured to everyone behind her. "These aren't *real* monsters; they're just kids with really good costumes. I know you've been playing your video game a lot, but you can't tell me you honestly think monsters exist?"

Dustin squinted at her. "You told me you were leaving camp early. Not LARPing. If they're dressed up to LARP, you'd be dressed up to LARP, and I know exactly how you look when you're playing a vampire. You wouldn't do that without fangs. Besides, those don't look like costumes." Then, he gestured to the team behind him. "We've had plenty of training. We know real monsters on sight."

Sylvie stuck to her narrative, experienced LARPer that she was.

"Dustin, it's pitch-black, and those are actual crossbows. They could really hurt someone. Take a moment to think about it."

Her voice was level, her body calm but defiant. Sylvie was almost proud that even as her heart wildly beat in her chest, she didn't tremble.

"What's more possible, Dustin? That I, Sylvie, your only friend who LARPs as a monster, would be at a camp specifically to do just that, or that I, Sylvie, your only friend who LARPs as a monster, would be at a camp with *actual* monsters?"

Dustin hesitated, and Sylvie grabbed that shred of doubt and yanked. "Here, I'll show you—hand me my bag."

"Why?"

"I'm going to prove I'm here for LARPing."

Again, Dustin hesitated. Sylvie held up her hands. "Fine, or search it yourself, Night of the Knight," Sylvie relented, very purposefully addressing him with his ridiculous character name. "I don't care—"

Just then, the clouds broke, and the whole clearing was bathed in the brightness of the full moon. The scene felt as if it were under a spotlight, and the weight of the discussion they'd had hit Sylvie like a ton of bricks. Her fingers began to shake, her skin itched like mad, and the suddenness of it swept the rest of her words away.

Still, her plea landed. Dustin dropped the bag to the grass, knelt, and began unzipping the main pocket.

That sick feeling was back. It roiled in Sylvie's gut, and she drew a breath that didn't seem to fill her lungs. "It's . . ."

What was wrong with her voice? There was no power behind it.

Sylvie gritted her teeth and balled her hands into fists,

ready to will the rest out, but . . . something wasn't right with her physical body either. Her incisors bit into her gums as if they didn't fit in her mouth. Her fingernails tore into the flesh of her palms.

On reflex, Sylvie thrust her hands out in front of her body. Her nails *were* longer and sharper. She'd never had hair on the backs of her hands, had she? That had to be a trick of Monster Camp's heavy nights, the fog, the full moon—

"Okay, so you brought your books . . ." Dustin's lantern hung over her bag, the LARP guides, with their well-loved covers, curling in the light. Sylvie gaped at him as he inspected the pages, her tongue thick and clumsy. Panic stiffened her features. Her attention narrowed again to her changing hands. He couldn't see the hair from there, could he? "That's hardly conclusive—"

"Check the side pockets." Vera stepped in front of Sylvie. Dustin glanced up and blinked at her. "Hi, Knight of the Night, I'm Vera, half vampire and Sylvie's roommate." She gave a little wave. "The pocket closest to you should have Sylvie's stick-on fangs and pouches of the fruit punch she has in her 'You Suck' tumbler. Such a classic vampire LARPer, this one."

Vera cocked a thumb back at Sylvie but stayed angled in front so Dustin couldn't see Sylvie was struggling to stay upright as shock zipped through her. Her mind was processing all of this at half speed as the hairs on her hands began to ladder up her arms.

This wasn't Vera. She didn't put herself out there. She didn't draw attention.

Dustin started digging, and suddenly there was someone else stepping up next to Vera, crowding Sylvie's malfunctioning further out of view and butting into the conversation. And someone stepping up behind her. Two someones. Lenny, his broad body stealing some of the moonlight off her back, and Milo, whispering in her ear. "Stay strong. Breathe."

A hearty guffaw from Chad.

"So classic that she's got a binder full of LARPs too. Can you believe that? Such a nerd!"

"I'm familiar with the binder in question," Dustin answered carefully.

"It should be beneath the manuals," Vera cut in, and Sylvie's too-slow brain realized that her roommate had packed her bag.

"Oh yeah, you have to see this, man." Chad took a step forward, obviously eager to help. "It's got—"

"Stay back!" the girl from Camp SLAY barked, pointing her crossbow at Chad's chest.

Chad's hands flew up in surrender. "Geez, I was just going to show him the LARP we've been working on." The girl wavered but didn't put down her weapon; Dustin, though, glanced up toward Chad, his expression a question mark. "The first page. You'll see all of us listed and the quest."

It hit Sylvie's shocked mind then: they were LARPing.

Vera and Chad were live-action role-playing this scene in real time with real humans. Real, dangerous humans.

Sylvie's knees wavered weakly beneath her, and she leaned back onto Lenny for support. She couldn't believe it.

The monsters were LARPing as humans pretending to be monsters.

Dustin searched under the manuals and pulled the binder into the light. He flipped it open, his lantern illuminating the first page. His partner lowered her weapon ever so slightly to bend down and read over his shoulder.

"Sylvie the Vampire, Vera the Half Vampire, Lenny the Kelpie . . . What's a kelpie?"

"Scottish water horse man," Lenny shouted from behind Sylvie with a wave and an up nod. "Like your fatigues, bro."

"Uh, thanks," Dustin said slowly. "And you must be Milo the Werewolf?" he asked, regarding Chad.

"Nah, that's Milo." Chad tipped his chin over his shoulder toward his cousin. "I'm Prince Hairy. Sounds good with Knight of the Night, doesn't it?"

Sylvie's skittering heart lurched. He *could* pretend. They all could.

And Dustin was buying it.

"Um, yeah."

Bought it.

Dustin squinted at the group, lips moving soundlessly as he assigned personas to the remaining monsters. As his eyes slid over her, Sylvie was sure the cold sweat on her face was visible as she fought not to sink to the grass and scream, because literally everything hurt and pulsed with each breath. Her knees were so soft now that she'd wedged herself between Lenny and Milo, her lips sealed shut over her clamped jaws and her arms wound behind her back.

Dustin closed the binder and discarded it back in the yawning pocket, which he didn't zip. He stood up. "Weapons down, Alpha Group."

Sylvie audibly exhaled with relief. All around her, the postures of her monster friends loosened. For a fleeting moment, she felt okay . . . before the pain rushed back, the itching, the sprinting heartbeat. Within, her adrenaline pumped with a roar that made her fingers shake, twitch, hurt.

"Sarge isn't going to like that his intel is wrong," the girl who was Dustin's partner said as she disengaged her crossbow and clipped it back on her belt.

Dustin wrinkled his nose. "He shouldn't like that we could've really hurt someone." He pulled the radio from his belt, and he hit the button. "Radio one-two, this is Private Dustin of Alpha Group. Sarge, do you copy?"

The speaker crackled under the weight of every set of eyes under the moon, now full and bright in a way that made Sylvie sweat.

"Radio one-two, this is Sarge. What's going on, Private?"

"Sarge, we've confirmed a large number of civilian

campers in the west quadrant past the border. They are humans pretending to be monsters. I repeat, they are humans pretending to be monsters."

There was a pause on the other end. Then came a fevered adult voice. "*Pretending? Are you sure? That seems terribly convenient given our credible intelligence.*"

Dustin nodded to Sylvie as he answered. She held her breath. "I know one of the kids from school. She's a hundred-percent human but pretends to be a vampire a lot."

Sarge spouted an aggrieved bark on the other end. "A vampire?! Why would anyone *pretend* to be a vampire?"

Dustin rubbed a hand down his face, smearing the paint. "Sarge, have you heard of something called LARPing?"

"I don't care what it's called. It's ruined this mission!" Then, in a voice that seemed to be aimed in another direction, everyone heard Sarge yell, "Calling all units! Calling all units! Retreat! Do *not* engage with the enemy! They are civilians in disguise! Everyone back at base. Now!"

There was another mass exhale from the Monster Camp side as Dustin radioed in, "Sarge, Alpha Group in retreat, over."

The radio popped, and Dustin clipped it back to his belt.

That sick feeling roiled in Sylvie's stomach, her heart skittered, and her skin was on fire. Suddenly, she was afraid she might just fall over with relief, even with Lenny partially holding her up. Drawing a breath that didn't seem to fill her lungs, she found the voice to croak, "Thanks."

For as well as she knew him, Dustin seemed a little surprised. He nodded. Held out the radio. "Did you still want to get ahold of your dad?"

She shook her head, opened her mouth . . . Sylvie's knees finally buckled. Vera was right there with her, holding her hand, which felt strange and tingly. Sylvie tried to blink, to speak, but something was wrong with the muscles in her face now, not just her voice. She'd never had a panic attack like this one before. But she'd also never saved her friends from a literal hunting party.

Suddenly, Sylvie couldn't keep her eyes open. The moon was just too bright. Over the rush of blood in her ears, she heard that one hunter girl ask at a distance, "Uh, is she okay?"

"Oh, man—Sylvie?" Dustin's voice.

Sylvie dug into the grass, her new clawlike nails sinking into the sod as she willed words to form. Anything. Just a simple response was what she needed. But she couldn't.

"Um, it's just all that fruit punch," Vera announced, pivoting on her toes toward him with a little humanlike giggle. "Blood-sugar swings are the pits. Let's go inside the cabin, huh, Sylvie? I've got a bagel tucked away in there."

"Are you sure?" Dustin's voice again. Marginally closer. Concerned. Sylvie's face was sweating. Itchy. She still couldn't open her eyes. What was happening? Was he coming her way? She needed him to leave. Them to leave.

"Nope, we're good, man. She's good. We've got her." Lenny's voice. "Have a stellar night."

"Uh. Okay."

More footsteps. The snap of twigs, the murmur of more than one distant discussion, and the crackle of the radio.

Then, they were gone.

After several beats, Vera's voice came again. "Chad? Milo? Um, we need you."

Sylvie had to be hearing things. Vera never needed either of them. And she said "we" . . . why would she say "we"?

Then, just as suddenly as it'd started, the roiling in Sylvie's stomach was subsiding. Her skin didn't feel itchy anymore, but somehow it felt . . . blanketed? Like she'd slipped on a too-small sweater, and her sweat had glued it in place. The blood rushing in her ears evened out, and it was like she could hear everything—every breath from the people around her, every blade of grass shivering in the warm wind, every shade of movement.

And movement was coming. More than one set of feet. The rustle of wings.

"The shield is up." Amos. That was Amos.

"Good. Rupert's on recon. He'll stay next door tonight." Master Gert. "Scott, get your team sweeping for stragglers."

"Consider it done." Running footsteps receded with the manticore's voice.

When Sylvie finally had the energy to open her eyes, it wasn't just Vera and Lenny leaning over her—instead it was a full circle of faces she knew.

The witches, the ghosts, Tatiana, Vivian, Bebe, Francis, Fade. All with mouths hanging open. Vera's eyes were black holes, and the grip she had on Sylvie felt . . . muffled or weak or waning. Something.

She tried to sit up, and Vera helped her, and then her vision landed on the remaining adults.

Amos, Yeti, Mummy G, Master Gert.

It was Yeti who broke the silence with a grin as he said, in a voice that sounded almost underwater to Sylvie's newly sensitive ears, "Well, I'll be."

The others said nothing, just joined him in a smile.

Sylvie didn't know why they were so amused. She just felt weird.

Blinking, she looked down at herself . . . and promptly blinked again.

Once. Twice. Three times.

Something was wrong with her eyesight. It'd gone fuzzy. No, that wasn't right.

She looked fuzzy, but no one else did. Fuzzy and . . . furry.

Sylvie stretched out a hand to touch her knee, which to her confused eyes seemed to be covered with a *coat* the same dark color as the hair on her head. The moon glinted across the glossy, short, dense strands, and when her hand made contact . . . it wasn't a hand.

It was a paw.

Covered in the same fur and tipped with actual claws.

Sylvie stared at her hand—paw. Stared at her nails—claws. At her clothing, which hung ripped over her very hairy legs.

Just then, her newly super hearing caught hold on a sound. Her head snapped up, another threat bursting through her confusion.

There, two figures stepped from the shadows. Sylvie recognized the color of their hair and the sharpness of their smiles and the clothes that were now half-shredded and hanging from their bodies like rags. In their paws, the silver glint of their matching bracelets, removed.

Chad and Milo. The same, but different.

Instead of boys, they were now, in the light of the full moon, totally, a hundred-percent werewolves.

They blinked at Sylvie with too-human eyes, and their snouts broke into toothy grins. They took in her fur. The shape of her face. The twitch of her ears.

Then, they sat back on their haunches, and those grins widened until the one on the left with the brown, shaggy hair tilted his head and revealed a mouth full of spiky teeth. *Fangs*.

"Hey there, furball," Chad said. Not in words, but in a howl. One she understood.

Sylvie gasped.

"Did you bite me?" she asked in a voice that was both hers and not.

Chad laughed a wolf's laugh. A true laugh, not the pretend one he shared with Dustin. "Nope. We had nothing to do with it."

And now she understood everything.

Sylvie Shaw was a monster after all. Not a vampire, but a werewolf.

CHAPTER 36

A Secret Hidden Within

When morning came, Sylvie's fur receded, her claws shrank back, her fangs—she really had fangs!—retracted, and her senses faded to be more human.

Sylvie suddenly looked the same as she had before, but she was forever changed.

A werewolf.

She was a werewolf! Not in a million years would she have guessed. She didn't look like Chad or Milo; she didn't know the lunar cycle or really even look up when the moon was full. Yet she'd run all night with them in a series of tunnels that let them go wild as their wolfish selves without endangering any other campers or wildlife.

It was totally awesome.

And now, she was back in Master Gert's office, waiting for an answer.

Daylight streamed in through the windows, and somehow the office looked different than it had the night before, when Sylvie had been certain it was her first and last time inside. Now every square inch of the room told a story.

And Sylvie wondered how last night would fit in.

Had it been remarkable—a narrow escape from a monster's greatest enemy? Or was it just something unfortunate that happened every few years? Like a minor fender bender or a bad haircut?

Before Sylvie could wonder more, the door behind her closed, Master Gert dropped to the seat across from her, and Sylvie realized they had a file folder in one hand. The label was upside down, but with the neat print of a label maker, it was easy to read upside down.

SHAW.

Sylvie rubbed her hands on her jean shorts, which were black as always.

The director didn't open the folder. Instead, they laid it before them, took a sip of their tea, and folded their long hands one on top of the other.

"Sylvie, last night I was purposefully a bit vague. That was unfair to you, but I now have permission to explain it better now."

Permission? From whom? Other werewolves? Some overarching monster council? Sylvie waited, her hands immediately clammy yet again. She resisted the urge to wipe another sweaty streak down her shorts.

After a pause, Master Gert said quietly, "I knew your mother."

They did? Her heart began to pound loud enough that her ears started to ring. Sylvie swallowed, trying to blunt the noise. She needed to hear what came next.

Master Gert seemed to recognize both Sylvie's shock and the fact that she literally could not respond. They went on, voice gentle.

"As you may have guessed by connecting the dots—you are half werewolf, half human. Your werewolf half belonged to your mother, who was a full-blooded were-wolf. Rose attended Monster Camp many years ago and was even a counselor while in college. She became one of my dearest friends. And I was enough of her friend that . . . I'm your godparent."

Well, now, Sylvie was gobsmacked.

"You . . . what? I'm sorry. I . . . I didn't know. Have I met you before? I feel like I would've remembered. Or Dad would've said something, or . . ."

As Sylvie trailed off, Master Gert smiled, tight-lipped like Vera. Like something inside them might break if they revealed the whole of their emotion.

"I am aware you didn't know. And you only met me when you were very little—before you might have remem-bered. There's a reason for that."

Sylvie tried not to gape, but she'd been up all night, gallivanting around as a werewolf, and so, well, she gaped.

"Rose—your mother—wanted me to look after you. To protect you." Surprisingly, they turned to the walls and waved a hand over the many pictures featuring people and that beloved big black dog. "It's something I'm very good at. Sylvie, I'm known as the Gurt—G-U-R-T rather than G-E-R-T—Dog of Somerset. Have you heard of the legend?"

Sylvie shook her head.

"There aren't many benevolent black dogs in monster history. In fact, I may be the only one." They toyed with their tea bag, took a sip, reset. "For a thousand years or so, I watched over the children of Somerset, in the Quantock Hills of England. I kept them safe, maybe guided a lost traveler or hundred, and really just kept the peace. Then, as the world changed, I decided I would keep my fellow monsters safe. I flipped the 'u' in my name to an 'e' to invite fewer questions, crossed the pond, and founded this camp."

Sylvie's eyes misted as she looked at the photos now. That was Gert—er, Gurt?—playfully shepherding children and adults and monsters of all stripes. Here and there.

"You're not the only godchild I have. I'm a popular choice in the monster community, and I will always and forever accept the request of anyone who asks. So, when Rose did, I of course agreed right away to take care of you in the event that anything happened to her . . . and, as we both know, something did."

Again, Sylvie swallowed, this time to quell the lump that was forming in her throat.

Master Gert's voice dipped, but their dark eyes never

left Sylvie's face. "After Rose left us, I contacted your father about helping out."

"You *know* my dad?" The "human" was implied.

"Yes, I know your dad. I've known him for a long time." Now their smile was sad—wider, but still breakable. "And I respect Ethan and his choices when it comes to you. So, when he told me he'd like to wait and see if your monster DNA came through, I assured him I would step back and wait for him to make the call."

A curl of anger flared in Sylvie. And as if they sensed the spark, Master Gert nodded once and continued.

"I'll admit, I mostly abided by his rules, though I did *happen* to start sending a Monster Camp brochure to your house once you were old enough to attend. It was a little rebellious of me, I know, but I wanted to keep the door cracked open for you."

Now . . . that made sense. Amos had said something at check-in about how she'd "finally decided" to attend. And her dad had acted like he'd seen the Monster Camp brochure before when Sylvie never had.

The tears began to spill over as Sylvie sniffed and shook in her seat. "Am I . . . like her?"

Master Gert smiled softly now. They pushed the file carefully forward.

"Why don't you see for yourself?"

With trembling fingers, Sylvie accepted the folder and opened it.

There, clipped together neatly, were pictures of her

mother. At her age. Older. As a smiling girl and a grinning wolf. With Master Gert and Rupert—ageless as ever. With ghosts and vampires and mummies and witches.

And there Sylvie was too.

Pictures and mentions clipped from the *Evermore Gazette*. Her birth announcement. When she'd been a toddler eating watermelon under the brim of a too-big hard hat at her dad's construction site. Honor roll.

Then, a shot she didn't know about . . . one where she was walking around on Halloween, dressed up as a witch in that ridiculous hat her dad had wanted to draw from before she'd picked a camp. It was a picture of her and her mom in dusk light, walking hand and hand, Sylvie's jack-o'-lantern bucket already overflowing. Her mom was midlaugh, eyes glistening at the camera, cheeks pink, teeth showing. Maybe they were a little sharp. . . . At their feet was a much younger Magnus and a leash that led in the direction of the camera.

Sylvie's dad had taken the picture.

On the back, in her mom's handwriting, were the words: *Sylvie, age 3.*

Then, below, a little note:

> *Gert—*
>
> *Thought you'd love to know my little pup*
> *loves monsters and magic.*
>
> *—Rose*

Sylvie drew in a shuddering breath and wiped at the wetness across her cheeks. She really was a monster. She couldn't believe it. But if that was true, then . . .

"Master Gert? If I'm a monster, why did you tell me I didn't belong at Monster Camp? Why did you throw me out?" Sylvie felt a little flame of anger flicker to life in her stomach. All those days feeling scared! And, maybe even more importantly, all those days feeling like she might finally fit in somewhere! Why hadn't Gert told her the truth?

"What are the two rules of Monster Camp, my dear?"

"Be kind and be yourself," she spit out, almost automatically. Then, her thoughts spun back into motion. "But why—"

"Sylvie, over the last few days, you made it clear you weren't interested in following those two rules. You lied to everyone at camp. I know you must have been scared when you first arrived. But I think you realized rather quickly that no one here was going to hurt you. And you had *many* chances to be honest with everyone here about who you were—even if, as I now know, you still weren't aware about Rose's true nature—but instead you chose inauthenticity. Inauthenticity that made several campers concerned for their safety. Playing pretend is one thing, but lying to the point that you hurt others? That's something else altogether."

Sylvie licked her lips, but before she could even attempt a rebuttal, a knock came at the office door.

"Come in," Master Gert called.

Her dad.

He was dressed as always in jeans and a T-shirt, his hat pulled roughly over wet hair. His face lit up.

"Sylvie!"

And then, as he wrapped her in a hug, Sylvie's shoulders began to quake. He pulled away, concern etched in his face and voice. "Why are you crying? The hunters didn't . . . Are you okay?"

Sylvie's eyes fell to the picture in her hands, absently wrapped around his back. He followed them, his lips falling open as he saw the photo.

"Oh, Rose . . ." Sylvie was surprised to see his fingers were shaking as he gently touched the corner of the print. He didn't snatch it away. He just . . . looked at it. After a long swallow and a squeeze of Sylvie's shoulder, he rubbed a hand down his face and addressed Master Gert. "She knows?"

"I've told her about Rose. Though I suspect you'll have more to say."

Sylvie's dad nodded. Then, he looked at her. "You really changed? With fangs . . . and not the kind you buy in packs of twenty?"

This made Sylvie gulp out a laugh and sent a few more errant tears streaming down her face with the movement. "Yeah. Fangs and fur and a *tail!*"

His Adam's apple bobbed. "Huh." His gaze found Master Gert. "You were right; there's no way to hide it if that's who you're meant to be."

Master Gert simply, sagely nodded. "I think I'll leave

you two to talk for a moment." They rose gracefully from their seat before slipping out the door.

"Syl-Bear, Gert's totally correct. It's time we talked about some tough things." He looked down at his hands, then reached for Sylvie's. "What do you remember about your mother's death?"

"It was an accident." Her lungs stuttered. "A bad accident."

"Not quite." Sylvie's eyes jumped to her dad's. "Sylvie, it wasn't an accident. And it has everything to do with why I kept your monster DNA from you."

Her dad's gray eyes didn't waver, even as they grew heavy with sadness.

"I won't go into the details, but . . . changing on a full moon is always dangerous for werewolves. Sometimes hunting accidents happen on the night of a change—a human looking for a bear or a deer and catching a wolf instead. And sometimes those accidents aren't accidents at all."

Sylvie's breath caught on all the words her dad wasn't saying.

"Hunters? Like . . . like the ones from next door?"

Her dad's gentle nod was a bomb going off in Sylvie's mind.

All the air left Sylvie's lungs in a whoosh. She had so many questions, they piled up from her quivering gut to clog her windpipe. How did she not know? Why did no one tell her? Why had her dad—

"Sylvie." Her mind skidded to a halt at her dad's soft

drop of her name. Long fingers tipped her chin up so she'd look at him. "I love you as much as I loved your mother, if not more. I knew your mom was a werewolf, and I knew what kind of risks came with joining that life. But it wasn't until I lost Rose that the possibility of losing you also became real. And, as Gert probably told you, some children who are half monster never show their monster side."

Vera's too-human teeth flashed in Sylvie's vision.

"It's a recessive trait and can just live inside you, dormant. I was worried it would make you miss your mother more to know what she was and what you could be." He swallowed hard. "I knew you were fragile after we lost your mom. I didn't want your heart to break again if you weren't like her."

Tears pricked at Sylvie's eyes.

Of course.

That's why he'd always pushed her away from her monster obsession. From her insistence on pretending to be a monster every day. From LARPing and fangs and . . . more than a passing interest.

"But," he started, his voice dying after the word. He paused and looked down for a moment before he lifted his gaze back to meet Sylvie's. "If I'm being honest, I just couldn't bear the idea of losing you too. And I thought if you never showed your monster DNA, we'd never have to worry about monster hunters. They could never take you away from me."

In that moment, Sylvie broke. She knew exactly how

he felt. How many times had she started panicking that she might lose her dad too, the same way she lost her mom? If one parent could be stolen away by a horrible accident, couldn't another? Wouldn't she have done anything in her power to prevent that from happening? Sylvie launched herself at her dad, wrapping her arms around him in the tightest hug she could manage.

"I'm right here, Dad. And I understand."

It wasn't a reassurance—monster hunters were real. The night before was a closer call than she'd like to admit. But she was here, he was here, and for the first time, they *both* understood what lay between them where her mom should be.

With a rib-crushing squeeze of his own, her dad pulled away. He did absolutely nothing to sop up the tears that were smeared across his stubbly cheeks. He punched out a long, wobbly exhale and pressed his big hands over the tops of her shoulders; they were warm and grounding.

"Syl-Bear, I need to talk with Gert. There are things I have to do now to make sure you're safe—the monster world has a lot of safeguards that, well, I didn't need up until now for you. But I can't ignore that any longer, and without Rose . . . I need an expert to make sure you're as protected as possible."

"Okay." Sylvie didn't know what else to say.

"There's paperwork beyond all my questions, so it might take a little while. Why don't you go see your friends? I'll come get you when we're finished."

"Okay," Sylvie said again. Then, she handed the folder over to her dad. "You should look at this. . . ."

He accepted it and kissed her on the forehead—right where she usually added to her widow's peak. Today, the little dip was bare and natural. It might be from here on out.

On shaky legs, Sylvie stood. Out of habit, she reached for her throat, only to stop short—it would take some time to remember her necklace was lost to the forest and the foggy blanket.

But it was okay.

She had so much more of her mother now. She could work it out with her therapist and find a new way to calm herself. Sylvie batted at her wet cheeks with the heels of her hands and walked to the open office door.

Master Gert slid past her back into the room. As the door was closing, she heard them ask, "Ethan, it's been a long time, but if I recall, you take your tea with three sugars?"

"Is that very unusual or very common?" Sylvie heard her dad reply, a little awe in his voice, clearly unsure why Master Gert would remember with such clarity after what seemed to be several years and hundreds of other meetings with parents taking tea.

Something waded in Sylvie's throat as she heard Master Gert's reply over the whisper-snick of the door going flush to the frame. "What was important to Rose is easy for me to remember."

CHAPTER 37

Lost and Found

Sylvie stepped onto the porch on the back of the Monster Camp administration building.

She had no sense of how long she'd been in Master Gert's office.

The common was full of shouts and voices, much like that first day. Except instead of everyone enjoying themselves separately, Sylvie noticed there was a rollicking game of something like kickball using the massive acorn ball the witches had made during the fireside role-playing demonstration.

Every camper seemed to be playing, and most of the grown-ups were scattered around. Laughing. Relaxing.

Sylvie was so engrossed in watching them that she nearly jumped out of her skin when a voice appeared right next to her ear.

"I believe this is yours."

Sylvie spun in surprise. There, next to her and silent as a whisper, was Vera.

Extended in her slim hand was a familiar crescent moon.

Sylvie's shock broke into pure, surprised joy.

"You found it!"

Sylvie's eyes met Vera's big dark ones in amazement, and her fingers reached forward, but then they stopped, hovering over the arc of silver. "I didn't even tell you it was missing—how'd you know to look?"

That favorite tight smile of Vera's lit up her heart-shaped face. "I didn't. I went hiking, and it was lying on the trail like it was waiting for me—or you. Chad told me it was probably why you'd never changed before. Silver like this wards off the change. He and Milo have bracelets that do the same thing. It's a safety thing for werewolves when away from their packs. They took them off when it was obvious you were changing."

Sylvie stared at the necklace.

Her mom had been protecting her all this time.

Several thoughts piled into Sylvie's mind, but when she finally pinched the necklace out of Vera's cool palm and clasped it back around her neck, a surprising one lay atop the heap.

"Wait, you went hiking with *Chad*?"

Somehow, Vera blanched. "Well, no, it was all of us!"

"Oh, sure it was—"

"It was!" Then, Vera glanced at her shoes. "We *think*

all the monster hunters made it outside of the shield last night—Scott set the zombies loose just to make sure, because they're really good at human detection. But just in case there are some unwelcome eyes, we don't want to appear any different than a human camp. So, a morning hike."

Sylvie swallowed thickly. "Um, I never got a chance to thank you last night during my change. I know you don't like speaking up, but you thought fast and kept Dustin from figuring out what was happening to me and that could've been really bad and—"

"Sylvie, I was happy to."

Was that true? Sylvie hoped so.

Something like hope clawed in Sylvie's stomach that their differences and similarities were enough to make up for her actions that hadn't been so good.

And just like that, words started spilling out of Sylvie's mouth. "I'm sorry. I'm so very sorry. I should've told you the truth the moment I realized this wasn't LARP camp. It was on the tip of my tongue to say something on Sunday night—I knew with a human mom that you'd understand . . . but I . . . I freaked. I freaked, and I lied more, and I just lied and lied until I'd even convinced myself that I belonged here."

She'd realized this herself in the time since she'd been banished from camp. But the person who needed to hear it most was Vera.

Vera, who she'd betrayed in more ways than one.

Vera, whose friendship felt the best and hurt the most as it lay at her feet in pieces.

Vera, who shared the pain of being singled out among the monsters as being different when the thing that made her different made Sylvie completely whole.

Nerves rising in her gut, Sylvie swallowed and said, "Um, I know I made some really bad decisions, and now I'm a half werewolf of all things, but . . . do you think we can still be friends?"

Sylvie couldn't look up, not even through her lashes, as the weight of the question drained her heart. Vera was quiet, and at first, Sylvie was terrified she wouldn't get an answer, not even one that hurt, when, suddenly, she felt a set of long arms wrap around her and pull her close.

Vera's touch was cold, but the hug was the warmest one Sylvie had ever had.

It struck Sylvie then that her dad had been right back when he begged her to try camp—she *did* have a new best friend out there, waiting for her to just show up and be herself.

It was a quest to get there, but she'd done it. And Sylvie didn't regret a bit of the journey along the way.

When Vera pulled away, that tight smile of hers showed—with teeth.

"How long do you have?"

Sylvie looked over her shoulder to the closed door of Master Gert's office.

Sylvie fought the urge to shrug. The time left was

precious. Precious should never be counted in a shrug.

"I don't know."

Vera took Sylvie's hand in hers. "Whatever it is, let's make the best of it."

Then, together, Sylvie and Vera stepped down the stairs and into the light of a Monster Camp day—humans, monsters, friends.

Monsters After All

Sylvie Shaw was officially a monster.

It wasn't like there was a secret handshake or anything, but now that she was official, there was a super secure server that Fade set up where her Monster Camp friends could chat about all things monsters. Not only that, but they made plans to meet up in places monsters could easily be themselves in the open—Halloween and the Frankensport Comic-Con in the spring, right across the river.

It was amazing.

And it became possible, because, with her dad looking on, the Monster Camp attendees and staff publicly forgave Sylvie, thanked her for her bravery in saving them from the monster hunters, and voted to reinstate Sylvie as a camper.

To say Sylvie was thrilled was an understatement.

Admittedly, maybe even better, many of the monsters had committed to LARPing. And a few weeks after camp, on the eve of the Fourth of July, which also happened to be her twelfth birthday, Sylvie was able to call a special summer LARP session at Evermore Glade Park with some pretty awesome special guests: Vera, Chad, Milo, Lenny, and Freya.

Milo lived just outside Evermore, so he hosted Chad and Lenny—and invited Sylvie to run with his familial pack on the full moons—while Vera's parents agreed to let her stay a whole week with Sylvie. Freya even got to take the bus from Frankensport to Evermore for a sleepover.

It was great fun, but it was also a great opportunity.

So, Sylvie made signs that said "MONSTER LARP-ING IN SESSION"—the perfect cover for why a group of monsters might be hanging out in the middle of a human park. They'd even managed to get a round of s'roars going at the communal grills in the park (carefully overseen by Sylvie's dad, of course). This time, Sylvie even added a beetle to hers. After Chad had convinced her to try one, Sylvie realized they were pretty delicious. And she'd learned from Milo that it wasn't just monsters that ate bugs anyway—plenty of people around the world ate them too. Sylvie was happy to join their ranks. Funny how quick she was to dismiss something great just because it was a little unfamiliar. She didn't think she was ready to try the toxic sludge, though.

Everyone was preparing for the LARP when a familiar voice called across the park lawn.

"Draculette! Where's Dust-Mop?"

Sylvie spun, and there, just as he'd been the first day of summer break, was Fisher Loggins, palming a basketball. He was flanked by his minions, Kiefer and Kyle, and they all grinned in an identical, mean way. Like they'd practiced it in a mirror.

So much had changed for Sylvie since she'd last seen him, but Fisher was the same one-note bully he always was. He hadn't changed an inch.

Sylvie gave him a good, fangy smile, sidestepped the question about Dustin—she hadn't invited him because she didn't need another close call—and, because she was only a little petty, asked, "Did you guys come to LARP?"

She gestured toward their group, which was twice the size of his little bully party of three.

"There's still time to join, if you want." She tried very hard to keep her voice light and nice. "We've got a bunch of people here today. We were just about to start."

Sylvie hoped Fisher would see he was outnumbered and simply leave. But Fisher was a bully and thought it was his job to be a monster. So, he matched Sylvie's open tone and rubbed his square jaw as if he were actually thinking about it. "What's LARPing again?"

The definition loaded itself onto Sylvie's tongue, even though she knew this was a setup.

"It stands for 'live-action role-playing,'" Vera answered,

coming forward and beating Sylvie to it. "You play a character and complete a quest with others who are also playing characters."

The second Fisher smelled a way to bully Sylvie while humiliating a new target, he did.

"Draculette! You made another friend. Congratulations!" Fisher whooped, completely fake, with a slap to the basketball in his hands. Then, he pointed at Vera as if recognizing a celebrity on the street. "Let me guess . . . your name is Vladmira?"

Vera smiled—with teeth. With fangs, to be exact.

They'd come in within the last week, and even though she could retract them—which was soooo cool and very convenient to keep up appearances at human school and swim team—there wasn't a question that they'd be around during the day's LARP.

Vera glanced at Sylvie. "He does know vampires can drink him dry, right?"

"Sure, sure, and you can fly, and you're superstrong too; I know the drill, O fanged one." Fisher waved a hand at the other monsters. "Draculette, I don't know how you did it, but you recruited a band of idiots even worse at being monsters than you."

Chad took a bold step toward Fisher, his eyes narrowing and pointed teeth flashing. Like Sylvie and Milo, he couldn't change for this LARP because there wasn't a full moon, but being full-blooded werewolf, in that moment, he very much didn't look *totally* human. Which was the point, Sylvie realized, the moment he tilted his head and asked, "How do you know we're not real monsters?"

Fisher scoffed. "Pshaw, yeah. Right. Monsters aren't real, losers."

Vera moved to be shoulder to shoulder with Chad, fangs out and obvious. "You know Sylvie, but you don't know us. How sure are you that if I bite you, I won't drain your life away?"

"Or that we won't turn you into a werewolf?" Milo asked, stepping in line and gesturing to his cousin with a squint beneath his glasses.

"Or that I won't turn you into a toad?" Freya challenged, coming in line, looking every inch the witch she was.

Fisher's face was still set in a scoff, but Sylvie saw his fingers flex on the ball in his hands, as if readying to throw it in self-defense.

Suddenly, Sylvie realized her monster friends truly looked *monstrous*.

In that moment, tight in their circle, there was no question what they were. It was right there, plain as day.

They were monsters in the open, for all the world to see.

Fear flickered in the eyes of Fisher's minions, who broke ranks and looked to their leader for permission to retreat. But Fisher held firm and, because it was the only move in his holster, reacted in a way that was supposed to hurt. He rolled his eyes at his minions. "They're all delusional. Let's get going before it spreads."

But before he turned, there was a blitz and a flash, and suddenly the basketball in Fisher's hand was *AFLAME*.

"What the—"

Tendrils of bright orange fire cut him off, leaping straight for his nose. Face contorted, Fisher's head whipped back, away from the light and heat. But his athlete's reflexes didn't get the message, his meaty hands still holding tight to the burning ball despite being completely engulfed in magical flame.

Instead of helping him, Kyle and Kiefer both screamed and ran away. With one massive yelp, Fisher flailed into a twist to follow them—but tripped over his own two feet and face-planted. The flaming ball hit the ground, extinguished, and rolled into a nearby bush.

Pawing at his face, Fisher pushed himself up and sprinted after his minions. They all shrieked so loud and high that Sylvie was sure even old Magnus could hear the worst tones from their screened-in porch.

They were scared and didn't even try to hide it.

It was literally the most beautiful sight Sylvie had ever seen.

"That was awesome!" Sylvie high-fived Freya, and the little witch grinned, her trick from the sand-volleyball game at Monster Camp proving to be incredibly useful in real life. Plus, it didn't actually burn Fisher, so not only was he okay, but he also had zero proof that the flaming ball had actually happened.

Genius.

It might have been possible that Sylvie was so thrilled that she also beamed at Chad.

In response, Chad laughed a little, shifting that growling grimace into a toothy smile that Sylvie was getting to know quite well. He rubbed the back of his neck with a shrug. "What's the point of being a werewolf if you don't get a chance to scare somebody every once in a while?"

Vera waggled her eyebrows. "Well, we are monsters after all."

"So scary," Lenny added, making a *wooo-wooo* sound with his voice as he retrieved the basketball. The kelpie victoriously hoisted it over his head in a movement so fierce his hat fell off, exposing his horse ears. Milo laughed as he scooped up the ball cap and placed it back on Lenny's head.

"Indeed," Sylvie answered him, grinning so hard her cheeks hurt. "Now that we've vanquished Fisher and his trolls, who wants to finish our quest?!"

With a joyous cheer, the monsters huddled together and began.

ACKNOWLEDGMENTS

absolutely love writing for kids. It's a joy to connect with readers as they grow up and tell stories in which they hopefully see a little bit of themselves and feel at home. After putting seven (!) young adult novels into the world, I'm just thrilled that my middle-grade debut turned out to be *Monster Camp*.

I had more fun than should be allowed at something designated as "a job" writing about Sylvie, Vera, Chad, and their monster buddies, and I cannot thank my editor Kate Prosswimmer enough for trusting me to tell this tale. Kate is a gem to work with—enthusiastic, clever, and so very savvy about the art of storytelling. Her insights into this world and the characters were invaluable, and I appreciate every note and thoughtful Zoom session. Kate understood exactly what I was trying to do with the story and was so encouraging every step of the way. I truly hope we get to tell more stories together!

Furthermore, this book would not exist without the best partner in crime, Whitney Ross, my agent at Irene Goodman Literary Agency. Whitney has been with me for the majority of my author journey, and she did not bat an eye when I told her I wanted to write for the middle-grade category. She knows my capabilities and champions them in ways I wouldn't even be able to imagine, and I'm forever grateful and thankful to have her by my side. Thank you for being there!

Thank you to the team at Margaret K. McElderry for your dedication and hard work in the production, design, promotion, sales, and all-around love for making Monster Camp happen! To Kaitlyn San Miguel, thank you for your unerring eye in copy edits (and for getting the joke about the bookish tastes belonging to Vera's mom). To Pablo Rodriguez, thank you for your incredible artwork; to Greg Stadnyk and Irene Metaxatos for making the outside and inside of the book beautiful; and to the production team for getting Sylvie and her friends out into the world.

And, finally, thank you to those of you at home who were with me and Sylvie every step of the way. To my Kansas writers' group—you're the best werewolf pack in the world. To my talented therapist friend Sharah, thank you for your invaluable insight to Sylvie's anxieties. To my family—Mom, Dad, Justin, Nate, Amalia, and Emmie—thank you for being the best hype team in all the world. And, last but not least, to Dash—the Cardigan corgi rep is for you, our very good boy.